The Backup Plan

ALSO BY JILL SHALVIS

SUNRISE COVE NOVELS

The Family You Make • *The Friendship Pact*
The Backup Plan

WILDSTONE NOVELS

Love for Beginners • *Mistletoe in Paradise* (novella)
The Forever Girl • *The Summer Deal*
Almost Just Friends • *The Lemon Sisters*
Rainy Day Friends • *The Good Luck Sister* (novella)
Lost and Found Sisters

HEARTBREAKER BAY NOVELS

Wrapped Up in You • *Playing for Keeps*
Hot Winter Nights • *About That Kiss*
Chasing Christmas Eve • *Accidentally on Purpose*
The Trouble with Mistletoe • *Sweet Little Lies*

LUCKY HARBOR NOVELS

One in a Million • *He's So Fine*
It's in His Kiss • *Once in a Lifetime*
Always on My Mind • *It Had to Be You*
Forever and a Day • *At Last*
Lucky in Love • *Head Over Heels*
The Sweetest Thing • *Simply Irresistible*

ANIMAL MAGNETISM NOVELS

Still the One • *All I Want*
Then Came You • *Rumor Has It*
Rescue My Heart • *Animal Attraction*
Animal Magnetism

The Backup Plan

A Novel

Jill Shalvis

HARPER LARGE PRINT

An Imprint of HarperCollinsPublishers

THE BACKUP PLAN. Copyright © 2023 by Jill Shalvis. All rights reserved. Printed in the United States of America. No part of this book may be used or reproduced in any manner whatsoever without written permission except in the case of brief quotations embodied in critical articles and reviews. For information, address HarperCollins Publishers, 195 Broadway, New York, NY 10007.

HarperCollins books may be purchased for educational, business, or sales promotional use. For information, please e-mail the Special Markets Department at SPsales@harpercollins.com.

FIRST HARPER LARGE PRINT EDITION

ISBN: 978-0-06-329707-4

Library of Congress Cataloging-in-Publication Data is available upon request.

22 23 24 25 26 LBC 5 4 3 2 1

Dedicated to The Bean and The Spicy Peanut.
Having a one- and two-year-old in the house during
the writing of this book was complete chaos but also
the most wonderful, amazing time of my life.
Love you both to the moon and back.

Chapter 1

Alice's To-do List
Buy potato chips. The family-size bag. If
anyone eats them, act appropriately grief-
stricken at their funeral.

After two days of driving, Alice Moore needed to make a pit stop to stretch her legs but ended up in a drive-thru instead. Hey, it wasn't her fault that exercise and extra fries sounded alike. She'd just finished licking the salt off her fingers when she realized she was nearly at her destination.

She was either experiencing heart palpitations or her tummy had regrets about supersizing her order.

Probably it was both.

What was it people said about the past—don't look back? Well, she'd tried not to. Valiantly. But as she drove along the north shore of Lake Tahoe, surrounded by 360 degrees of sharp, majestic, still snow-covered peaks, she felt her past settling over her as heavily as the storm swirling overhead.

It'd been four years since she'd been in Sunrise Cove, the small mountain town where she'd been born and bred. She'd spent most of her adolescence at her dad's work, the Last Chance Inn, nestled in the hills above the lake. But that'd been a long time ago. She'd been braver back then, full of hope. These days she was more of a slap-an-out-of-order-sticker-on-her-forehead sort of person.

She'd been driving for two days, blasting old 1980s rock so she wouldn't think too much. But the closer to Lake Tahoe she got, the more her heart began to pound in her ears. Or maybe it was just the squealing of the clutch in Stella, her 1972 Chevy Blazer, proving that she needed a throw-out bearing replacement even more than she needed gas.

Turning off Lake Drive, she headed up Last Chance Road. At the end of the street, the ostentatious gate in front of her was wide open. She drove along the muddy and still snow-patched land surrounded by thick groves of towering pines that made the place smell like perpetual Christmas.

The old Wild West Last Chance Inn had been standing tall and proud since 1885, complete with a wrap-around porch and wooden signs above the windows labeled SALOON, JAIL, GRAVEYARD, etc., all making her feel like she'd just stepped back in time. She knew every nook and cranny of the place like the back of her hand. She'd learned to drive here, and was proud to say she'd only hit the mailbox three times. She'd ridden her bike here, and had helped her dad fix up anything with an engine. Convinced she could fly, she'd climbed the trees and jumped from the high branches. It'd taken a broken ankle at age ten to figure out that maybe she wasn't meant to be airborne.

She parked in front of the inn, but her gaze went to the barn, a hundred yards to the south. Beyond that was a creek where inn guests had once panned for gold, but it was the barn that had always called to Alice. Along with her car racing older brother and dad, she'd lost hours and weeks and months working on the inn's incredible collection of antique and old muscle cars.

If there was a heaven, it looked just like the inside of that barn. At least in Alice's mind. With a sigh, she stared out her windshield at what had once been the very best part of her childhood. Not the buildings, but the searingly intense woman who'd lived in them. Eleanor Graham had been a lot of things to Alice; pseudograndmother, teacher . . . enforcer. Her recent death had blown Alice's heart into little bits, leaving her feeling a whole bunch like the inn in front of her.

Badly in need of fixing.

And now she, a woman who owned little but the big, fat chip on her shoulder, also owned one-third of the Last Chance Inn and all its surrounding property. Boggling, and . . . *terrifying.*

The stipulation of the will stated that all three inheritors needed to come to the inn for the necessary renovations, or forfeit their individual one-third of the holdings. Today was the deadline in which to show up. Decisions needed to be made.

Not exactly Alice's forte, at least not *good* decisions anyway.

She slid out of Stella just as a light snow began to drift down from the turbulent sky. Par for the course for April in Tahoe. Or maybe it was because her armor of choice, three coats of mascara, wasn't waterproof.

There was a metaphor about her life in there somewhere, and her stomach tightened the way it did whenever she had to go to the dentist, murder a spider, or face her past, because it seemed no matter how hard she tried, the past *always* caught up with her. And right on cue, hers pulled up in an electric Nissan LEAF, a big decorative sunflower on the dash.

Lauren Scott.

Her one-time BFF got out in a clear rain jacket, hood up over her shiny blond hair, a pretty white sundress with pink tights, an open matching pink cardigan, and dainty ballerina flats. The heart-shaped sunglasses perched on her nose were a nice touch. Lauren was cute and adorable as ever. In contrast, Alice wore faded, ripped jeans and a beloved old Bon Jovi concert tee, her wild dark brown hair pulled back in a ponytail, feeling decidedly not cute nor anything close to adorable.

Just getting eyes on Lauren after all this time made her ache for the days when things had been easy. And good. Back to when they'd been each other's person through thick and thin, when Lauren had been in love with Will, Alice's brother, and they'd all felt like a family. A real family.

But Will was gone.

She missed him. And she missed Lauren, so much so that she felt both a little nauseated and unbearably happy at the sight of her.

"Wow." Lauren leaned back against her car. "You actually showed up. I'm shocked."

And obviously *not* the good kind of shocked.

Lauren drew a deep breath, like just looking at Alice pained her. "The last time I saw you," she said, "you made it quite clear that you were never ever coming back."

Yep, Alice had definitely said that, and a whole lot more. She'd said and done some horrible and unforgivable things, and the pain in her chest told her she wasn't going to escape her own demons anytime soon. "I can't do this, not right now."

"Or ever, right?" Lauren asked.

Truth was truth. "Look, we've got a lot to figure out here, and we can't do that if we're fighting. Let's just do what we're here to do. For Eleanor."

"You know how I feel about Eleanor."

Yes, and Alice knew why too. "And yet you came."

"I had to." A little bit of Lauren's carefully neutral facade crumbled as she searched Alice's gaze. "I have questions."

Questions Alice hoped to avoid.

Lauren pulled off her sunglasses. "So you still like to avoid talking about any *real* problem, especially between us."

Alice laughed roughly. "The real problem between us is that Will is dead." Something she still blamed herself for. "But you're right, it's not something I want to talk about, *especially* with you, and—"

And shit. Lauren's eyes went suspiciously shiny, causing guilt and grief to slam into Alice. "See, this is why we can't do this." Rocked by the emotions battering at her, she spun on a heel toward the front door, noticing for the first time the nice, brand-sparkling-new dark gray Chevy truck parked off to the side. Perfect, because she could guess who it belonged to—the third inheritor. Even as she thought it, the front door of the inn opened, and there Knox Rawlings stood in the doorway, casual as you please.

Alice, head still spinning from seeing Lauren, stopped dead in her tracks, her brain skidding to a complete halt. Apparently her feet too, because Lauren plowed into her back.

Giving her a dirty look, Lauren moved around her and kept going.

Not Alice. Her feet had turned into cement blocks. She'd expected Knox to be here. She'd warned herself, promised her awkward inner tomboy teenager that certainly he'd have lost his easy, effortless, charismatic charm by now, that maybe he'd also grown out of those good, rugged looks as well, hopefully having gained a beer belly and lost some hair, and maybe also a few teeth.

But nope, none of the above.

Knox was six-feet-plus of lean muscles and testosterone, and damn, of course he'd gotten better with time. Alice, on the other hand, felt like a train wreck. She could only hope he didn't remember her as the creeper teen, four years his junior, who'd once spent every free second she had spying on him as he worked for Eleanor too.

Lauren hit the front steps first, swiping at her tears. Alice followed, fighting her own. Stupid sympathy crying gene.

"I'm so sorry," Lauren murmured to Knox. "It's awful to meet you under these circumstances. I'm Lauren Scott."

"Knox Rawlings," he said and turned to Alice with absolutely zero recognition in his eyes.

Just what she'd wanted, so why did that irritate her? Ordering her feet to move, she promised herself ice cream, cookies, pies, whatever, as long as she moved with grace and confidence. *Lots* of confidence.

Instead, she tripped over a loose rock and had to catch herself. Stupid feet. "Alice Moore," she managed, as if she were completely calm. But the truth was, she'd not been calm a single day in her life. "Maybe we could get out of the crazy storm and get this over with?" With that, she brushed past them both and into the inn.

She got a few feet into the wide-open living room, but before she could process her emotions, she was greeted by a huge, scruffy brown mutt, who ran straight at her with exuberance.

"Pickle," Knox said calmly behind her, and the dog

scrambled to a stop, sitting politely in front of Alice, tail swishing back and forth on the floor, a wide smile on his face.

She melted. It was her heart, it beat for animals. Her heart was as stupid as her feet.

"Meet Pickle," Knox said. "When I rescued him, he went by Tiny, but for obvious reasons the name didn't stick."

Alice looked the dog over, a good hundred pounds past "tiny," and let out a choked laugh.

Pickle tilted his head back and "woo wooed" at the ceiling.

"He's sensitive about his size." Knox ruffled the top of his head fondly. "When I first got him, he was skinny and sick and, well, tiny. Good thing he loves food. Oh, and if you're ever eating a pickle, be prepared to share. He lives for them."

Alice absolutely refused to be moved that he'd rescued a dog.

"Oh my God." Lauren stopped in the doorway behind Alice and gasped dramatically. "Tell me that's not a dog. Tell me it's a bear or something."

"Okay, he's a bear," Knox said. "Or something."

Lauren sneezed and backed up, right into the wall while pointing at Pickle. "That's a *dog*!"

They all looked at the oversize scruffy fur ball.

"I mean, it's kinda hard to tell the difference, isn't it?" Alice asked.

Pickle gently headbutted Knox's hand, asking for love. Knox obligingly bent down to hug him, and Pickle licked his face in thanks.

Lauren, looking like she was afraid she'd be next, tried to back up some more, but she was already against the wall.

"He's harmless," Knox assured her. "I rescued him from Puerto Rico last year on a job site. He'd have ended up on death row."

"Okay, that's very sweet," Lauren said. "But maybe he could wait in the car, since I'm deathly allergic."

"It's a phobia," Alice said. "A well-founded one, but it's definitely not an allergy."

Lauren gave her a keep-talking-and-die look. "I'm *allergic*." And then, as if to prove it, she sneezed three times in a row.

"I hear if you do that seven times, it's as good as an orgasm," Alice said.

Lauren narrowed her eyes, but before she could respond, Knox spoke. "I had him tested for breed. He's a Samoyed, and Samoyeds are hypoallergenic."

"Wuff!" Pickle said, clearly proud of himself.

Lauren tried to back up some more, but a wall was . . . well, a wall. "If he's hypoallergenic, why am I still sneezing?"

"Because you got bit by your dad's evil girlfriend's dog when you were ten," Alice said. "I'd be afraid too."

"I'm not afraid!"

Knox stepped between Lauren and Pickle. "I promise, you're safe with Pickle. He's never bitten anyone. He can be shy, but that's because he's a rescue. He's actually drawn to shy people."

"I'm not shy. Nor am I scared of dogs."

Alice raised a brow and nudged her chin in the direction of Lauren's hands. Which were now gripping Alice's arm tight.

"Whatever," Lauren said, jerking her hands off Alice. "I'm a grown woman. *And I'm not scared of dogs!*"

Uh-huh. And the tooth fairy was real. Alice dropped to her knees and opened her arms. Pickle walked right into them, nuzzled his face at her neck, and she promptly died and went to heaven. "Oh, look at you," she murmured. "So handsome. So sweet."

"Okay, all of that, but he's not going to stay, right?" Lauren asked, her voice registering at least three octaves higher than normal.

Alice wouldn't mind if Pickle stayed, but hoped Knox would go, for no reason other than just looking at him reminded her of a time she didn't want to think about.

Knox patted his leg, and Pickle immediately deserted Alice for his numero uno. Both man and dog turned to the door. "You going to leave?" Alice asked hopefully. "What a shame. A terrible, horrible, no-good shame."

Knox gave her a long, unreadable look. "I'm putting Pickle in my truck and coming right back. But nice to know where you stand."

Chapter 2

Alice's To-do List
Put gas in Stella so you're prepared for a quick
getaway.

As Knox and Pickle shut the door behind them, Alice realized she was staring out the window at them, right along with Lauren.

Who sneezed again.

"They're gone," Alice said dryly. "You can stop with the fake sneezes."

Lauren sniffed. "Maybe I'm getting a cold."

Shaking her head, Alice forced herself to turn from the window and look around. Memories bombarded her, along with the heavy weight of all the emotions that came with them.

The inn had been made infamous by two TV shows.

First was the early 1960s Wild West TV show *Last Chance Inn*, a depiction of life on the range in the 1800s, hence the old sets leaning against the barn. The second show, *Last Chance Racing*, had been a late-1970s reality show before that was even a thing. The long, private road up to the inn had been used for filming what had been—and still was in most states—illegal street racing. They'd used the barn to store the cars.

Back in the day, the property had been a hugely popular tourist stop until the inn had closed a few decades ago. Now it had a run-down, neglected look to it that hurt Alice's heart.

Six months ago, Netflix had started streaming the original *Last Chance Inn*, bringing in a whole new generation of fans.

As a direct result, a restoration of the inn had been in the making, planned by Eleanor Graham, star of the original *Last Chance Inn* and owner of the property. She'd had a general contractor ready to sign on the dotted line and, with high hopes, had advertised a grand opening a month from now.

But then the grand dame had died, and all plans of renovations had been abandoned. The general contractor had moved on to another job, leaving everything in flux until Eleanor's inheritors decided what to do.

A genuine descendant from an infamous Wild West

outlaw, Eleanor had grown up on this property too. Self-assured, never wanting to rely on a man in an era when that hadn't been a thing, she'd never married or had children of her own. The inn had been her baby.

As a result, her stamp was everywhere. She'd believed in history and had picked decor that made you believe you were walking into the wild, Wild West. It hadn't been hard; the property had been in her family for generations. The front room was centered around a huge stone fireplace. The walls were beadboard—wood fiber and resin melded together, a common wood wall paneling in the late 1800s—with old lanterns hung for lighting. The ceiling was wood with rustic beams, the furnishings reupholstered antiques. Taken together with the old leather-bound books packed in the bookshelves and the hand-painted china replicas, the throw blankets on the couches in front of the fireplace, it all made quite the picture.

But unlike in the glory days, everything was covered in dust and stacks of unread mail and newspapers. Nothing to suggest any renovation work had actually begun. Only, Eleanor had hated dust and junk, so Alice took it all in with a heavy heart. What had Eleanor's last few years been like that she'd let go of her obsessive need for perfection?

Knox had built a fire in the huge stone fireplace, but

the room was still frigid, telling her he hadn't been here long. She actually had no idea where he'd even come here from. Lauren had never left Sunrise Cove, a fact Alice knew only because she'd somehow gotten on the subscriber list for Sunrise Cove's newsletter. She'd tried to send it to spam a bunch of times, but it kept faithfully showing up in her email box on the first of every month.

Written by Lauren Scott, town historian and librarian.

Knox returned sans Pickle, and the three of them stood there, looking at each other. Lauren was outwardly distraught, Alice doing her best to hide her feelings, even though she'd never been any good at it, and then there was Knox, blank faced, emotions locked up tighter than . . . well, Fort Knox.

"We should talk," Lauren said softly. "About what we should do." She pushed off her hood and unzipped her jacket, still wearing more pink than Alice had ever seen in one place.

"What's to talk about?" Alice asked. "Obviously we sell, ASAP." She'd let her boss know she might need a month off, but the thought of staying with Lauren and Knox for that long had her sweating in some uncomfortable places.

When neither of her coinheritors said anything, an uneasiness settled in her gut to go along with the rising panic. "Selling is the only logical choice."

Lauren shook her head. "You can see that the renovations never got started. We've got the big opening coming up, we can't just sell."

"I agree with Pink," Knox said.

Pink, aka Lauren, beamed at him.

"If this is all about Eleanor," Alice said with what she hoped was a reasonable, agree-with-me tone, "she made her mark a long time ago. She has nothing left to prove, and neither do we. There's no reason for us to reopen, when the only person it meant something to is gone."

"Not true," Lauren said. "There's been a lot of press, and the fans of the shows are super excited. And if this is, as you've said, *all about Eleanor . . .*" She actually used air quotes for the *all about Eleanor* part. "Well, then we should do this in her honor. Carry on with her wishes and reopen the inn."

"Again, I agree."

At Knox's low, quiet voice, Alice turned her head to stare at him.

"Eleanor gave me my first job," he said.

She held his steely gaze with difficulty, because same, and at the reminder of all Eleanor had done for her, her heart ached.

"She took care of a lot of people," he continued. "*And* the town, providing revenue and employment to hundreds over the years."

Alice turned her head and looked out the window, pretending that she was anywhere but here. Maybe on a deserted South Pacific island . . .

Then she realized the room was silent and both Knox and Lauren were staring at her. She cleared her throat. "I didn't hear the question, but the answer is chocolate."

Knox shook his head, clearly annoyed.

"I don't know if either of you know," Alice said, "but the place is a hot mess. Which means it's our hot mess. To open in a month, it would take the three of us working day and night to pull off, and even then, it might not be possible. Do you really want to put your own lives on hold for the next four weeks and be on top of each other?" She looked at Lauren, who had zero emotional ties to Eleanor for a bunch of very complicated reasons.

Lauren was looking around her, taking in the sights, making Alice remember she'd never been inside the inn. "There's a lot of history here," she murmured.

And as Alice well knew, Lauren loved history. The irony didn't escape her, that Lauren, Eleanor's grandniece, loved history as much as Eleanor had.

"Nearly one hundred and fifty years of history," Knox said. "And as for leaving or staying, I'd do anything for Eleanor, dead or alive." He said this in the same quiet, husky tone he might have said it's still snowing, which perversely made Alice want to see him lose his temper. But if he was anything like the younger Knox, he wouldn't. He didn't shy away from a problem, instead always facing it head-on. He'd certainly weathered enough of them in his life, same as she had.

But where *she* was a storm in her own right, always a swirling mass of tangled, wild emotions, he was the calm eye of any storm that came his way. "And our personal lives?" she asked, hoping she was the only one who could hear her desperation. "Are we supposed to give those up?"

Knox shrugged. "I run a general contracting company. I've got business partners who can hold down the fort while I work from here, handling both my business and finishing Eleanor's dream for her."

Okay, so Alice was reluctantly impressed in spite of herself. The summer after he'd graduated high school, his mom had died, and he'd left town. She'd never seen him again. Clearly, he'd come a long way. But . . . "I don't have the luxury of staying for emotional closure."

"Okay," Knox said. "If there's no emotional appeal for you, then how about monetary. The architecture of this structure is amazing. The moldings and baseboards alone are worth a fortune. The inn is shored up with redwood beams, also original. They don't make 'em like this anymore. With a little TLC, this place would be worth a lot of money, not to mention the barn full of muscle and antique cars, and the nostalgia of the show sets. A renovation is in our best interests."

Alice hadn't heard much past "if there's no emotional appeal for you . . ." Because was he kidding? There was nothing *but* emotional appeal here for her. In fact, her chest was so tight at the ball of emotions sitting on it that she could scarcely breathe. She'd taught herself how to stay calm, but to do that, she needed to get into her backpack and pull out the scarf she was knitting. She sucked at knitting, sucked bad, but the craft was the only thing that seemed to quiet her brain. Well, okay, so that wasn't strictly true. Food also calmed her brain, but she didn't have any at the moment.

So . . . the three of them staying for the next month? The thought nearly caused a full-blown panic attack, and she'd finally given those up. "And how about you?" she asked Lauren. "You can just walk away from your career at the library? Because I sure can't."

"I'm sorry, your career is what again? Last I heard, you were a nanny in Santa Fe."

"That didn't work out." Nor had waitressing, bar-tending, or landscaping, but that wasn't important now. "I work in a lumberyard in Flagstaff."

"Ah." Lauren nodded. "So much upward mobility there."

Ignore the 'tude. You deserve the 'tude. "I like it," Alice said. Wood didn't need looking after, it didn't have feelings or expectations. It just needed to be moved from point A to point B. The end.

"What are you doing wasting your talents in a lumber-yard anyway?" Lauren asked. "Why aren't you restoring cars, which you were born to do. *Literally.*"

Alice was actually almost content at the lumber-yard. The guys had all become her friends; Miguel and Steven, and especially Eddie, who often worked con-struction on the side and had taught her enough that she sometimes worked with him on those extra jobs when she needed money. They were all so good to her. It was the closest she'd come to belonging anywhere since she'd left Sunrise Cove.

They hadn't wanted her to leave but had under-stood. They'd extracted the promise that she'd be back when she finished here, which had warmed a teeny tiny corner of her cold dead heart. Because of that alone, she intended to fulfill her promise and get out of here ASAP. She met Lauren's gaze. "I find it ironic you want to commit to helping fix this place up, since you recently hired someone to plant flowers for your patio so you wouldn't get dirty."

Lauren pointed at Alice with a pleased gleam in her eyes. "You stalk my IG."

Alice grimaced. Stupid, rookie move.

Lauren grinned but it faded quickly. "And no," she said. "I can't give up my job at the library, but I'll have plenty of time to help. I can handle the accounting for the renovations, keep track of the expenses, and create an inventory of what we have, figuring out ways to use that inventory to increase our guests' enjoyment of the place. For instance, people are going to love coming out to see those old TV sets. We just have to set them up in a safe and manageable way."

Okay, all of that would be valuable, Alice could admit. "Great for you two. You can fix up the inn and keep your jobs. But I can't. You guys can buy me out."

"Yeah, what part of small-town librarian are you missing?" Lauren asked with a rough laugh. "I'm a dollar over the poverty line at all times. Besides, one of us leaving isn't what Eleanor wanted. I assume that's why she set things up so that the money in the inn's accounts is dedicated to the inn only, not to be distributed as cash to any of us. According to the will, only once the inn's up and running *and* in the black can profits be split among whoever stuck. If you leave, you get nothing."

Not if Knox would buy her out. She looked at him.

He gave a slow shake of his head. Apparently the man didn't do anything fast. "No can do, Tumbleweed."

She stiffened, and not because he'd just used the nickname her dad and brother had always used for her—well earned, by the way—but because he *so did* remember her!

Focus.

She'd been counting on getting out of this. Not for the money. Hell, she'd been poor most of her life. She had no real expectations for that to change, though a fresh start would have been . . . everything. As would the means to fuel a very specific dream that had been living deep inside her for years, way back to when she'd been her dad's little monkey wench, working at his side, renovating the antique cars. She'd always wanted to start up a women-run mechanic shop. Alice herself could never get under a hood again, *ever*, but she'd also never get cars out of her system entirely. She'd be more than happy running the show and hiring female mechanics to get the jobs done.

"Okay, how about this," Knox said at the standoff. "Let's do a walk-through and see what exactly needs to be done. We'll go from there."

Hating that it was actually a good idea, Alice gestured around them. "The Eleanor I knew was meticulous. She hand-mopped the floors, she hated dust, and never tolerated clutter. This cluttered mess wasn't at all like her. Something was wrong, very wrong."

"She was sick," Knox said. "She moved all her favorite stuff down here from the second floor because she couldn't get around much."

Alice walked through the front open room to the wide-open hallway that led to a den, dining room, and a huge kitchen that she remembered so well it almost hurt just to peek her head in. Off the kitchen was what used to be the office. The second floor held seven guest rooms, each decorated and made to look like a character's bedroom from the 1960s TV show.

All of it . . . messy, with that same sense of neglect. Eleanor had tried to turn the den into her bedroom. A hospital bed, a recliner, and some other bedroom furniture had been squeezed into it, every last surface covered with pill bottles, cups, books . . .

"This huge property," she murmured, "and her entire life shrunk down to one tiny room." It had been bad, and she hadn't even known. A sense of sadness weighed her down for the infamous old broad who'd once been the center of her universe.

"There was no pain in the end," Knox said from right behind her, making her realize she was standing still with a hand to her chest, aching, worrying that Eleanor had suffered.

She turned to face him, forgetting until she met his dark green gaze that there'd been a time she couldn't look right at him without making a fool of herself. "You were here with her?"

His eyes were impassive pools as he looked at her, but something flickered in them. "No. But we were in touch."

And she hadn't been. He didn't need to say the words for her to hear the reproach. She felt guilty enough all on her own.

"We need to talk about what we're going to do," Lauren said.

"Yeah." Knox turned to a cabinet on the wall that Alice hadn't known existed. He pulled out a bottle of whiskey.

Lauren nodded in approval. "Definitely."

He handed over the bottle, and Lauren tilted it to her lips. Town Librarian Takes a Walk on the Wild Side. She passed it back to Knox, who then offered it to Alice. She took two long swallows, figuring she was entitled. The first shot was pure fire. The second pleasantly numbing.

Knox drank after her, then sprawled in a chair, long

legs stretched out in front of him, his stubble two days old, maybe three, his pose suggesting a bone-deep exhaustion.

Understanding that all too well, she reluctantly took a seat on the couch across from him. Lauren sat on the couch with her, but as far away as possible.

For a long moment, they all just stared into the crackling fire. "I can't stay," she said.

Lauren looked over. "Because of me?"

Alice closed her eyes for a beat, and when she opened them, Lauren's were shimmering with tears again. And damn if Alice's didn't do the same. Throat too tight to answer, she just shook her head.

"I told you that I can't buy you out," Lauren said quietly, her voice thick with tears. "But you should know that even if I could, I wouldn't."

Alice's heart took the hit.

"Not for the reason you think," Lauren said. "I *want* you to stay."

If Alice had been standing, she'd have fallen over in surprise. She stared at Lauren, who stared right back.

Stunned, Alice looked at Knox.

"Three is better than two," he said with a shrug.

Lauren was sniffling and patting her pockets. She came up with a tissue. She'd been like that as a kid too. Always prepared for anything. Beneath that buttoned-up look beat the heart of a Girl Scout, one who'd loved Will "Speed Racer" Moore as much as Alice had, and would've done anything for either of them.

"If you stop crying, I'll stay," Alice heard herself say. "Just until we open one month from now. After that, we hire someone to run the place for us, and I'm out."

Knox rose to his feet without a word and began rummaging around in the desk against the one wall that wasn't beadboard but wallpapered. Most of the paper had peeled away so that the wall was basically down to drywall. He came up with a Sharpie.

"What are you doing?" Lauren asked as he turned to the drywall.

"That's permanent marker," Alice said.

Ignoring them both, he began to write.

"What does that say?" Alice asked, squinting at the messy scrawl.

He looked at the words, as if surprised they weren't legible. "You can't read it?"

"Not even a little bit."

He looked at Lauren. She bit her lower lip. "I can make out *some* of it," she said.

"She's lying," Alice said. "She's just incapable of hurting someone's feelings. Trust me, she can't read your chicken scratch either."

"I can so," Lauren said. "It says . . . 'down range'?"

Looking to be grinding his back molars, Knox crossed it off and wrote slower this time:

THE GROUND RULES

Then he underlined it, twice.

"Seriously?" Alice asked dryly. "We need ground rules?"

Not answering, he wrote beneath Ground Rules:

1. *No tears.*

Or at least she was pretty sure that's what it said. "What the hell."

He ignored this too, and moved over to start a new list, writing even slower this time, clearly wanting them to be able to read it. This one was labeled TO-DO. He then wrote for a full three minutes.

1. Handrails on deck.
2. New inside stairs.
3. Clean and condition inside beadboard.
4. Replace missing trim.
5. Light fixtures.

6. Clean and condition and restain furniture (sandpaper, putty, Spackle, stain for the molding and baseboards).
7. Sand shutters and paint.
8. Do something with the disgusting carpet.
9. Plumbing retrofitting in bathrooms and kitchen.
10. Replace rusted-out galvanized pipes.
11. Upgrade electricity to code.
12. Replace missing moldings.
13. Clean and condition the beadboard, replace the missing ones.
14. Windows: Replace rotten sash cords.

"That looks costly," Lauren said.

"Yeah," Knox said. "But it has to be done. The inn's account should cover it."

Alice snatched the pen from his hand, and turned to the Ground Rules list. Beneath the No tears, she wrote:

2. This is about Eleanor.

She then underlined Eleanor—twice—and turned to glare at him.

He held her gaze, his looking as if he was holding

back a smile. Before she could translate what that meant, Lauren grabbed the pen from Alice and wrote:

3. Open, honest conversations with actual words.

Then she paused and added:

DAILY.

Knox held out his hand and Lauren pointed to the with actual words.

He sighed. "Fine. Can I have the pen back?"

Lauren tilted her head and cupped a hand around her ear.

Knox gave an almost imperceptible shake of his head but said "please."

With a smile, Lauren dropped the pen into his hand, and Alice had to hold herself back from offering Lauren a high five for standing her ground with him.

Knox circled the open, honest conversations and drew an arrow to the No tears. "As long as it doesn't violate rule number one."

Alice tried to take the pen from him, but he simply held it above his head. At five foot seven, she was fairly tall for a woman, but not tall enough, which turned her right back into the sullen teenager she'd once been. "What are you, the keeper of the pen?"

"You were going to write down something argumentative and not wall worthy," he said.

That it was true didn't help. "Give me the pen." She smirked. "Please."

When he did, she added:

4. Do not kill your partners.

"That one's a reminder for me," she said.

Knox promptly put a line through it. "That's in the Commandments, which makes it redundant here."

Alice rolled her eyes. One of these days she was going to roll them so hard she'd go blind. She began a new list called Need. On it, she wrote:

Alice—A new life

"Good luck with that one," Lauren murmured.

"You know what?" Alice asked, tossing up her hands. "I need food to deal with this."

Lauren nodded and turned to the door.

"Hey, if anyone gets to walk, let's make it me," Alice said.

"I'm not walking away. I'm going to get my new and

cranky partners some food." And with that, Lauren slammed the front door behind her.

A shelf above the desk fell from the wall. It hit the wood surface and then the floor at Alice's feet.

Look at that. *Yet another* metaphor for her life.

But she'd upset Lauren, which felt a whole lot like kicking a puppy. Suddenly chilled, she hugged herself. Looking up, she found Knox eyeing her with an unfathomable expression on his darkly handsome face. "What?"

He shook his head. "Nothing you don't already know."

That didn't sound like it was a compliment, so she moved on. "Why did you pretend not to know me?"

He strode to the fireplace, crouched before it, and with a few economical movements that had the muscles in his broad shoulders and back flexing in a way that shouldn't steal her breath but did, he had the fire blazing. She nearly jumped in surprise when he finally answered her. "Because I *don't* know you. I suspect no one does."

A sentence that almost had her violating Ground Rule number one.

Chapter 3

Need
Alice—A new life.
Lauren—I second that.

You're *a strong, independent woman, Lauren Scott* reminded herself. *You've got this.* She stood on the front porch of the inn, their surprise spring storm gaining strength. The tall pines swayed in the wind, the snow flying off in slow motion waves, making the trees look like three-hundred-foot ghosts. *One month and everything will be okay . . .*

She blew out a breath. Apparently adulting was saying that sentence—everything will be okay—to herself over and over. Until she died.

She stared at the front door, the takeout bag in her hands getting cold. She was no one's errand girl, but she'd offered to get the food because she'd needed a moment. A moment to lose the urge to smother Alice with one of the living room throw pillows.

She realized the murderous urges suggested that she, in fact, did *not* have this, but hey, no one was perfect.

The fifteen minutes into Sunrise Cove for food and back had been good for her. The temptation to go home to her own little condo that she'd paid too much for was strong, but hiding out wouldn't make this go away. So instead, she'd stopped at the locals' favorite place to eat, the Sunrise Cove Diner. She loaded up on her own personal comfort foods. If her partners didn't like it, well then, that meant more for her.

And yet here she stood, on the porch, unable to summon the courage to walk into the inn for the second time today and . . . the second time ever.

Yes, her great-aunt Eleanor had willed her one-third of this place even though she'd never had Lauren here, not once. She was working really hard at ignoring that right now.

She felt a headache coming on. From her dog allergies, maybe. Or maybe she was getting a brain bleed. Were those deadly? She started to google it, but recognizing the stall tactic, put her phone away and sighed. Plenty of time to die a tragically early death later. So she walked into the place like she owned it—at least a third of it—chin up and everything.

The front room was empty, so no one saw the show. Just as well, since without the two big force fields of energies that were the personalities of Alice and Knox, she was able to get her first good look around. Moving slowly through the admittedly beautiful if neglected room, she could admit to seeing potential here, and she gave her inner historian and writer geek free rein to peek into every room.

Nothing was as her father had described it from his childhood. Lauren had expected something straight out of *The Shining*, but the inn didn't seem scary, haunted, or evil at all. In spite of the clutter and dust, the place, with all its Wild West charm, was really . . . incredible. It made her want to write about it, delve deep into the past, the shows, the memorabilia . . .

And, shockingly, Eleanor herself, whom she'd been taught to hate.

When she entered the kitchen, she stopped short at the sight of Alice sitting at the table looking completely at home. Which, of course, she probably was, since she'd spent so much of her earlier years in this house. Lauren's ex-BFF, with her signature long ponytail and a myriad of tiny earrings running up both ears, a baseball cap tugged low over her face, was wearing faded, ripped jeans, kickass boots, and a tank top—with an emoji of a frowny face on her chest—all of it emphasizing the toned, willowy body that Lauren had always been so envious of.

Once upon a time, Alice had been the most important person in her life, but that had changed, and it still hurt. Swallowing the remnants of resentment, Lauren plopped the bag of food onto the table. "Dinner."

"Thanks." Alice leaned forward to reach for it, but Lauren grabbed it back. "Don't thank me yet. I still have questions."

Alice stilled, then slowly raised her gaze to Lauren's. "You're holding the food hostage?"

"Yes. Why, after we lost Will, didn't we turn to each other?" She was working hard at keeping her voice even, not wanting to get emotional, which was a little bit like trying to breathe without air. "You were like my sister, but when I needed you the most, you were smoke. You returned only a fraction of my calls and texts." She made herself zip it, needing to hear Alice say something. Anything.

The briefest of emotions crossed Alice's face, but they were gone in a blink, and then she was sniffing at the bag. "Do I smell burgers?"

"Vegan, but yes."

Alice grimaced. "But there are fries, right? Crispy?"

"Maybe. You'll see when you answer my question."

Alice leaned back and met Lauren's gaze. "I think we both know that after all this time, my answer is irrelevant. Besides, we're here for a very limited time and have a huge job to pull off. After that, I have to go, so what does it matter?"

"You have to go? Or you want to?"

"Both," Alice said firmly.

Lauren tried to be cool about that, but who was she kidding? She'd never been cool, not a single day in her life. "If this is about Ground Rule number two . . ." She jabbed her thumb over her shoulder in the direction of the living room. "This being all about Eleanor, we both know she'd want you to stay."

"Maybe," Alice said. "But she knew me well enough to understand I probably wouldn't."

Lauren started to speak, but Alice held up her hand. "Look, I said I'd stay the month and see this place up and running. After that, we'll either sell, or hire someone to manage the inn, and go back to our lives. Right, Knox?" she asked as he walked back into the room, followed by Pickle, who was nose in the air, dramatically sniffing out the food.

Lauren took one look at the dog and sneezed.

Alice shook her head. "He's a bear, remember? And if he wants to eat one of us, I volunteer as Tribute."

"I don't want you to get eaten either!"

"Nothing's getting eaten except the burgers," Knox said with as dramatic a sniff toward the bag of food as his dog had given. "I'm starving."

Lauren handed over the bag and he pulled out six wrapped burgers. "Perfect," he said. "Two each."

"Heads-up," Alice said. "They're fake."

"*Vegan*," Lauren corrected, unable to stop eyeing the dog anxiously. "I thought Pickle was going to stay in your truck."

Knox grabbed a burger, unwrapped it, and flipped Pickle a pickle.

The dog snatched it out of thin air, wiggling ecstatically, like he'd just won the lottery.

"You didn't even taste that," Knox said in reproach, then looked at Lauren. "He can only be in my truck for so long before he starts to eat things. Like the steering wheel. My insurance company is still pissed off."

He flipped the dog another pickle, which was also inhaled whole. Knox just shook his head.

Pickle gave a happy "woo-woo!" and tap-danced for more.

"You weren't kidding when you said his name suited him," Alice said.

Knox nodded and, still standing, brought his burger

to his mouth. At the first bite, he winced, but then gamefully carried on.

Pickle whined, and Knox shook his head. "That was it for the pickles. I'd share the burger, but I fed you earlier, and also, trust me, you'd hate it."

Pickle "woo-woo'd" again, pleading his case.

"All right, but remember, I warned you." Knox tore off a bite and tossed it to Pickle.

It hit Pickle in the forehead and fell to the floor.

"He's still learning to catch," Knox said.

Pickle snatched the faux burger from the floor.

"But the floor's dirty," Lauren said.

"I can promise you that's not the worst thing he's licked today."

Pickle chewed the vegan burger, then froze, the whites of his eyes showing. He made a "gak" sound and spit out the food.

"Told you." Knox scooped up the bite with a napkin and tossed it across the room and directly into the trash can.

Pickle flopped onto the floor and heaved out a sigh.

Knox kept eating like he hadn't eaten in three weeks.

"You really were starving," Alice said.

He slowed his chewing and swallowed, eyeing his audience of two as if he'd almost forgotten they were in the room. He swiped his mouth with a napkin before shrugging. "Been a busy two days, haven't had any breaks."

"Eleanor's attorney mentioned you were coming in from Seattle," Lauren said.

Alice looked up from her burger, clearly unable to hide her curiosity about her teenage crush in spite of herself.

Lauren smirked.

Still holding her burger, Alice tucked three of her four fingers against her palm, leaving just her middle finger to wave at Lauren.

This only made her smirk all the more. She'd have liked to tease Alice about her teenage-crush-turned-grown-up-crush, but she didn't feel like dying today. "Did you have a travel issue?" Lauren asked Knox.

"Put in a sixteen-hour day on the job yesterday," he said. "Drove through the night. I arrived here just before you both did." He shrugged. "Skipped a few meals during that time."

Or all of them, Lauren guessed, pushing a second burger his way, as well as the fries.

"Back to the problem at hand," Alice said.

"Wait." Lauren stood and walked to the light switch. The sun was starting to set and they were practically in the dark. Not a fan of the dark, she hit the switch, but nothing happened. "Oh no."

"Don't panic." Alice set down her burger and crossed the room to the other wall.

Knox began his second burger. "Why would you panic?" he asked Lauren.

"Because she's afraid of the dark," Alice said before Lauren could answer. "Not as much as she's afraid of dogs, but close."

"Excuse me," Lauren said testily. "I'm *allergic* to dogs."

Alice looked at Knox. "She's also afraid of men in sandals, but hey, everyone has their own idiosyncrasies, right?"

Lauren considered throwing a fry at her, but she was fundamentally opposed to wasting food.

Alice flicked the other light switch on and off. Still no lights.

Lauren took a big gulp of air and held it because it was suddenly very *very* dark. "My palms are getting sweaty."

"Breathe," Alice said. "It's okay."

She said this genuinely, without her usual sarcasm, but since she couldn't in fact know if it was going to be okay, Lauren did not breathe. Instead, she quickly accessed her phone's flashlight and raised it high to look around nervously.

Knox was mowing through his second burger. "Are we worried about the things that go bump in the night?"

Lauren hugged herself because she was now, but before she could further deny it, Alice spoke.

"Some asshole bullies once locked her up in the high school gym in the dark and left her there overnight."

Huh. That sounded an awful lot like maybe Alice was still angry about that, angry for Lauren. She glanced over, but Alice wasn't looking at her, she'd turned on her phone flashlight too and was trying to pry open an old cabinet.

Knox turned to Lauren, eyes sympathetic. "Were you hurt?"

"Traumatized," Alice said for her, which was really starting to piss her off. "The dickheads left her there for eight hours." This was said grimly while she fought to get the cabinet open.

"Jesus," Knox said.

"It was a long time ago," Lauren said, her face hot. "And I'm *not* traumatized." Just utterly mortified, because fine, yes, she was terrified of the dark now. Whatever. "What are you even doing?" she asked Alice. "What is that?"

"An electrical panel," Knox said with approval in his voice, moving toward Alice. He reached in and added his strength to hers, and the stubborn door finally opened.

Both Alice and Knox studied the rows of switches like they were reading them, but it was all Greek to Lauren. "So?" she asked, voice a little high, but hey, it was getting really, *really* dark now.

Knox shook his head. "I don't think this panel is for the main house. It looks ancient and unreliable. I think it's probably the original electrical panel. There's got to be another newer one somewhere."

"In the attic," Alice said.

Lauren was boggled. "And we know this because . . . ?"

Even Knox looked curious.

But Alice took a bite of her burger. It was unlike her to evade, but then the reason why hit Lauren and she suddenly felt so much better about herself. "Because she used to hide up there."

"You did?" Knox asked.

Alice sent Lauren an eat-shit-and-die look that made her want to laugh for the first time today. When they'd been teens, Alice used to tell her about going up to the attic to stare out the window at Knox, who'd be outside doing whatever chores Eleanor threw his way.

"Why?" Knox asked.

"Yeah, Alice," Lauren said innocently. "Why?"

Alice pointed at her as she moved to the door. "I'm going up to the attic."

Lauren's smile faded. "You can't go up there in the dark." Mostly because she didn't want to be left here alone.

To her surprise, Alice stopped. "Yeah, you're probably right. The access is a bitch to get to. Best to wait for morning for that adventure."

"Morning?" Lauren's heart rate tripled as she realized the implications. "You mean . . . no electricity until morning?"

"Don't you have a place in town?" Knox asked.

Oh. Right. Good thing she hadn't gotten caught up in her fears beyond reasonable thought. She grabbed her purse and looked at her partners, feeling compelled to say, "I've got an extra room and a couch . . ."

"Thanks, but Pickle and I will be fine here," Knox said.

Lauren looked at Alice, hoping she'd take her up on the invite so they could have a four-year-overdue-talk-slash-fight.

"I camped out on my drive up from Flagstaff," Alice said. "I'm still all set up in the back of my Blazer, I'll be fine."

"It's snowing," Lauren said. "And your top leaks."

"How do you know?"

"Because you were wearing snow when you got out of it earlier."

"I'll be fine," Alice said. "Seize the day and all that."

Lauren wasn't much on seizing the day. She tended to just sort of poke it with a stick. But she was going to call BS on Alice. "You stalk my IG. Why not take the opportunity to stalk me in person?"

Alice grimaced. "I only stalked you once or twice."

"Uh-huh." But wow. She *really* didn't want to talk to her, and hell if Lauren would beg. She was tired of begging people to love her.

"It really is still pretty cold," Knox said to Alice, who just shrugged, like a little chill didn't bother her.

Probably because she had ice in her veins.

Knox rolled his eyes and Alice narrowed hers. "You got something to say?" she asked him.

"Nope."

"He thinks you're stubborn as hell," Lauren said. "And ridiculous for turning down my warm place, but I can take a hint." She turned to the door. "Good to know you'd still cut off your own nose to spite your face."

Alice stilled, looked stricken, and for a beat, Lauren felt bad. For a single beat. "I'm out, but before I go, do we have a plan?"

"We can't even agree on what good food is," Alice

said. "How are we supposed to do this?" She looked at Knox. "You really going to let your partners run your business for the next month?"

"I'll be Zooming in daily. I'm not worried."

Alice looked at Lauren. "And you. You can't seriously tell me your librarian job is going to wait a month for you."

"No," Lauren said. "I'll have to put in my hours. But I work from seven to two. I'll come straight here if that's what you're worried about. I've got lots of ideas, like getting media attached to the opening, checking in with any of the original stars of the TV show to see if anyone's interested in making an appearance, and the show has a fan club that's dying to come out and get social media pics, for starters."

Alice sighed. "I'm not worried about you putting in hours and you know it. You're a hard worker with a great work ethic. You'll pull your weight. I'm worried about . . ." She shook her head, falling silent.

And Lauren knew. Alice was worried about being back where she had spent her formative years with her dad and Will and Eleanor, which had molded her into the woman she'd become. Lauren knew this place was filled with memories for her, good memories, maybe the best in her life. But Will was gone. Her dad too. And now Eleanor. And she'd clearly avoided facing any of that. But she wouldn't be able to avoid it while living here.

As for Lauren and *her* teen years . . . well, *Alice* was her single best memory from that time. And the truth was, Lauren wanted her back in her life, however she could get her.

"This so-called plan isn't easy for me," Alice said. "Unlike you two, I can't work from here. And I can't *not* work. I need to keep earning money, just like both of you will be."

"Then we'll put you on the inn's payroll," Knox said easily. "From the renovation fund." He looked at Lauren. "You okay with that?"

"Absolutely," she said, hoping her inner smile didn't show. It was a perfect solution for all of them, and it would keep Alice here. Well, for the month anyway.

Knox looked at Alice. "You're hired."

"No."

He arched a brow. "No?"

"It has to be equal," Alice said. "If we're *all* going to be working, then we *all* get paid."

Lauren nodded in gratitude, because truth be told, she barely made ends meet. She wanted to hug Alice, but she'd gone back to eating, stopping to toss Pickle her pickle. The only sound in the room was the dog licking its chops.

"So it's settled." Knox eyed the two remaining burgers. Lauren pushed hers toward him, and with a nod of thanks, he grabbed it and snapped his fingers for Pickle, who leaped happily to his feet. Then he strode from the room, the dog trotting happily after him.

Alice tossed up her hands, but followed as well.

Lauren rounded off their little parade behind the Pied Piper.

With the daylight nearly gone, the rooms were surprisingly dark and Lauren's heart kicked. They found Knox in the living room, keys in hand. His key chain had a red pointer light, which he flashed at their lists. "We start tomorrow," he said, flicking the light at Ground Rule number two. "And we keep *that* in mind at all times."

This is about Eleanor.

Lauren nodded grimly. "It's always about someone, isn't it." Which left her wondering . . . would it ever be about her?

Chapter 4

THE GROUND RULES

1. No tears.
2. It's about Eleanor.
3. Open, honest conversations with actual words. DAILY—as long as it doesn't violate rule #1.

When Knox awoke, he instantly knew three things: it was still dark, he hadn't woken of his own volition, and he and Pickle weren't alone in the room he'd ended up in late the night before.

"I can't find a ladder," a female voice said. "So I need you to boost me up to the attic access door, which is in the ceiling of the laundry room."

He opened his eyes and was immediately blinded by Alice's flashlight. Muttering every oath he knew, he threw up an arm to protect his eyes and glared at Pickle, who was playing possum at the foot of the bed. "Some watchdog you are." He shook his head and looked at Alice, who'd thankfully lowered her light. "What could you possibly need in the attic in the middle of the night?"

"It's not the middle of the night. It's six a.m., and I want to check the wiring to see if the electrical problem is an easy or hard fix, so hustle. I'm on the clock, you know." Then she snapped her fingers at him, just like he always did for his dog. "Let's go, Fort Knox."

"Excuse me?" he said.

"You heard me."

Pickle rolled over and showed his belly. It's what he did when he sensed tension. He was so positive he was cute enough to make things all better. And it was hard to argue because it always worked. Worked now too, because Alice began to rub him down.

Pickle had been found alone on the streets as a puppy. As far as the Humane Society had been able to tell, he'd never had a home. This had left him gun-shy, but right now he was practically purring. Knox had never been jealous of a dog before, but he was thinking about being jealous now.

"Time to roll," Alice said.

Pickle jumped from the bed. Then, as if on second

thought, he jumped back up and . . . kissed Knox right on the mouth. "Thanks, buddy." He sat up and scrubbed his hands over his face, the scruff he encountered sounding rough in the silent room. Without electricity, hot water wasn't happening—something he'd learned during his very short shower last night. "And we're up this early why . . . ?"

"After today, we have only twenty-nine days before opening."

And she already had one foot out the door. Good reminder that no matter what his body *thought* it wanted, his brain didn't actually want Alice to rub his belly and make him purr. "You mean before you leave."

"That too," she agreed, *not* averting her eyes when he tossed off his covers and sat up. In fact, she boldly took her time studying the fact that he wore only a pair of knit boxers, which didn't hide much, especially first thing in the morning.

"Guess you know your way around a gym, old man," she finally said.

He had to laugh. At thirty-two, after a long day of physical exertion on the job, hauling beams and other equipment around with his crew, he sometimes felt ancient. But the way she looked at him actually made him feel a little bit like Superman. Standing, he scooped up the jeans he'd left hanging over the footboard of the bed he'd tumbled onto last night. He'd been exhausted beyond reason or he'd probably have taken the time to choose a bedroom different from the first one he'd come to. In the dim glow of Alice's flashlight, it was rustic, but also . . . lacy and feminine. Great. He was in the frilly, froufrou, over-the-top feminine boudoir designed for the show *Last Chance Inn*, done up in Eleanor's "signature color" . . . pink. The curtains were lace, and the comforter was lined in lace, as were the pillows.

Alice was smiling wide at his grimace.

"Nice choice," she said.

Ignoring her, he went through his duffel for a clean shirt. Then he grabbed his ball cap and shoved it on his head.

"Under construction," she said, reading the saying on the hat. "Funny."

And true . . .

And since fair was fair, he took his turn to take a good look at his unwelcome alarm clock. Alice was tall, lean, and sexy as hell in faded jeans, work boots, and a snug long-sleeved Henley. The sleeves were shoved up to the elbows, revealing a barely there, delicate scripted tattoo around her right wrist, too tiny to read from where he stood. Her shiny mahogany hair was pulled back and her eyes, the exact color of her hair, stared at him, a swirl of emotions swimming in their depths.

He'd always heard a person's eyes were windows to their soul, but he'd never believed that until now. Because by the glow of nothing more than her flashlight, her gaze revealed a lot more than her witty sarcasm had. It revealed something that looked a lot like . . . anxiety? "You okay?"

"Always."

Uh-huh. The things he knew about her were pretty basic. Her mom had bailed. She'd been raised by her dad, practically in the barn here at the Last Chance Inn. And by the time she was a freshman in high school, she could handle herself in or on anything with a motor.

Oh and he knew one more thing—she'd sure grown up right nice.

"You always this slow in the morning?" she asked. "Because wow. My boss would have my ass fired."

"I'm the boss. And normally a morning person." But he'd underestimated what it would feel like to face the past he'd purposefully turned his back on. "Coffee would help," he said.

"Yep, and so would a personal chef, but neither is going to happen for us."

Grinding his teeth, he headed into his attached bathroom, shutting the door on her smug face.

He would've taken his time in the shower just to spite her, but he stepped into the water and yelped before he could stop himself, adding a "holy shit" as the icy spray hit him full-on frontal.

It brought him back to his youth, when his mom hadn't always paid their utility bills. There'd been lots of cold showers in those days. He wondered if he would drive by the old place, and how he'd feel if he did.

Shitty, he decided, and walked back into the bedroom to find a smirking Alice. "Oh, good. You're still here."

"Didn't know a guy your size could hit that note." She held up a can of soda. "Not coffee, but it's the only caffeine I could find."

He tossed the towel onto the bed and gratefully took the can. "It'll do. Thanks."

She waited until he was on his last gulp of the soda. "'Bout ready, princess?"

He choked, then pointed at her. "That is *not* going to be what you call me. And not Fort Knox either."

She just smiled. And damn, it was a killer smile. Shame she was so evil. He moved past her and out the bedroom door.

"First, sleeping in," she said to his back. "Then crying in the shower. You used to be so tough, so badass. And now you're sleeping surrounded by silk and lace."

"Maybe I'm just gender secure."

She laughed and he stopped short, making her plow into him, swearing as she nearly tripped. Turning to face her he looked down into those expressive eyes. "Are you baiting me for a reason?"

"Is that what I'm doing?"

He smiled at her innocent tone, not fooled for a second. "It's that, or you're flirting with me."

That shut her up. She pushed past him and led him wordlessly to the attic access, which was indeed in the eight-foot ceiling of the laundry room.

"There are ladders in the barn," he said.

"Now that you finally decided to get up, a ladder isn't necessary." She hopped onto the machine with a sexy, flexible ease and looked down at him. "Come on. I need you to give me a boost."

"I'm the one going into the attic."

She went hands on hips, expression dialed to 100 percent obstinance.

He sighed. "You're going to fight me on this, aren't you?"

"Of course I am. It's not like I can hoist your two-hundred-pound ass up there."

"One hundred and seventy-five," he said.

"Whatever, just get me into the attic. And don't worry, I've done some work for an electrical contractor."

"Fine," he said. "But that washing machine is ancient. It won't hold the both of us. Let's just go out to the barn and—"

"No!" She drew a deep breath before speaking purposely quieter. "We don't need the barn."

There was something in her tone, and most definitely something in her eyes, that had flashed right after he'd said *barn*. And then the reason for that slammed into him like a two-by-four upside the head.

She probably hadn't been inside the barn since the night her brother had died. It would be a land mine filled with memories for her.

"This old machine will hold us just fine," she said. "They don't make them this sturdy anymore." Finding her rhythm again, her brow quirked upward in a challenge.

Not smart enough to refuse the bait, nor ruthless enough to make her face a past she wasn't ready to, he jumped up onto the washing machine, his hands automatically going to her hips to balance them in the same two square feet. He held his breath, waiting for the whole thing to break apart and send them crashing to the floor.

When it didn't, she smiled. "See? Not our day to die."

"Good to know. Pickle, we're all just fine, I promise," he told the dog, who'd begun barking the second he'd jumped onto the washing machine.

Pickle stopped and smiled up at him, all right in his world because Knox told him it was so. Not for the first time, Knox wondered how different *he* might be now if he'd had someone to tell him that once in a while. He looked at Alice. "Your plan?"

They tipped back their heads and eyed the attic access.

"Easy," she said. "I climb you like a tree and you hoist me up."

A part of him that he really didn't want to think about right now stirred at the "climb you like a tree." Before he could dwell on that, she put her hands on his shoulders and jumped him. He caught her and then there was a beat with their faces only an inch apart as he worked to balance them so they didn't tumble onto their asses. All while a current seemed to run through them both.

"I think I found the missing electricity," he said.

Alice rolled her eyes. "You are such a guy." And then she hiked herself up his body until her knees were on his shoulders, he had her ass in his hands, and a view that stopped his heart. He could also now read the tat on her wrist. Unbreakable. She had another on that tantalizing inch just above the waistband of her jeans, near her left hip bone. This one, in the same tiny beautiful script as on her wrist, said:

You are braver than you believe, stronger than you seem, and smarter than you think.

He had the irrational urge to put his mouth to the words.

"Balance," she ordered. "You're wobbly."

No shit. And if she'd had his view, he'd like to think she'd be wobbly too. He gripped her tight, planting his feet more sturdily.

"Oh my God! Hold still!"

"I'm trying," he muttered, his hands digging into her ass, her legs practically straddling his face. This was officially now the most intimate he'd been with a woman in recent memory.

Lauren walked into the laundry room and gasped—not at Knox and Alice's compromising position, but at the dog just in front of her.

"Pickle, *stay*," Knox managed to grit out.

Pickle, deprived of the opportunity to lick Lauren to death, stayed with a whine.

Lauren's gaze jerked upward to Alice and Knox, and she gasped again. "Oh my God. Is this some kinky sex thing?"

Knox would've laughed except Alice snorted derisively, and damn. That wasn't the usual reaction he got from a woman when it came to such matters.

"Never happening," Alice said and shifted her weight. In the next beat, she was doing a pull-up into the attic access.

Lauren's mouth was open. "How did she do that? That was . . . *ninja*."

Yeah. And sexy as hell. But . . . "never happening"? *What was so bad about the idea of having sex with him?*

Lauren was watching them both carefully. "I don't think anyone should sleep with anyone while we're here."

"Duh," came Alice's muffled voice from the attic. "And let's make it real easy—no ties, physical or emotional. Period."

Knox watched the blow of that cross Lauren's face. He knew even less about her than he did Alice. But she was Eleanor's grandniece and clearly Eleanor wanted her here, and that was enough for him.

"We need a new circuit board," Alice called down, oblivious. Her long legs reappeared, then that enticing strip of skin as her shirt rode up a bit while she hung, suspended. Knox put his hands to that skin, gripping her waist as he lowered her to the washing machine.

"Got it," she said and jumped to the ground.

Right. She got it. He just wished he did.

Pickle barked when she jumped. Lauren jumped too. Then sneezed.

Alice rolled her eyes and hugged Pickle before walking out.

Knox, Lauren, and Pickle followed her to the living room, where she turned to their Need list and added: circuit board.

"Okay, and I've done some stuff," Lauren said, pulling out her phone to access her notes. "I started a spreadsheet for expenses, contacted media outlets about attending our opening—"

"Wait," Alice said. "What if the inn isn't finished in time?"

"It has to be," Lauren said. "Because . . . drumroll please . . . I also have some of the original stars of the show willing to make an appearance, which will bring the fans out in droves for pictures!"

Knox stared at her, impressed. "What time did you get up?"

She smiled. "I don't need much sleep."

"Great idea," Alice said, moving closer to the board to write in some other things they needed, missing Lauren's brilliant smile at the unexpected praise.

Knox added a few things to the list too. After, Lauren pulled out her phone, took a pic of it, and thumbed around for a minute. Then both Knox's and Lauren's phones pinged. "That's our shared list," she told them. "Add to it at will. We can all access it."

Knox read what Lauren had just sent. She had re-arranged the items by the job so they could easily see what they needed for each task. If he had any lingering doubts about either of his partners pulling their weight, those doubts were long gone. "I'll go to the hardware store."

"I'm coming with," Alice said. "No offense, but guys don't manage lists very well. Which I know from being the only woman at the lumberyard."

He shrugged. "Suit yourself."

"Always do, Fort Knox."

He went back to the general rules and added a fifth Ground Rule:

No nicknames.

His and Alice's gazes locked and that entirely unwelcome emotion hit him again.

Attraction.

He must be losing his damn mind.

"I'm coming too," Lauren said. She started toward the front door, but stopped and turned to the list of Ground Rules. She wrote:

6. No one sleeps with anyone.

"Do *not* worry," Alice said.

"Seriously," Knox said. "Standing right here."

Alice laughed. *Laughed.* Then she added rule number seven:

No ties, emotional or physical, period.

Again, Lauren's smile dimmed some.

"Let's do this," Alice said, either not noticing, or pretending not to.

Knox had zero idea what the problem between them was, but he did know one thing—it was going to be a very long month.

Chapter 5

THE GROUND RULES
1. No tears.
2. This is about Eleanor.
3. Open, honest conversations with actual words. DAILY—as long as it doesn't violate rule #1.
4. Do not kill your partners.
5. No nicknames.
6. No one sleeps with anyone.
7. No ties, emotional or physical, period.

Two minutes later, Knox was squished into the front bench seat of his truck with Lauren and Alice, wondering how he'd gotten himself into this. They were shoulder to shoulder, Pickle in the backseat, face pressed to the window, panting with joy. Pickle loved nothing more than a good outing. Well, okay, maybe he loved crotch sniffing strangers more, but a car ride was definitely high on the list.

The radio was blasting 1980s rock, thanks to Alice, who'd appropriated the radio before even securing her seat belt.

"How about something from this century?" Lauren asked, yelling to be heard over the heavy drums of Metallica and today's rain—well, half rain, half snow, which equaled slop—hitting the roof.

Alice didn't respond, she was busy singing along.

"Rule number three!" Lauren yelled over the music. "Open, honest conversations with actual words, remember?"

"I do," Alice said. "I've just got nothing to say."

"Since when?" Lauren asked.

Alice just rolled her eyes.

Lauren leaned forward and turned on the heat. "Nice truck!" she yelled to Knox. "Is it new?"

He turned down the music before his ears bled. "Yes." He and his business partners had done well enough last year to trade in their old, falling-apart trucks for new ones. "I was due."

Lauren looked impressed. Alice did not. "They don't make them like they used to" was all she said.

"What's wrong with this one?" he asked.

"Nothing, if you like overpriced and not built to last."

"Well, I like it," Lauren said diplomatically.

"I liked that 1970 Dodge truck you used to have," Alice said.

Yeah, he'd liked it too. It'd been beat-up on the outside, but under the hood she'd been all grit, guts, and speed. Until she'd been hit and totaled one day while parked at the grocery store. He'd grieved her ridiculously. "May she rest in peace. But this truck will last me a good long time, or so the market claims."

"The market doesn't know what it's talking about," Alice said. "The best was made in the seventies."

She was not wrong. He loved old cars too. But a work vehicle was about practicality, not pleasure. Still, he had to laugh. He was more successful than he'd ever been, and she'd liked him better when he'd been as poor as dirt with no future, no place to belong to, no forever home, nothing.

Not that it mattered what she thought. The three of them had a mission, and it was all about Eleanor right now. He greatly appreciated what she'd done for him, even if it meant facing his past demons. His dad had walked before he was born. As for his mom, Knox had loved the whimsical, sweet, funny woman more than anything, but she'd been a barely functioning alcoholic.

He could sometimes still feel that sick helplessness over his inability to stop her from drinking herself into an early grave. It'd been his biggest fear, that loving him wasn't enough to keep her clean or sober, and she'd leave him too.

And she had. Just not by choice.

How he'd hated being that kid everyone felt sorry for. Back then, it'd given him a rough, dangerous edge, like he had to prove he was so tough so that no one would pity him, ever. He'd been all hard-ass on the outside, and scared on the inside—not a constructive combo.

"Did anyone remember to add painter's tape to the list?" Alice asked.

"I don't know," he said. "I wasn't allowed to make the list."

"Because no one can read your writing. Painter's tape, yes or no?"

When they'd both been at the inn as teens, they'd never interacted, so he had no idea what it was about her that got beneath his guard. He couldn't quite say he liked it, but somehow he liked *her*, which couldn't be good for either of them.

Alice looked at Lauren, who was sitting in the middle all serene and calm, today's sweater—pale pink, but still pink—buttoned up practically to her nose, dark jeans, and boots that were not meant for April's slop.

She didn't answer Alice's question.

Alice looked over Lauren's head to Knox. "Will you ask her if she added painter's tape to the list?"

Knox responded by sliding her a glance that would've had any of the men on his crew shitting themselves, but she didn't appear bothered in the least.

"Knox," Lauren said. "Will you *please* tell Alice that I heard her the first three times. And yes, I've added painter's tape to the list—which she would know if she accessed our shared list."

"This has been the longest ride of my life," he said. "And I've driven across three of the continents."

"We've gone two blocks," Alice said.

"*Exactly.*"

"Maybe it's because you seem to be allergic to the go pedal, Granny."

Lauren eyed the dash and frowned. "He's going the speed limit. Some of us like to avoid trouble with the law, you know."

Alice opened her mouth, undoubtedly to say something to set Lauren off, so Knox took a left turn.

Hard.

Alice's head bounced off her window. "*Hey!*"

"Sorry," he said, not even a little sorry.

"Move over," Lauren said to Alice. "You're squishing me."

"I offered to take Stella," Alice said, rubbing her head.

"Stella needs some TLC," Knox said. "Like a throw-out bearing, and I'm assuming a new reverse gear, since I saw you attempting to back out with one foot out your driver's door last night."

"I needed potato chips," she said defensively. "And you know what? Stella's never let me down. I mean, okay, yeah, maybe she's a *little* beaten up by life, but she's scrappy and tough."

Knox slid her a look. "Are we talking about the car, or you?"

She gave him an eye roll.

"And for the record," he said, "I tried to do this by myself."

"We are not letting a man decide paint colors," Lauren said.

"Hell no," Alice agreed.

Then the two of them stared at each other, clearly shocked that they appeared to agree on something. Knox almost laughed. Except he was stuck with them both, so it really wasn't all that funny. He was going to need more caffeine, a *lot* more, plus some actual food. Making an executive decision, he detoured into a drive-thru. He placed his order, added an extra sausage patty for Pickle, then looked at Lauren.

"They don't have a vegan option."

Knox turned to the speaker. "Add an Egg McMuffin, minus butter, cheese, and the egg."

"Wait— So just the muffin?" a disembodied voice asked through the speaker, sounding horrified.

"Yes."

"Sir, I don't know if I'm allowed to do that."

Knox put a finger to his left eye, which was developing a twitch. "Charge me for the whole Egg McMuffin, just leave everything off it."

There was a long pause, during which Knox managed not to bang his head against the steering wheel. He was going to have to learn to pace himself, because it was obviously going to be that kind of a day. He'd no doubt have plenty of opportunities to bang his head later. He looked over at Alice, brows up.

She leaned across them both and ordered the same thing he had for himself, plus some sort of cinnamon roll.

"How in the world do you eat like you do and stay so skinny?" Lauren asked, sounding irritated. "If I even *looked* at your order, I'd gain five pounds."

"I'm not skinny," Alice said a little defensively, which surprised Knox. He hadn't thought she gave a damn what anyone thought of her.

For the record, though, she was right. She wasn't skinny. Her legs were a mile longer than the legal limit, and okay, maybe she was slender, but she had a toned look to her that he now knew came from manual labor and not a gym pass. Basically, she was a long, lean drink of water with curves that he absolutely needed to stop thinking about.

A long, lean drink of water who, after eating all her food, then ate one of his Egg McMuffins, which she *claimed* was an accident.

Accident his ass.

Five incredibly long years later, they parked at the local hardware store. They left Pickle snoozing comfortably in the backseat and *finally* walked inside, where Lauren grabbed one of those little hand baskets.

"Seriously?" Alice asked.

Lauren frowned. "What?"

Knox gently took the basket out of her hands and grabbed a big cart.

They started in the light fixtures aisle, where he and Alice stopped to look at their choices. Lauren had her attention on the indoor plant section right behind them. She picked up a small plant with red flowers.

With a smile at the guy in a blue work apron watering the plants, she set the pot in the cart.

"That's an indoor plant," Knox said.

"I know."

"We don't need plants yet. It'll just get in the way," he said.

Apron Guy came closer, eyes on Lauren. "Need help?"

"No, thanks," Knox said. "We're not getting any plants today."

"I was asking the lady," Apron Guy said, then smiled at Lauren.

Lauren craned her neck to look behind her, as if trying to see who he was talking to.

"He means you," Alice stage-whispered. "*You're* the lady."

Lauren blinked, then smiled tentatively. "I do need help, thank you. Would this plant be okay with a temporary outdoor living situation until we got our kitchen fixed up?"

Knox had to give the guy credit—he took the question seriously.

"No," Apron Guy told her, his voice easygoing and kind. "That plant won't like being outside at all."

"Even if I showered it with love?" Lauren asked.

The guy smiled. "The showering with love is nice,

but it'll still die. We do have some beautiful indoor/ outdoor plants against the wall there."

Knox realized he knew him. They'd gone to the same high school. His name was Ben Westmoreland, and he'd run track and had broken his leg in the state championships.

"Thanks so much," Lauren said, eyeing his name tag. "Ben."

Ben smiled. "Anytime." He looked over at Knox. "Knox," he said in greeting, revealing he at least vaguely remembered him as well.

Lauren moved toward the wall of indoor/outdoor plants. Ben followed her.

"Guys always did fall at her feet," Alice said almost wistfully. "It's because she's so friendly and draws people in, not to mention all those gorgeous curves."

She said this like she had absolutely no idea how stunning *she* was, even when she was scowling. Hating the almost haunted look in her eyes, he said, "If a guy fell at your feet, it'd be because you knocked him there."

As he'd hoped, she laughed. "You got that right."

Two aisles later, Lauren caught up with them, a plant in each hand. Alice was currently arguing with Knox over their various shutter choices.

Lauren pushed her way between them and pointed at a set of shutters on display. "This one," she said, and because it was the set Knox wanted too, he grabbed the card with the order/purchase information to show at the checkout.

A few aisles later, Knox looked into the cart to find . . . "Yarn?" he asked with incredulity, then immediately shook his head. "You know what? Forget it. I'm not even going to ask." He had no idea when Lauren thought she was going to have time to knit, but it wasn't worth the argument. He consoled himself with the fact that surely it couldn't get worse.

He should've known better, because karma really was a bitch. At the end of the next aisle stood a petite little blonde. Nikki Waters, the first woman to ever break his heart. Yep, this trip was just a barrel of laughs, start to finish. If they ever finished, that is. "Maybe you two want to go ahead of me and check out the paint colors in the next aisle."

"*You're* going to let us mere women pick out the paint?" Alice asked, heavy on the disbelief.

"Yep, go nuts. I'll be right there." He waited until they'd gone around the corner before heading Nikki's way. He could've made himself scarce and not faced her at all, but apparently he wasn't that smart.

Nikki had been the sweetest girl in his class. Hell, the whole town, and back when he'd been going through the worst time of his measly existence, she'd tempted him with a future he'd never dared dream of. They'd become high school sweethearts, and she'd been the one soft spot in his life.

At the moment, that soft spot was dressed in yoga pants and a cropped sweatshirt, hair falling straight and blunt to her shoulders as she looked over a display of window screen choices. Catching sight of him, her eyes lit up.

His heart stopped. Not because of her surprised smile, but because as she turned toward him with her jogger stroller, he saw a little girl in it, maybe four years old, looking exactly like her mom.

"Knox!" Nikki practically bounded toward him, all happy, warm smiles, like it'd been yesterday when she'd last seen him, not fourteen years. "Wow, now I'm *happy* it's raining outside! Priscilla and I"—she smiled down at her little girl—"we were out for a walk, and well, you know what humidity does to my hair, so we came in here to wait it out. I've been hoping to run into you."

"How did you know I was back?"

"Oh, you know how Sunrise Cove is." She laughed softly. "No sense of secret. All one thousand five hundred of us know everyone's business." Then she leaned in and hugged him, a big, warm hug that had her entire body pressed up against his.

He closed his eyes. How many times had he imagined

this moment? Imagined holding on tight and never letting go, but instead all he wanted to do was go be with his two bickering bickersons partners. Disentangling himself, he took a step back. "Nikki—"

"I know! It's so great to see you too!"

Huh. Maybe she'd forgotten she'd fallen into bed with someone else the summer after high school. The summer his mom had died. The summer Eleanor had gotten him a two-week job out of town so he could get away for a bit. Two weeks. That was it, and the only reason Nikki had told him what she'd done was because she'd discovered she was pregnant.

Priscilla was attempting an escape from the stroller. Nikki expertly grabbed her, holding her on a hip. "Priscilla, honey, say hi to Knox. He's . . . an old friend. Knox, this is my youngest, Priscilla."

How she said "old friend" without an ounce of irony was beyond Knox, but he smiled at the little girl. "Hello, Priscilla."

"Mommy, I want an ice cream! We need to bring Sissy one too."

"She won't be home from school yet."

So she had two kids. *And* the life he'd thought they'd have together. And since just listening to her felt a whole lot like torture, he turned to walk away.

"Knox, wait!" Nikki grabbed his hand. "Silly, we've

got to exchange information. You've changed your number, and I'd love to keep in touch. Here—" She thrust Priscilla at him and pulled out her phone. "I'll airdrop you my contact." She grabbed his phone from his back pocket to do just that while he held Priscilla, receiving her stink eye loud and clear.

I get it, kid . . .

Nikki slid his phone back into his pocket with a brow waggle. "Now we have each other's info so there's no excuse not to have a little get-together."

Actually, there were a *million* excuses *not* to have a little get-together, starting with how she'd treated him, and ending with the fact that it didn't matter anyway, because he no longer trusted her with his heart.

Nikki took Priscilla back and looked him over for an inappropriate amount of time. "You look good, Knox," she said, and made the universal gesture of *call me* with her pinkie and thumb before walking away with her fancy jogger stroller.

Knox turned back to his cart to find both Alice and Lauren watching from the other end of the aisle. When they saw him looking, they both mimicked Nikki's *call me* gesture.

Nice. And wasn't it just great that his misery would turn out to be the thing that brought Alice and Lauren together.

Chapter 6

Need
Alice—A new life.
Lauren—I second that, preferably in Bali.
Knox—this is for WORK-RELATED NEEDS
ONLY, LADIES!

As Alice pushed their cart down an aisle, Ms. Librarian was at her side, reviewing her list, looking serene and cool. How did she do that? Alice tried, but after thirty seconds, she knew the truth— serene and cool weren't in her repertoire.

Knox had vanished. Maybe he'd gone after Nikki.

Nikki. Ugh. Back in high school, she and Knox had been the golden couple. Alice had been a freshman when they'd been seniors, but she'd stalked Knox's every move, her wild teenage heart leading the mission. She knew all about the perfect Nikki Waters, who could do no wrong. But she *did* do wrong. She'd broken Knox's heart, and for some dumb football jock. Alice was so lost in those memories that it took her a moment to realize Lauren had stopped short with what sounded like a "fuck me" under her breath. Alice stared at her in shock. "Did you just drop the f-bomb?"

Lauren whipped around to face her. "Hurry. Turn the ship around! Abort mission! *Repeat, abort mission!*" When Alice didn't move fast enough, Lauren grabbed the cart herself and attempted to turn, clipping the front corner of a display of artfully arranged paint cans.

All of which cascaded to the floor in a symphony of clanging, and nearly took out Alice as well. "Are you kidding me?"

Lauren was still desperately trying to get out of the aisle with the cart, but the chaos she'd left in her wake was slowing her down.

An elderly woman with blue hair and more wrinkles than an apple doll put a hand on their cart, smiling at Lauren. "Honey! It's so good to see you out and about. You're so brave, soldiering on without the love of your life. Agnes! Agnes, look who's here! It's our lovely town widow, bless her heart."

Agnes was a beanpole with a ski cap on her head,

red lipstick on her wrinkled lips, and smiling rheumy eyes. "Oh, sweetie." She clasped Lauren's hands. "I remember when I lost my Herbie. It was months before I could even get rid of his things."

The first woman nodded at Agnes. "You two were a real Lauren-And-Will."

Alice was confused. "A 'Lauren-And-Will'?"

"Yes, apparently we're a noun," Lauren said.

Both the older women sighed in unison. "You two were practically engaged," Agnes said. "That boy was over the moon for you. It's so hard to move on from true love. You've kept his memory alive for *all* of us."

Alice was stunned. Lauren . . . *bravely soldiering on*? What, did they expect her to stay single forever? Who'd ever expect that of a twenty-eight-year-old woman? She looked at Lauren, who wasn't seeming so serene anymore. Her cheeks were red, and Alice was pretty sure steam was beginning to come out her ears.

"I gotta go," Lauren murmured and walked off, sans the cart, which she left for Alice. As well as the mess of the paint cans at their feet, not to mention the two little old ladies.

"Poor girl," Agnes murmured in her wake. "Being a widow is so hard, and at such a young age too. A real shame. No parents, no Will, and now no Eleanor. The dear is all alone in the world."

"She's *not* alone, she's got me." The words were out before Alice could think about what she was saying, surprising even herself.

An employee came down the aisle to begin the cleanup. Alice bent to help, but she was waved off. "So sorry," she said and pushed the cart to go in search of either of her partners. It was a sad day when she was the most mature of their little trio.

It took her ten minutes, but she finally found Lauren muttering to herself in the garden tools section. "It's been four damn years," she was telling a small hand rake. "And I'm *still* the town widow."

"People loved him," Alice said quietly. "They love you."

Lauren whipped around, her face pale now, and there was something in her gaze that read like sheer grief. "I want it to stop."

"Gotta slay your own dragons, princess."

Lauren rolled her eyes. "Go away. I want to be alone."

Alice looked around them. "You mean you and the hundred or so people wandering this store?"

Lauren made a noise of annoyance, then tossed up her hands. "Why do people think I'm brave? I didn't do *anything*. I *never* do anything."

Alice drew a deep breath and reminded herself that

she'd once cared for and loved Lauren as deeply as she'd cared for and loved her brother.

And you just left her . . .

At the time, Alice had believed she'd contributed to Will's accident. After all, she'd been the last one to work on his car. She'd replaced the brakes just that morning. There'd been an investigation, and her dad, who'd owned the car, had lost everything in a lawsuit and left town.

Alice had felt like leaving would be the right thing for her to do too, but now she wasn't so sure. What she wouldn't give to be able to go back in time, back to when they'd all been teens, their biggest decision being what they'd do after school that day. Will had been the best brother. Two years older than her, he'd taught her how to catch M&M's with her mouth, sneak out of the house to go night sledding, and how to look someone right in the eyes and lie. All good skills. Even back then, Lauren had loved the guy, though it'd taken him years to catch up. She looked at Lauren now, wondering if her heart was still broken. Hoping not.

Ben was stacking clay pots about ten feet away. Finishing up, he straightened, dusted his hands off, and smiled at Lauren. "Is it okay to ask if you need any more help?"

Lauren smiled like the question had made her day.

"Of course," she said. "Knox was just hangry because Alice ate his second Egg McMuffin."

"Well, who knew he'd be a big ol' baby about it," Alice said in automatic defense.

Ben blinked. "So, the three of you are . . . together?"

Lauren, who'd just taken an unfortunate sip of her iced tea, choked, then began to cough.

Looking worried, Ben came closer and gently patted her on the back.

"No," Lauren finally wheezed.

Ben took a step back, hands up.

"She meant no, the three of us aren't together," Alice said, laughing harder than she had in forever. Lauren was still blushing, but also smiling at Ben.

Okay, so he was a good-looking guy, Alice could admit. Just under six feet, he had sun-kissed brown hair and a lanky, lean build that looked good in unassuming jeans and a polo. But it was his mischievous smile, including a cute dimple on his left side, that topped off the package.

Lauren looked at Alice. "Do people really think we're . . . together?"

She looked so horrified that Alice felt a little insulted. "Who cares what people think?"

Lauren turned back to Ben. "We're not. Together."

He smiled, kicking it up a notch, adding a wink. "Good to know."

Lauren tilted her head, looking concerned. "Do you have something in your eye?"

"Uh," Alice said. "I think he winked at you. It means he's flirting."

Lauren looked at Ben, startled.

Ben laughed roughly. "Guess I'm out of practice, because I thought we were *both* flirting."

Lauren bit her lower lip, like she was into the flirting but unsure how to join in.

"Let me help you out here," Alice said to a mystified Ben. "If you think she's flirting with you, chances are she's just being friendly. If you think she's weird and makes you uncomfortable, then she's probably flirting with you."

"Hey," Lauren said, then sighed. "Yeah, okay. That's fair." In typical form, she changed the subject by pointing at a display of succulents. "I could probably handle keeping one of those alive, right?"

"Succulents play by their own rules, and no one's got a copy of the rule book," Ben said. "But they're adaptive, and can survive in harsh environments, going long periods of time without attention."

"Sounds like me and this plant are kindred spirits

then." Lauren picked one up and set it in the cart before smiling at Ben. "Thanks."

Then she took the cart and walked off.

Ben looked disappointed.

"She doesn't get out much," Alice said sympathetically. She turned to go and found Knox standing there, waiting for her with a look on his face that she couldn't quite track. Not wanting to think about it, or the fact that she still had twenty-nine very long days and nights in front of her, she headed his way. Their gazes locked and held, and something in his made her knees wobble. Annoying.

"Tumbleweed," he said.

"Fort Knox," she said, and kept going.

"Chicken," she thought she heard him murmur, and he was right. When it came to him, she was indeed one big chicken.

Chapter 7

Lauren's To-do List
Water succulents.
~~Ask Ben out on date~~ (I know this was you,
Alice, and it's not funny!)

Lauren slept deeply. She was exhausted from es-
sentially working two full-time jobs, so it wasn't
a surprise. But what *was* a surprise were the dreams.
Suddenly she was having adrenaline night fantasies—
skydiving, deep sea-diving, things she *used* to dream
about all the time but had never tried in real life.

Yes, hello, her name was Lauren and she'd always
had a deeply buried desire to walk on the wild side.

Once, Will "Speed Racer" Moore had been that wild
side. He'd been wild and free and dangerous, and she'd

thrilled to it. Until she'd realized he'd loved someone more than her.

Himself.

They'd never done any of the things she'd wanted. It'd always been about building cars, street racing them, rebuilding them, rinse and repeat. But still she'd stayed because she'd loved him.

She'd always loved him.

It'd started in middle school, a terribly embarrassing unrequited crush. He'd been so far out of her league, but that hadn't bothered her heart one little bit. It'd taken years, but when Will had finally noticed her at her twentieth birthday party on a hot summer night at the lake, she'd been so flattered, she'd practically fallen into his bed. She'd been young, immature, and certainly not prepared for a guy like Will, who lived life in the fast lane.

For four years, she'd done her best to keep up, but deep down she'd craved a deeper connection with him. The truth was, the thrill had begun to wear off by that long-ago night when he'd asked her to marry him. She'd had to follow her heart.

And break his.

But what she hadn't known was that he'd stupidly go street racing alone in the rain to blow off steam.

And die.

She'd had time to come to the understanding that she'd sold herself short for too long. It was time to live, especially seeing how colorful both Alice's and Knox's lives seemed when compared to her own. It was her turn now.

When morning came, she sat up and took stock. A few days ago, a cute guy had sort of flirted with her at the hardware store. Today she was signing herself up for zip-lining in South Tahoe. Not quite skydiving, but sometimes a girl needed training wheels. Sitting there in her bed, she grinned.

Lauren Scott was back.

Feeling good about herself for a change, she walked into the cool, calm, quiet library an hour early for her shift—per a text request from her boss. This sometimes happened on Story Time days. If they had too many kids sign up, she'd arrive early in her Mother Goose costume to chitchat and keep everyone calm before the actual Story Time began.

As she headed through the front room toward the children's section, she drew a deep breath, inhaling the sweet, lingering musky smell of old books that wafted into her nose. Because here, like nowhere else, she was always at home. Here she had all the books in the land, along with fellow bookworms, and peace and quiet. She loved peace and quiet. It filled her soul.

After an unhappy, chaotic childhood involving her mom's early death, her dad losing his office supply business due to a string of bad investments and then falling into a depression, things had been rough. Rougher still when her great-aunt, who'd raised her dad, had refused to help him get back on his feet. He'd passed away last summer after a long battle with pneumonia, but before that, and for most of her growing-up years, Lauren had learned to be quiet, good, and need nothing. She hadn't really come into herself until she'd started seeing Will, but no matter how crazy her life got, being in this building was her calm. Her center.

Always.

She was stopped before she got far by Mr. Goldmann, who was somewhere between eighty and the Ice Age.

"Morning, Chickie," he said in his smoking-for-decades voice. "You decide you can't live without me yet?"

She smiled. "You just might be too much man for me, Mr. Goldmann."

He beamed. "Aren't you the one."

This was a weekly ritual. She patted him on the arm and started walking again, only to be stopped by someone else. Her dentist, Dr. Martine, and her four-year-old daughter, Casey. "Lauren," Dr. Martine said. "How are you doing?"

"Good, thanks. Hi, Casey."

Casey, super shy, flashed a quick smile before burying her face in her mom's neck.

Dr. Martine cupped her daughter's head and smiled as she spoke to Lauren. "Don't forget, now, when you're ready, I've got a nephew to set you up with. I'll even give you a deal on teeth whitening before you go out with him."

Wait—did her teeth need whitening? She ran her tongue over them. She'd just read about a woman who'd lost all her teeth due to stress. They'd turned yellow and then all just fallen out. Oh, God, did her teeth feel loose? They did! She waved away the Mother Goose feather floating in front of her face. "I'm already seeing someone." She shocked even herself with the lie.

"Oh, that's great! Someone from town?"

The picture of Ben's smile filled her brain. Flustered, she made a show of checking the time. "Would you look at that? I've gotta get the show on the road!" With a wave, she walked into the children's section, where she was immediately greeted with a chorus of happy voices that soothed her soul more than her secret stash of not-vegan chocolate—and that was saying something. The kids rushed over, so excited to see her that she couldn't help but smile. Here, if nowhere else, she was loved.

Silly as it might be, the kids were a connection to a

childhood she'd never really had. There were at least a dozen kids here today, and though she adored them all, her favorite was five-year-old Hope. The girl was tiny but mighty, always making sure the smallest kids got the front row, glaring down the bigger boys who were sometimes too rough.

Hope, sitting in her grandma's lap, beamed wide at the sight of Lauren, who waved her over. Hope came running. She had dark hair, dark eyes, and the brightest smile of any child here.

"Your two front teeth finally fell out!" Lauren said, happy for her, as Hope had been talking about getting to meet the tooth fairy for months.

"Yesth!" Hope lisped with a wide grin.

"And? Did you get to meet the Tooth Fairy?"

"I fell asthleep before she came." Hope looked momentarily crestfallen, but then instantly cheered up. "She left me thith bracelet. It wasth my mommy's!"

Lauren looked down at the thin, delicate macramé bracelet around Hope's wrist. "It's beautiful."

"My mommy made it. Before she had to go. Just like Quack."

"Quack?"

"My duck." Hope's lower lip quivered. "They live together in heaven, with unicorns and fairies. Grandma says that Mom gets to ride the unicorns."

Lauren's heart squeezed so hard she could scarcely breathe.

"Excuse me, Lauren?"

She turned at the sound of her boss's voice. Naleen stood in the doorway, her gray-streaked black hair piled on top of her head, her reading glasses hanging on a beaded necklace around her neck, her sensible black flats not daring to show a single sign of wear and tear. "Can I see you in my office?"

"Of course." Lauren squatted and hugged Hope. "I'll be right back, okay?"

"Okay!" And Hope skipped to the reading circle.

Lauren followed Naleen to her office, her pulse leaping. This was it. Her promotion. She'd dedicated the past two years of her life to this library with the goal of becoming head librarian. Her name had been on the short list. In fact, the whispers around the library said that she *was* the short list. The job was hers to lose.

Naleen sat behind her desk and Lauren took one of the two chairs in front of it. As she sat, a few feathers floated around her. "Sorry. It might be time for a new costume."

"Yes, well, thanks for coming in early."

"No problem. I love this place, you know that. I'm looking so forward to the future."

Naleen winced, and Lauren's Anxiety Meter began to beep.

"Honey," Naleen started slowly. "We *love* how dedicated you are. I want to say that up front."

Beep, beep, beep . . .

"Your devotion to the kids is remarkable," Naleen went on. "My Clifford always says so."

Naleen's husband, Clifford, had passed two decades ago, but Naleen visited his grave weekly and had long chats with him.

As for Lauren, she was having trouble breathing. It had to be the costume. Or her life.

"*Everyone* here loves you so much, Lauren." Naleen pushed a few things around on her desk. A stapler, a pencil sharpener—even though no one ever used either anymore—and her box of Clorox wipes. "I'm sorry," Naleen said. Her boss drew a deep breath. "I've been putting this conversation off for weeks . . ."

And just like that, Lauren's Anxiety Meter ran out of batteries. "I didn't get the promotion," she said flatly, sagging back in her chair, legs boneless.

"Honey, and I say this with a *very* heavy heart . . ." Naleen's eyes filled. "There's been budget cuts, and we are no longer going to have the position available."

"Oh no," Lauren breathed softly, saddened but at least relieved she wasn't being let go. "Oh Naleen, I'm so sorry, this must be devastating for you, you worked so hard for the grants to open that new position."

"Yes, I've been absolutely heartbroken, and haven't slept since I got the news. With everything you've been through, I didn't want to add another loss to your plate."

Lauren felt touched to have the woman be worried about her, but . . . "Everything I've been through?"

"Losing Will and all."

She drew a deep breath. "It's been a long time, Naleen."

"Yes, but you're still mourning."

"I'm okay. I'm going zip-lining in June. On one of my days off," she added quickly.

"Oh. Um . . ." Naleen paused. "To be clear, when I said the position is no longer available, I meant your current position. It's the budget cuts. I was forced to pick seniority over work performance, but believe me, I sent a very sternly worded letter about it." Her eyes still had tears in them. "I'm so sorry, Lauren, but we have to let you go at the end of the month."

Lauren sucked in a breath, feeling things she couldn't name, all of them so heavy it was hard to keep her head up, but that might have been the costume.

"I really hope you'll stay on until then," Naleen said.

The gut punch made it difficult to speak, but somehow through that and the buzzing in her head, she said, "I'd never leave you in the lurch."

"Oh, you're so incredibly sweet. I'm just so sorry, dear. I worry so much about you."

She'd been biting her lip up until that point, trying not to cry, but at Naleen's words, she felt her spine snap straight. Because hell no. She might not have much in her life, but hell if she'd admit it. "Don't worry about me. I'm going to be okay. In fact, I've got a huge opportunity in front of me . . ." Assuming Alice and Knox hadn't set fire to the inn while she was gone, that was. "And now I can dedicate all my efforts to that." She even managed what she hoped was a confident smile as she nudged a box of tissues toward Naleen.

Her soon-to-be ex-boss drew three tissues out to dab at her eyes. "But without your librarian friends, who will be your emotional support?"

Okay, so it was true that she didn't have family and she hadn't had a BFF since Alice, and her current friends did *all* work here and were at least two decades older than her . . . but she *hated* knowing people felt sorry for her. "I'm going to be fine," she said and stood up. A couple more feathers fell from her, along with the last of her dignity.

"Please don't be a stranger." Naleen stood too. "Oh my goodness, I almost forgot, a package came for you today." She turned to her credenza, grabbed what looked to be a small old-fashioned wood and leather travel trunk, and set it on her desk in front of Lauren.

Lauren was stunned. No one ever sent her anything. She ran a finger over the box and found the lock unlatched. She looked at Naleen, who wasn't nicknamed Miss Nosy for nothing. "What's in it?"

"Oh . . ." Naleen's smile faltered. "I'm sure I wouldn't know, dear."

Right. Lauren nudged the opened lock and gave Naleen another look, not thrilled with this blatant invasion of her privacy.

Naleen had the good grace to look slightly abashed. "It's from Eleanor. The key came in the attached envelope with a note from your great-aunt's attorney."

Lauren froze and now eyed the box like it might be a bomb. "The box is from Eleanor? To me?"

"I think I'll give you a minute."

Lauren sank back into the chair in front of Naleen's desk, well aware that Naleen didn't actually leave. Which suited her just fine, because she didn't really want to be alone with this box. She'd done enough things alone in her life. And after today, she really needed a friend, even if it was a friend who'd just fired her while she was wearing a stupid Mother Goose costume.

Slowly, not at all sure she really wanted anything to

do with whatever contents the box held, she opened the envelope and pulled out the attorney's letter.

Dear Lauren,

Enclosed in the travel case you'll find some of your great-aunt's belongings from her brief stay in the advanced assisted facility where she passed. We're sending it all to you, her last living relative.

Including her remains.

Her urn is in the box. She did leave a request with me that you and your two partners take her to Hidden Hills, where she and her sister Ruth used to ice-skate in the winter. She wants you to go on April sixteenth, the date of Ruth's passing. She said Ruth would be waiting for her. They hadn't spoken in years, but it was Eleanor's greatest hope to be able to give her sister a piece of her mind in the afterlife.

Best of luck.

Lauren had stopped breathing. "Eleanor is . . . " She gulped. "In this box?"

"As well as some of her belongings," Naleen said. "She obviously loved you."

According to her dad, Eleanor hadn't ever had the

ability to love anyone or anything. The sole exception being the Last Chance Inn.

"Lauren? You all right?"

She wasn't sure. Oh wait, yes she was. She was sure she was *not* all right. "She wants us to scatter her ashes for her," she said slowly. "On April sixteenth. Which is . . ." Good God. "Tomorrow . . . ?" She looked up at Naleen. "How did that even happen?"

Naleen shrugged. "From what I understand, she gave the three of you a very purposeful date to be at the Last Chance Inn. She was a smart woman. Good at getting people to do what she wanted, when she wanted."

Lauren gingerly opened the lid of the box. Yep, that was an urn all right. She could feel the annoyance and impatience curling out from it, aimed right at her.

Tearing her gaze off the urn, she looked at the other things in the box. There was a clutch purse that looked as if it'd come straight out of the 1950s, and a beautiful antique diamond ring in a small black box that she recognized immediately.

It'd been Will and Alice's grandmother's ring, the very one Will had proposed to Lauren with. Dear God, she'd forgotten about it, and how Eleanor had come to have it. She felt herself flush because it wasn't a story she wanted to be reminded of in front of Nosy Naleen, especially since it involved Lauren's deep, dark secret. With shaking fingers, she put the ring in her own purse to give to Alice in a private moment when she was ready to explain it, and went back to the box's contents. There was an iPad, some jewelry, and a lipstick. The lid on the lipstick was a little loose, and oddly curious about the sort of shade Eleanor might have chosen—Evil Red?—she took the lid off, twisted it and . . . it started vibrating. Dear God.

It wasn't a lipstick.

Lauren dropped the small vibrator into the box like it was a hot potato and slammed the lid down. Horrified, she stared at the now vibrating box.

Naleen's eyes were wide with shock, her hands over her mouth.

Wow. Okay. The way she saw it, her new business partners should have to suffer this very bad no good day right along with her.

The box and its contents—*not* the getting fired from the best job she'd ever had. At the thought, her heart squeezed, but she shook her head. Nope. Now was not the time for a breakdown. She'd save that for when she knew how to handle the consequences.

Such as finding a new job to keep a roof over her head and food in the fridge. Because she really, *really* liked food in her fridge. Specifically dark chocolate with sea salt, because, sue her, but dark chocolate with sea salt fixed just about everything.

Chapter 8

Need
Alice—A new life.
Lauren—I second that, preferably in Bali.
Lauren—And also dark chocolate with sea salt.
Knox—this is for WORK-RELATED NEEDS
ONLY, LADIES!

Knox almost always got up early. It was a holdover from when he'd been a kid. He'd get up before the sun, check to make sure his mom was home and breathing, and then he'd walk or ride his bike the few miles to the lake. In summer, he'd swim or bodysurf for as many hours as he had. In the winter, when it was too cold to get in the frigid waters, he'd stand at the shoreline, with the swells lapping gently over the rocky sand, and look out at the mountains, which were the only sure thing in his life. It was there at the glorious blue lakeside where he'd learned to manage his emotions.

From the lake, he'd go to school, and then after that to the inn, where his mom worked as Eleanor's house-keeper. Eleanor gave him work too, doing whatever she needed, whatever it took to keep his and his mom's world together.

He'd failed at that, spectacularly. He'd been eighteen and just out of high school when she'd succumbed to alcohol poisoning. For years, he'd blamed himself, thinking if only he'd tried harder . . . But with some hindsight and the dubious honor of maturity, he knew no one could have saved her but herself.

When he'd left Sunrise Cove, he'd stayed in touch with Eleanor, visiting her whenever he could—though he'd not made time to stand at Lake Tahoe's edge, not once.

Deciding to remedy that, he got out of the ridicu-lously frilly bed. Yeah, he was still sleeping in the pink room. Alice had refused to switch with him, saying she was allergic to lace. If that was true, he'd eat the lace thong he'd caught a tantalizing glimpse of the other day when her jeans had slid to a dangerous, sexy low as she worked on the floorboards. "She's playing me," he told Pickle. "But I'm not playing back. I don't have a death wish. Time to get up." And doing his best to ignore the miles and miles of lace, he got up and dressed.

Pickle opened one eye, watching suspiciously from the foot of the bed.

"We're going for a run."

Pickle closed his eye.

"I will leave you here."

Pickle leaped off the bed. He wasn't fond of exercise in any form, but he had a serious case of FOMO and couldn't stand to be left behind.

They got to the lake just as dawn arrived and stood breathing heavily at the shoreline, Knox feeling vibrantly awake, Pickle plopping onto the sand.

Knox took in the deep azure-blue waters of one of the highest alpine lakes in the country and breathed in the almost unbearably familiar calm quiet. Just like always when he stood right here, his problems seemed so far away.

Pickle gave a startled "woo-woo" and took off after a gaggle of geese coming out of the water. With alarmed squawks, they scattered but regrouped quickly to begin stalking Pickle, flapping their wings at him in indignant anger.

Pickle dodged left and then right, trying to catch up with them, but they were smarter and stayed out of reach. Finally he sat, looking confused.

That was when the biggest goose came up behind him and bit him on the ass.

With a yelp, Pickle leaped straight up in the air, but by the time he came down, the goose was gone.

"Don't write checks you can't cash," Knox suggested.

When the sky was aglow with the sun's rays peeking over the tops of the rocky peaks, touching down on the glass-like lake, they headed back.

At the inn, he stopped at the mailbox because he was pretty sure no one had checked the mail in a couple of days. Normally Lauren did the chore, so he was surprised at the note taped to the outside.

Alice and/or Knox, but hopefully Knox because you won't laugh at me:

Inside is two days of mail being held hostage by a big fat hairy spider with googly eyes and a LOT of legs. Every time I try to reach in, he gives me the come-and-get-me gesture with two of those spindly legs. If one of you could convince him to move to a new home or brutally murder him, I'd so appreciate it.

Lauren

Knox opened the mailbox and pulled out the stack of mail. No big fat hairy spider with googly eyes and a lot of legs. He headed inside, dropped the mail on the table, filled Pickle's water bowl, fed him, then took a shower. He and Alice had fixed the circuit breakers three days ago now, and he'd discovered he could handle almost anything as long as he had hot showers. This morning, he happily stood under the hot steaming water for far longer than necessary before dressing and heading back to the kitchen and the coffemaker he'd bought the other day, needing to mainline some caffeine.

He was leaning against the counter doing exactly that when he heard Alice scream from the bathroom: "ARE YOU KIDDING ME?"

"Brace yourself," he warned Pickle.

Sure enough, Alice showed up in the kitchen doorway a moment later, wrapped in nothing but a towel and water droplets, her hair full of shampoo, the suds running down her face and shoulders, vanishing into the towel. "*You*," she ground out.

How the woman managed to irritate the hell out of him *and* turn him on all at the same time, he had no idea. "Looks like we need to add a bigger water heater to our list."

Not mollified in the slightest, she pointed at him. "*This is war*," she announced, and stomped off, leaving wet footprints on the wood floor.

Oh, good. War. "Careful," he called after her. "Wet wood can be really slippery—"

As he said the word, she indeed went slip-sliding and nearly fell onto her ass, but she caught herself *and* her towel.

Sometimes life was a bitch.

"*War*," she repeated at a higher volume this time.

Pickle whined, his heavy brow wrinkled in worry.

"Don't worry," Alice told him. "It's not you. *You* are adorable." Once again, she pointed at Knox. "You are not."

"Understood."

She adjusted her towel. "I'll be back after my cold shower. Oh, and there's a spider on top of the stack of mail. Don't let Lauren see it, she's more afraid of spiders than she is of dogs."

Knox turned, and yep, sure enough, a big, fat, hairy spider complete with googly eyes and a lot of legs sat on the mail on the kitchen table like it owned the place. *There you are.* "Right. I'll brutally murder it, right away."

Alice stared at him like he'd grown an extra head. "What is wrong with you? No murder. Relocate her, because maybe she's a mama. But if you want any peace in this house, take her far away from the house." Shaking her head, she started to walk away. "Oh, and we've got a leak in the ceiling of my bathroom."

When she was gone, Knox relocated the spider out in the field, then rinsed his mug, set it in the dishwasher, and snapped for Pickle. "You heard the woman. We'd better get to work."

Outside, he eyed the eaves. They appeared to be overloaded with dried pine needles and, given the droppings along the house, probably also field mice.

This wasn't a problem for him. He'd spent the past few years in literal hellholes. Being here was not only a piece of cake, it was also a reminder of where he'd come from. Eleanor had nourished his love of building things. She'd challenged him, saying, "Boy, I bet you can't fix those steps." Or "Fix the leaky kitchen sink" . . . and he'd figure it out.

The bottom line was that she'd given him a valuable skill, and a way to pull himself out of the gutter. She'd saved him, and there was only one way to repay her—save this inn. He was still standing there staring up at the roof when Alice came up next to him.

"What are we doing?" she asked.

He slid her an amused glance. "So we're speaking?"

"When required."

She'd braided her wet hair, which hung down her back. No makeup, torn-through-the-knees jeans, and a sweatshirt, scarf, and work boots, yet somehow she was the sexiest thing he'd ever seen.

"Wow," a woman said behind them. "The place looks just like it does on the show."

Knox and Alice turned in unison to find three women in their sixties, in various leisure wear and supportive athletic shoes, all of them phones up, snapping photos.

They each had a lanyard around their neck, their badges proudly claiming them as Last Chance Inn Fan Club Premiere Members.

"This is private land," Alice said. "You can't just come out here and start taking pictures."

"Oh, but they're for Last Chance's fan club's Instagram page," the first woman said. She beamed in her black-and-white polyester tracksuit. "I'm the president. We're based out of L.A., but we drove up here to get some pics. When we post them, all the other ladies are going to be so jealous."

The woman in the middle, wearing purple velour and matching lipstick, said, "We heard there might be a remake, filmed here. Are you two going to be the stars? You sure got the sexual chemistry down."

Knox slid an amused look to Alice. She narrowed

her eyes. "No," he said. "We're not actors, and there's no reboot happening, that's just a rumor."

"Bummer," the president said. "Do you think we could pretend you didn't tell us that last part and get a pic of you two?"

"Oh yes," the third musketeer said in migraine-inducing yellow terry cloth sweats. "And could you two stand closer together? And maybe kiss?"

"Seriously?" Alice asked. "We—"

Knox put a hand on her shoulder and leaned closer to the ladies. "We're the owners of the property, getting the inn ready for the reopening. If you want to post about that, we'd love to give you a pic or two."

Alice whipped her face to his, which he ignored, because the ladies squealed and had their phones back up and ready. He slid his arms around Alice and dipped her dramatically, pressing a chaste kiss to her cheek before bringing her upright again. He half expected her to knee him in the family jewels, or at least warn him to sleep with one eye open. He didn't expect her to dig her fingers into his biceps and close her eyes at the feel of his mouth to her soft skin like she enjoyed the touch.

When he brought her back up, she stared wide-eyed at him.

"More, more, more," the women chanted, practically vibrating with glee.

"That was plenty," Alice said tightly, stepping back from Knox.

"She's as grumpy as Eleanor Graham was," one of the ladies said cheerfully. "Love it."

"Now, Alda, we don't know. Look at her, maybe she just needs some carbs."

Alice opened her mouth, and Knox pulled her in tight against him, palming the back of her head and not so accidentally, smashing her face to his chest. "Okay, ladies, that's it," he said.

"You can bet your sweet ass that's it," Alice muttered into his shirt.

"Remember," he said, waving, "we open next month!"

"Well, isn't he the hottest thing since sliced bread," one of the three ladies said as they got into their car.

Knox was grinning as they drove off.

Alice shoved free. "Wow," she said.

Most definitely not a compliment. "You think you're ready to work now, or do you want to pander for some more future guests?"

"Are you saying you had no fun at all realizing how much this place means to people?"

"I'm saying the dip and kiss wasn't necessary."

"My apologies."

She narrowed her eyes. "You're not even a little bit sorry."

"Tell you what," he said. "Feel free to get even any-time you want."

"We're on the clock, funny guy. Tick-tock. Let's get on this. Paint, right?"

"We've got to handle the leak before we paint," he said.

She nodded.

He cocked his head, amused. "Did you just agree with me on something?"

"Don't get used to it."

He smiled. "I wouldn't dream of it."

"We need the ladder again. Tell me you didn't put it away."

"Of course I put it away," he said. "I never leave stuff out. But it's just leaning up against the side of the barn."

"Okay, *you* go get the ladder while I assess our situation."

"So you're going to avoid the barn the whole time you're here then."

She sucked in a breath but didn't ask him how he knew, just turned her head and stared at him with those whiskey see-all eyes. "Maybe."

He nodded, and when he didn't press, she looked surprised. "You're not going to tell me that's a stupid plan?"

He shrugged. "You're a big girl. You already know that."

This won him a very small, wry laugh, which felt a whole lot like winning the lottery. He and Pickle went and retrieved the ladder. The minute he set it against the side of the inn, Alice stripped off her scarf and sweatshirt and started climbing.

"Déjà vu," he said on a sigh.

"Look," she said, "I can get a look at the eaves and assess the situation. Because there's a lot of stuff coming up that I can't help you with, so I want to do everything I can to pull my weight."

He doubted she'd ever *not* pulled her weight, but before he could say so, her cell phone began vibrating on the ground next to the sweatshirt and scarf she'd tossed aside.

"Crap," she said, stopping halfway up the ladder. "Who is it?"

He looked at the readout. "Miguel."

She grimaced.

"Boyfriend?"

"Work," she said. "Answer on speaker so I can talk?"

"Yes, ma'am." Knox entered the four-digit code she rattled off and answered the call on speaker with, "Alice's phone."

There was a weighted pause. Then a gruff male voice. "Who's this?"

"Alice's phone," Knox repeated.

From above him, Alice rolled her eyes. "Miguel, it's me," she called. "What's up?"

"Oh, hey, darlin'," the voice said, softening, going flirtatious. "How's it going there? Ready to come home to Flagstaff yet?"

Knox looked at Alice in time to see her roll her eyes again. "I know I told you guys I'd be a month."

"Maybe you want to fly in for a visit then. Say this next weekend."

And maybe Knox should have accidentally disconnected the guy when he had the chance.

"Let me guess," Alice said dryly. "Steve or Eddie gave you overtime, and you've got a hot date lined up, so you want to foist your shift off on me."

"Come on, A, don't be like that. You know you're my first choice for a hot date. Only all you ever do is turn me down. Who's the guy? The one who answered?"

Alice met Knox's gaze. "Take the overtime, Miguel. You need the money, since you keep spending it like it's candy. Tell me you miss me and say goodbye."

"I miss you. We all miss you."

"Yeah, because I'm the only one who knows how to run the place," Alice said. "Listen, I've gotta go, but remind Eddie he owes you from that time he got so drunk on the plane home from Vegas, he couldn't work for two days. That should clear you so you can go on your date."

Miguel laughed. "You're right. Thanks." He paused. "You okay, A? Cuz me and Eddie could road trip up to visit."

"Wow, you really do miss me. But yeah, I'm good. Oh, and Miguel?" There was a smile in her voice now when she said, "I miss you guys too." Then she jerked a chin toward Knox, which he assumed meant please disconnect the call.

Alice started climbing the ladder again without another word. Apparently, they weren't going to talk about it. At the top of the ladder, she peered into the rain gutter. "Huh."

"Need help?"

"No, Fort Knox, I do not."

"I asked you not to call me that."

"No, you most definitely did not ask. You commanded. Hold on, I just gotta get past all the pine needles to find the problem."

"The leak's about six inches to your right."

"Is that real inches or penis inches?" She chortled at the grimace on his face and reached into the gutter. Coming up with a handful of pine needles, she tossed them down, barely missing him.

"Hey."

"Oops." She sent him a smart-ass smile that he secretly loved. "Sorry."

He pulled a pine needle from his hair. "Liar."

She grinned, then reached in for another handful and gasped, nearly tumbling off the ladder.

Not sure what the problem was, he raced up the ladder behind her to keep her from falling as she exclaimed, "A mouse!"

He was behind her now, pressed up against her, caging her in his arms.

She pointed across the roof. "It ran off."

"It's okay. It was probably just a field mouse. They're destructive, but meek. He won't hurt you, and I've got traps I can set."

"Oh, I know *she* won't hurt me." Her eyes narrowed to little slits. "And you're *not* murdering a field mouse."

Knowing better than to pick this hill to die on, he nodded. "Not murdering. *Relocating.* They're humane traps."

"No. You can't separate families!"

He paused, trying to decide how to approach this and still get his way. "Pretty sure our guests won't want to share the inn with mice, Alice."

She opened her mouth, no doubt to argue with him

about something, but then she suddenly paused. "Tell me that's a hammer in your pocket."

"It's whatever you want it to be."

She narrowed her eyes and he pulled the hammer from the tool belt on his hips, the one that had gotten caught between them.

With a snort, she snatched the hammer. "I've got this."

He backed down the ladder, but oddly, he didn't want to. Pressed up against her, he'd felt the same electric shock he'd felt standing on the washing machine with her. Interesting, and he wondered if she felt it too. Deciding that he didn't need that intel, he just watched her work.

"I see a problem," she called down a few minutes later. She'd used the handle of the hammer to clear the rest of the drain pipe of pine needles. "It's an ice dam from that storm the other day. But also, I think we need to divert the water away from here. We did this once down in Flagstaff with a sheet of metal." With that, she climbed down and turned to face him. "How did I do?"

He had to smile. "You know exactly how you did. I'm impressed."

"The things you learn when you need money," she said with a small laugh, as if uncomfortable with the compliment. The laugh had sounded a little rusty, and he realized that he hadn't heard her laugh much, if at all, but when she smiled, it lit up her whole face and transformed her completely.

"Do you need help with the ice dam?" she asked.

Did he? No. Did he want her company? Yes. So they went to the hardware store for the metal, then broke apart the ice and attached the sheet of metal in place.

After, he went to work on the downstairs bathroom. He had to demo so he could replace the floor, countertop, sink, and toilet over the next week. As he worked, Alice dragged out the pile of decimated bathroom. He learned she could swear like a sailor, and so creatively that he actually catalogued a few new oaths. After the demo, he took over cleaning up the mess, and Alice vanished.

He ended up in the kitchen late in the afternoon, starving. He'd hit up the grocery store a few nights back, picking up what he considered the essentials. He was getting ready to cook himself something to eat when Alice appeared as well, dusty from head to toe.

"I cleaned off the show sets," she said.

"For Lauren?"

She sighed. "Yeah."

Lauren had been adamant that they showcase the sets, that guests would want to take pictures of themselves on them. Knox agreed with her. He just found it funny that Alice always did Lauren's bidding, even when not speaking to her. Funny and touching, because at the end of the day, it was obvious that Alice cared about Lauren, deeply. But probably if he pointed that out she'd kill him with his own hammer.

Alice went straight to a cabinet. She had also made a store run, but near as Knox could tell, it was mostly fast, easy convenience food. She opened a bag of chips, poured each of them a bowl.

"Don't get used to this level of service," she said. "And just so you know, if I have to open it, pour it, or stir it, it's homemade."

He laughed, aware of her watching as he took ingredients from the fridge and then put together food in under ten minutes. She actually moaned when he set a plate in front of her. Hash browns, eggs, sausage, toast.

"I've died and gone to heaven," she said.

"Don't be impressed, it was a survival thing. And breakfast's the only thing I can make."

She looked up at him, studying his face for a moment. "You cooked for you and your mom?"

So she knew a little something about him too. Seemed fair. "Yes."

She nodded. "Childhoods suck."

He laughed wryly, liking her attitude and the fact she didn't feel sorry for herself. He watched as she inhaled the food he'd made, feeling oddly satisfied at her letting him feed her. "You're different today," he said. "You're different without Lauren here."

She froze, fork halfway to her mouth. "What does that mean?"

"You're less on edge. More at ease." And . . . sure of herself, he thought. So sure of herself. It was sexy as hell.

She shrugged. "I guess I'm getting used to being back." She paused again. Hesitated. "Not all blasts from the past are good ones, you know?"

"Very much so." He cocked his head. "You ever going to tell me about you and Lauren?"

"It's a very long story."

"I like long stories," he said.

"I . . ." She shut her mouth and looked away. "I'm not ready to talk about it."

He nodded. "I can understand that."

She looked relieved, then gave him a side eye. "Did we just agree on something else?"

"Go figure." He scooped up some food. "So you learned construction in Arizona?"

"Actually, it started with Eleanor," she said, a small smile on her lips, maybe at the memories.

Not much surprised him, but this did. "Eleanor? She used to make me do all the stuff around the house. She said she didn't know how."

Alice laughed again, less rusty now, an almost musical

sound that had him smiling back. "She enjoyed playing the evil queen, but the truth was, she collected lost souls and liked to make sure they were capable before she let them back out into the wild."

As he well knew. "So once you were released into the wild, where did you go?"

Her gaze was soft, inward, her expression reflective. "You first. You left when I was fourteen."

"I went to a trade school in Seattle," he said. "I didn't learn until later that Eleanor had secured me a sponsorship, which she made me pay back by volunteering for three months with an organization that rebuilds communities after natural disasters all over the world. I stayed a year. From there, I ended up going into business with two of the guys I'd been working with."

She smiled. "She was a sneaky, manipulative one. Do you like what you do?"

"Love it," he said and pointed at her. It was her turn.

She shrugged. "I bounced around, doing different jobs here and there. Nothing as exciting as you. I wasn't nearly as smart, and rebuked Eleanor's efforts to get me into college."

"You also left mechanics in your rearview mirror," he said quietly.

"Maybe I just grew up."

"That you most definitely did. Right nice, too."

She snorted. "If you only knew about the stupid crush I had on you."

"Oh, I knew."

Her mouth dropped open. "No way. We never talked. And I was *stealth*. The stealthiest of stealth. The queen of the stealthiest of stealth."

"Oh, you mean when you used to hide in the loft and watch me work?"

She grimaced. "Fine. So I liked when you used to chop wood. You'd get hot and take off your shirt." She slid him a sly smile. "Teenage Alice thanks you."

"Good to know." He cocked his head. "And grown-up Alice?"

She bit her lower lip while looking at his mouth. "She's . . . undecided."

What an adorably sexy liar. "You're flirting with me again."

She met his gaze. "Am I?"

He smiled. "Yeah. But you're also just playing with me right now. You let me know when you mean it."

She sucked in a breath but said nothing, clearly knowing the value of silence.

But he knew it too, so he simply looked right back at her. As it had several times now, the air seemed to crackle and pop around them. "Yeah, that pesky electrical problem is most definitely us."

This had her taking in another deep breath. "What's between you and Nikki?"

Out of the blue, but a fair question. "Nada."

She studied him, trying to read him. He hoped like hell he was broadcasting his truth, which was that he felt currently . . . messed up, but not because of Nikki.

He was mourning Eleanor. And also mourning both the best and worst time of his life. When he'd run into Nikki the other day, it should've been a gut bomb, but instead all he felt was an echo of a long-ago hurt. And if that wasn't confusing enough, he was feeling sparks for the woman who used to be a girl, running around here with a ponytail and dirt smudged on her cheek. In fact, she still wore a ponytail and had dirt on her jaw.

"If you ever want to talk about it," she said quietly, "I'm a pretty good listener."

"Noted." He held her gaze. "And same."

Her mouth curved in an ironic smile. "*Noted.*"

They were both still staring at each other when they heard the front door open and Lauren yell "Hey!"

Alice jumped a foot back from Knox, as if they'd been doing something naughty. Since they hadn't been, it meant the naughtiness had been all in her mind, which he liked. A lot.

Brushing past him, Alice headed to the living room

and he followed, both of them breaking into a run when Lauren suddenly screamed.

"What's wrong?" Alice demanded, pushing Knox out of the way to get to Lauren first.

She was standing on the foyer table in . . . a Mother Goose costume? And her feet were tap-dancing frantically. "A rat! It's under the table!"

"And there's a Mother Goose on top of our table," Alice said, stopping short.

"I'm not kidding!" Lauren yelled.

Before Knox could move, Alice got down on all fours and looked. "Aw, it's not a rat. It's a baby field mouse. Looks like the one Knox and I met earlier."

"What the—"

"Shh, you're scaring her." Alice came back up, hands cradled. She opened them just enough to reveal a black mouse the size of a quarter.

"*Oh my God!*"

"Shh! Minnie Mouse isn't used to screaming. Or a five-foot-two Mother Goose." Alice then carefully walked the mouse outside.

"She touched the mouse," Lauren said to Knox, not moving from her perch. "She just picked it right up in her bare hands. Is she crazy?"

Yes. But in the *very* best of ways. "Here." He gave her a hand down just as Alice came back in, sans Minnie.

"I set her in the flower planter right next to where we saw the droppings earlier," she reported.

He smiled at her and she did a double take. Note to self: try smiling more often.

Lauren strode straight to the lists on the living room wall, her Mother Goose posture one of indignation. She stopped before the Need list, blew a feather away from her face, and wrote: mousetraps.

Alice walked up to the wall, took the Sharpie, and . . . crossed it off. "We already know about the mice and are handling it," she said and smiled. "There. See what I did? I used Ground Rule number three and communicated."

"Since we're on the subject of Ground Rule number three," Lauren said, "there's something I need to tell you guys."

"You're allergic to mice as well as dogs?" Alice asked.

"You're not funny, and no."

"Is it about why you're in a Mother Goose costume? And you're seriously molting, by the way." Alice swiped a feather from midair. "Is this some sort of role-play thing?"

"What is wrong with you?" Lauren asked. "I'm the Story Time Lady at the library."

"That was my second guess," Alice said.

Lauren sighed, as if greatly tried. Knox understood the sentiment.

"I'm trying to tell you something," Lauren said.

Knox turned to her. "If this is about the yarn you sneaked into the cart, I already saw."

Lauren paused. "I didn't buy any yarn."

"Well, someone did," Knox said. "And it sure as hell wasn't me." He paused. "Not that there's anything wrong with knitting or anything."

Next to him, Alice shifted.

He looked at her and went brows up. "*You?*"

"Fine, I don't look like the sort of woman who knits, I get it!" She tossed up her hands.

"Wait," Lauren said. "You knit?"

Alice glared at them both. "*So?*"

"I just can't believe the badass tomboy knits. You hate stuff like that."

Alice crossed her arms. "You're standing there in a goose costume and you want to talk about the fact that I knit? And I'm not badass. You're just jealous because I'm . . ." She appeared to be searching for the right word. "Adventurous."

"Hey," Lauren said. "I'm adventurous too."

"Not a single day in your life."

Lauren looked at Knox, who gave an apologetic smile. "I didn't think you were either."

"Ha!" Lauren pointed at them both. "Shows how much you know! I just signed up for zip-lining!"

Now it was Alice who looked shocked. "You did?"

"Yes! Even though on the company's website, the lead guy was in sandals. So there! Tackling *two* fears at the same time!" Lauren looked pleased with herself. "Which means that now we're *both* adventurous." She fingered the scarf around Alice's neck. "I guess the knitting explains this thing."

Alice's eyes narrowed. "What's wrong with my scarf?"

They all looked at the variegated blue scarf around her neck. It was uneven, narrow in some spots and thick in others, and the stitches seemed mismatched.

"It's crooked," Lauren said.

"Said the woman in a Mother Goose costume," Alice fired back.

"Give it up about the costume!" There was something in Lauren's expression suddenly, Knox realized, something that looked suspiciously like grief, but it was gone in a blink. "Long story," she finally said.

"Yeah, well, apparently there's a lot of those floating around," Alice said, then hesitated, as if seeing the same thing Knox did. "Are *you* okay?"

"*Dandy,*" Lauren snapped.

Alice glanced at Knox, then back to Lauren. "I mean,

it seems like a nice time for a long story. I love long stories."

Lauren snorted. "*Not a single day in your life.*"

"Fine." Alice tossed up her hands. "But for your information, the scarf's *supposed* to be crooked. It gives it a homemade look."

Lauren opened her mouth to say something, but in the silence, the box on the table with her purse seemed to be . . . *vibrating?*

"Is that a bomb?" Alice asked.

"Yes, but not the kind you think." Lauren swallowed hard. "And I'm not talking about it until I have a bag of chips. The mesquite barbeque chips on the kitchen counter."

"Those are mine," Alice said. "And you looked at the ingredients and said nothing in there was fit for public consumption, and that you'd die before you touched them."

Pickle trotted into the room and stopped short in front of the vibrating box. The hair at the scruff of his neck stood straight up and he growled low in his throat.

Lauren moaned and covered her eyes with her hands.

"Seriously," Knox said. "What's in there?"

"Chips first!" Lauren yelled and stomped off to the kitchen.

"Quick," Alice said. "Get your keys, we gotta go."

Knox blew out a breath. "You ate all the chips, didn't you?"

"Days ago," she admitted.

"Just admit it."

"Are you crazy? You don't know what she's like when she's hangry."

They heard a muffled scream of frustration from the kitchen, but before they could make a run for it, Lauren was back, looking a little bit like an addict in need of a fix. She pointed at Alice. "I will get even."

"I'll get another bag," Alice promised cajolingly while backing up slowly.

"Now?" Lauren asked hopefully.

"The box first," Alice said.

Lauren sighed. "Yeah, you're right."

"I am?"

Lauren moved to the table and looked down at the box like maybe it was a coiled rattlesnake. "It was delivered to my work. It's Eleanor."

"What did she do?" Alice asked.

"No," Lauren said. "It's *Eleanor*. In the box."

Alice just stared at her. Knox joined in on the staring. "Excuse me?"

"Her urn's in there. We have strict instructions to take her up to Hidden Hills on Ruth's death date—which is *tomorrow*, I might add—and scatter her ashes there. I guess it's where Eleanor and her sister, Ruth, used to go and ice-skate. She's hoping to haunt Ruth for the rest of eternity."

Knox found himself speechless.

Alice appeared the same.

"I mean, if it'd been left up to me," Lauren said, "I'd have set her in the small cemetery on the far northeast corner of the property. I noticed some lovingly tended graves there, and it's actually quite peaceful. There's a gorgeous headstone with the name Chester on it. He must have been incredibly important to her."

Knox smiled, and Alice choked on a laugh.

Lauren narrowed her eyes at them. "What?"

"Chester was Eleanor's favorite golden retriever," Alice said. "That area you're talking about is a pet cemetery, because the dogs she had over the years were the most important things to Eleanor."

Lauren stared at her. "More important than people?"

"Yep," Alice said, with actual fondness.

Lauren shook her head. "What I don't know is why I got the box. We didn't have a relationship."

"Look," Alice said. "I love Eleanor, but she should have done better by you. Not contacting you, even after your dad's passing, was just wrong."

Lauren drew a deep breath but didn't speak.

Knox didn't understand how Eleanor could have

treated Lauren that way. "She never contacted you at all? That's not cool."

Lauren bit her lower lip.

"What?" Alice asked her.

"She tried to call me after my dad died. I . . . didn't pick up." Lauren grimaced. "I should have. I know that, but I didn't. I couldn't. I was still pretty messed up . . ."

"I understand," Alice said.

Lauren looked touchingly surprised, and after an awkward beat, changed the subject. "Along with the urn, there're also some . . . um, personal belongings."

"And the ticking?" Knox asked, looking at the box.

"Oh, that's one of those things you've got to see for yourself." Lauren picked up the box and carried it to one of the couches. She sat and put the box on the coffee table in front of her, waiting for them to join her.

Alice sat across from her, the coffee table between them, looking suspicious. Knox remained standing.

Lauren gestured for Alice to open the box.

Alice leaned forward and gingerly flipped it open.

Lauren reached in and pulled out the urn, setting it on the coffee table.

The box was still vibrating.

Alice and Knox leaned in to look at the same time, then recoiled in unison from the sight of a tube of lipstick having a seizure in the box.

Lauren cackled in sheer glee. "Yep. That was worth the price of admission."

Knox closed his eyes tight, trying hard not to let any thoughts go through his head. He failed. "You realize I can never unsee that, right?"

"Is someone going to turn it off?" Alice finally asked.

"Not it," Knox said.

Lauren held up her hands. She pointed at Alice. "She's the one on the clock."

"Wow," Alice said. "And we're *all* on the clock, remember?"

"We could just let the batteries die," Knox suggested.

"Oh for godsakes. Give me the damn thing." Alice yanked the vibrator out and turned it off. "I'm amending the open communication rule. I don't want to talk about this. *Ever.* The rule should state we only communicate about things pertaining to the inn's renovation. *Period.*"

Knox couldn't stop staring at it. "I really thought that was her lipstick."

"You mean you've seen it before?" Alice asked, sounding boggled.

"She used to tell me to go get a twenty from her purse." He grimaced and ran a shaky hand down his face. "I'm officially scarred for life."

Lauren nodded, looking both grim and grimly amused. "At least we're even."

Chapter 9

THE GROUND RULES

1. No tears.
2. This is about Eleanor.
3. Open, honest conversations with actual words.
   DAILY—as long as it doesn't violate rule #1.
4. Do not kill your partners.
5. No nicknames.
6. No one sleeps with anyone.
7. No ties, emotional or physical, period.

Alice would have enjoyed the look of torture on Knox's face a lot more if she hadn't suspected she was wearing the same one.

Lauren reached into the box for the next item. A pale pink cardigan with pearl buttons. "Huh," she said. "Cute."

Alice felt a laugh burst out of her chest. "That's because you have one just like it. You and Eleanor have the same love for all things pink."

Lauren blinked, as if just realizing that was actually true, and not looking thrilled to find she had something else in common with her great-aunt. Visibly shaking that off, she leaned forward and pulled out a delicate gold necklace with a small diamond-encrusted heart charm.

It made Alice's heart constrict. "I never saw her without this necklace. Never. Walter gave it to her, but she liked to say it was too pretty to blame the necklace for his behavior, so she kept it."

Alice was looking at Lauren, so she saw her jerk with surprise at the name Walter.

"Who's Walter?" Knox asked.

"My grandpa," Lauren said softly. "He and Eleanor were together when he fell in love with her sister, Ruth—my grandma."

"Walter was the love of Eleanor's life," Alice told him. "She never really recovered from losing him. But when Walter and Ruth were killed in a car accident, Eleanor took in their two-year-old son as her own. Evan."

"My dad," Lauren said. "Who was raised by a woman who resented his presence from day one."

Alice frowned. "Not as Eleanor told it. She loved Evan, but when he turned eighteen, he walked away from her and broke her heart all over again." She shook her head, unable to imagine the pain. Or, given her own life and what she'd been through, maybe she *could* imagine. "I always admired how no matter what knocked her down—betrayal, TV show cancellations, the inn closing—she always picked herself up and kept going."

Lauren was staring at the necklace with a whole boatload of emotion spilling from her gaze, so Alice handed it over.

"Can you really pick yourself up?" Lauren finally asked in a very quiet, very serious voice.

"Are you kidding?" Alice let out a rough laugh. "I've picked myself up so many times I've lost count. And you *know* who taught me how to do that."

"But . . ." Lauren looked so conflicted that Alice actually ached for her. "My dad always told me she was so hard on him, so unbending. She ruined his childhood."

"She left you a third of this place," Alice said. She tried really hard not to judge a person's choices, especially having made some questionable ones of her own. Plus, she'd been privy to a very different Eleanor from the one the rest of the world knew. Yes, the woman had been deeply flawed. And okay, also obstinate and mercurial, but for those few she chose to love, she'd go to the ends of the earth without hesitation. But as far as Alice was concerned, the misconception of Eleanor's character wasn't on Lauren. It was on Lauren's dad and Eleanor herself. Alice peered into the box for the next item. "There's an iPad. Anything on it?"

"I don't know," Lauren said. "I raced out of the library with the vibrating box and came straight here."

Knox flipped open the iPad cover and swiped on the home screen. "It's dead."

Lauren pulled a portable battery charger—in a pink case—from her purse and handed it over.

Knox plugged it in and swiped again. "No passcode. How unlike her."

"Maybe she wanted Lauren to be able to get into it," Alice said.

Lauren snorted. "Right."

"Maybe you could give her the benefit of the doubt until proven otherwise," Alice suggested.

Lauren didn't look convinced, but she didn't argue further. Still, when Knox tried to hand her the iPad, she shook her head.

So Knox began to swipe through it himself. "There're a few apps. The usual, nothing added though." Then he paused. "Huh."

"Huh what?" Alice asked worriedly.

"First of all, there's a doc with information on the inn."

"More words," Alice said, losing patience. Hell, who was she kidding? She had no patience to start with, never had.

"It looks like Eleanor planned on hiring a hotel management firm to run this place," Knox said. "She hadn't signed on the dotted line yet, but the info is all here. They'd staff and run the inn for us, so we wouldn't have to sell. We could keep it as a business venture."

They all stared at each other.

"Why in the world wouldn't the attorney have mentioned that to us?" Lauren asked. "Knowing this would've given us all peace of mind."

"Oh my God." Alice could picture Eleanor up on a cloud high above laughing her ass off. Or who knows, maybe from the top of a fire and brimstone mountain. Shaking her head, she plopped back against the couch cushions. "Damn, she was sneaky. And manipulative, even to the very end."

"I don't get it," Lauren said.

"The obligation of the inn being on our shoulders got us all here." Alice looked at her two partners. "Be honest, if we'd known about the hotel manage-ment firm from the start, one or more of us might've chosen not to come at all, and instead let them handle everything."

Lauren slowly raised her hand. "I'd still have come. For curiosity's sake, if nothing else."

"I'd still be here," Knox said.

They both looked at Alice.

"Look, the only question that really matters now is, what do we do? We could ignore, finish the renovations, and just sell, as we planned."

"Or," Lauren said, "we pay the hotel management firm to take over for us after the renovations are done. Let them handle the reopening and the day-to-day operations, and we keep the inn as an income."

Alice felt her stomach sink to her toes. In a vote right now she'd be outnumbered, though they were kind enough to not say it as they all just looked at each other.

"We have time for that decision," Knox finally said quietly, going back to the iPad. "There's nothing in her email inbox, sent, or trash folders. Either they've been wiped, or she never used the app— Hold on. There's a draft folder with emails that were never sent."

"To . . . ?" Alice asked.

"Her sister, Ruth. And every email has one of *our* names in the subject line, except the first one."

"*What?*" Alice and Lauren asked in disbelieved unison.

Knox tried to hand Lauren the iPad. "This iPad came to you first. You should be the one to read them."

"No."

Alice turned to her, knowing that while her own default mood was stubborn, Lauren's was fear. Of everything. But Alice couldn't help but feel that in this case, Lauren needed to be pushed through the fear to face the past. The *real* past. "Lauren—"

"I can't," she whispered, looking stricken.

Alice looked at Knox. "Read the first letter."

Knox nodded and began to read out loud:

Dear Sister to Whom I'm Not Speaking Even Though You're Dead,

And it's a damn shame you're dead too, because I could really use your advice right about now. I'm not going to live forever and I'm thinking about what I'll do with Granddad's inn. I know you got his money and I got the property, and I've always been grateful for that. I also know you probably don't give two flying hoots, but I really do wish I had your ear, just so I could do the opposite of what you suggest. After you ruined my life with your selfishness, I cut myself off from others. But somehow, in spite of that, I've let three people become family to me—even though at least one of them has no idea. So I'm leaving the inn to them. Huh. Look at that. I didn't need your opinion after all.

Signed, The Way Better Graham Sister

When Knox finished reading, there was a beat of stunned silence. Alice didn't know about the others, but she was way too choked up to speak. She'd known Eleanor considered her family, but it was sure good to hear it. Given the look on Knox's face, he felt the same. She could only hope that Lauren realized that Eleanor's love language had been actions. Leaving Lauren a third of this place had definitely been a show of love.

"What a crock of bull-pucky," Lauren finally said. "She never even spoke to me, much less treated me like family."

Alice drew a steadying breath, trying hard to sound even, but suddenly she was both missing Eleanor and yet also furious with her for not telling Lauren about her own past. "She was trying to honor you and your dad's wishes to stay away from you."

Lauren looked surprised. "What?"

"Apparently after your dad made some poor investments and Eleanor wouldn't bail him out again, he told her to stay away from the both of you. That you didn't want to see or talk to her either."

Lauren blinked. "Again? What do you mean bail him out *again*?"

"I'm actually not sure," Alice said slowly. "But I got the impression that years and years ago, he had a habit of making bad investments and she'd bailed him out a bunch of times before. He said that you and he didn't want her sticking her nose in your lives at all. Ever. She didn't like to talk about it, but I think she resigned herself to only watching you from afar, and you said she tried to contact you after your dad's passing."

"But . . . why didn't he ever tell me any of this?" She looked at Alice. "Why didn't you ever tell me any of this? We were best friends. Unless we weren't."

Alice closed her eyes for a beat at the wealth of pain in Lauren's voice. "It wasn't my place to tell you, but I did try a few times. You never wanted to talk about her—"

Standing up, Lauren turned her back on them, hugging herself. "Well, guess what? I still don't."

"There are more email drafts," Knox said. "We should read them."

"Maybe," Lauren said, hugging herself. "But not now."

"Yeah." Knox snapped the case closed. "We could

probably use some breathing room between them. Maybe we do one every night that we're all here together, after work."

Alice nodded.

They both looked at Lauren. She grimaced. "Yeah. Okay."

Knox stood up. "I'm going to take out Pickle." He turned to go, then pivoted back. "But I really hope you two figure your shit out in a way that Eleanor and Ruth never managed to do." And with that, he walked out of the living room, Pickle on his heels.

A minute later, they heard the back door open and then shut.

Lauren went to the wall, where she wrote Ground Rule 8:

Read Eleanor's emails together.

Then, without another word, she also walked out.

"Great," Alice said to nobody. "I'll just be here fixing this inn up all by my lonesome in order to regain my freedom."

Chapter 10

Dear Horrid Sister,

In case you were wondering, I'm still dying. Apparently, I'm just doing it really slowly. I just wanted you to know I'm still leaving this place to the three people who deserve it the most, including your granddaughter.

Signed, The Nice Sister (okay, so nice might be the wrong word . . .)

Alice couldn't fall asleep to save her life, probably because she knew what the day would bring. By mutual decision, the three of them were going to get up at dawn and go to Hidden Hills with Eleanor.

The dawn part hadn't been by mutual decision.

Knox had decreed it so, saying that was the best time to put Eleanor to rest. Late last night, he'd sent out a text telling them to be ready to go by five.

In the morning.

Dread filled every single corner of Alice's heart and soul. So much so that she'd decided to ignore the decree.

A few minutes before five, her overhead light came on, blinding her.

"Time to go," Knox's gruff morning voice said.

She fumbled around, searching for the handy, dandy baseball bat she usually kept with her.

"What are you looking for?" he asked, leaning against her doorjamb, appearing to enjoy her morning stupor.

"My baseball bat, but I left it in Stella."

He actually dared to flash a grin. A sexy grin. She solved that problem by closing her eyes.

"Who's the morning person now?" he asked smugly.

Eyes still closed, she pointed in the direction of his smug-ass voice and said slash yelled, "*Get out!*"

"Five minutes."

Since he wasn't the boss of her, she pulled the blanket over her head. A moment later, she heard the front door open and then voices. Knox and Lauren. Of course, Lauren had arrived like a good girl, right on time.

Suck-up.

Grumbling, Alice shoved herself into some clothes, secured her wild and crazy hair in a ponytail, and then brushed her teeth. "Good enough," she told her exhausted-looking reflection in the bathroom mirror. "Just go get it over with."

Easier said than done. She tended to avoid funerals like the plague. Not that she'd been to many. Her grandma's, but she'd been three and didn't remember anything about it other than her dad had told her she'd cried all the way through it. Not because of her grandma's passing, which she hadn't been old enough to really understand, but apparently because she couldn't blow out the pretty candles in the church.

Years later, as a young teen, she'd gone to a funeral with her dad when a fellow racer had flipped his car and died on impact. Her dad had sat there stoically, head bent over his folded hands, eyes closed, looking devastated, never making a sound or shedding a tear. But the moment the minister had started the eulogy, Alice had lost it, sobbing big, ugly tears that she couldn't control, no matter how hard her dad hugged her. She just hadn't been able to get it together. She'd been politely asked to wait outside.

Eleanor had once asked her to escort her to a friend's funeral. Alice hadn't known the woman. Had never even met her, but right on cue she'd sobbed through the whole thing. She couldn't really say why, other than everything about the experience made her feel unbearably sad to the depths of her soul.

And then there'd been Will's funeral. She'd pregamed with some pilfered anxiety meds from Eleanor's medicine cabinet. She'd barely survived it. Once again her uncontrollable sobs had been loud and embarrassing, but it was, after all, her brother's funeral, so no one evicted her that time.

She'd offered to go to Lauren's dad's funeral, but he'd left a request for no services at all. Good thing, since they were her kryptonite.

This isn't a funeral, she told herself. Like Evan, Eleanor hadn't wanted any sort of service or celebration of life, nothing. She'd put it in writing, and no one dared cross her, not in life, and certainly not in death.

Alice made it down the stairs to find the place empty, and for one hopeful second, she thought she'd gotten lucky and they'd left without her.

Then she heard them on the porch.

"Nice of you to finally join us," Knox said when she came out the front door. "Who's got Eleanor?"

They all looked at each other's empty hands.

For some reason Alice found this hysterically funny and she started laughing. And then couldn't stop.

"Inappropriate laughing is her coping mechanism,"

Lauren told Knox. She looked at Alice. "The last person ready has to get the dearly departed."

Knox nodded. "It's the rules."

She was so *never* going to secretly lust after him again. "I hate you both." She went back inside, picked up the surprisingly heavy urn, then stomped onto the porch again. "We're doing this at the ass-crack of dawn because . . . ?"

Knox shrugged. "From the stories I've heard, the little lake always froze over, but no authorities ever checked it out or cleared it for skating. As a result, Eleanor and Ruth's parents thought it was too dangerous and forbid them from skating there."

"Let me guess," Lauren said. "That didn't stop them."

"They used to go early in the morning, before school," Knox said.

Alice found a small smile. "Fine. Let's do this. Hopefully Ruth's spirit is ready for the incoming." She headed toward Stella.

When she realized no one was following her, she turned and lifted her hands. Well, one hand, since the other was holding on to Eleanor.

"We're walking like Eleanor and Ruth used to do," Knox said. "It's actually not far if we go out the back of the property. A mile and a half tops."

"Driving would be so much easier," she said with what she thought was great diplomacy. "Stella will love the road up there."

"Did you fix that noise she makes yet?" Lauren asked.

"Or fill her up with gas?" Knox asked.

So . . . they walked. Knox took the heavy urn as they headed to the far south end of the property, then climbed over the fence at the same place Alice had climbed over it for years and years. They walked a single-track trail she knew better than the back of her hand.

It was indeed a mile and a half to get to the very small lake. Knox wore threadbare Levi's and, maybe in deference to the morning chill, a long-sleeved black T-shirt instead of short sleeves, stretched taut over his broad shoulders, which Alice was absolutely not staring at. Nope, her eyes were too busy taking in his ass. He moved with easy efficiency and a long, loose-limbed stride that was both sexy and addictive to watch.

Lauren was in a navy-blue long-sleeved sweater dress, thick matching tights, and pretty black boots that were not meant for the trail. She walked with a carefulness that said she was far more used to walking in the library, and had spent little time out in the wild. And yet she pulled off the whole thing with absolutely zero dramatics, managing to look adorably cute as she made her way along.

Alice didn't feel adorable or cute. She sure as hell didn't feel sexy.

She felt . . . nervous.

Already, her chest was tight. Her hands clammy. Her throat turning. *If you cry,* she told herself sternly, *zero cookies for a week.*

No, *a month!!!* "Is it too early for alcohol?"

Lauren handed her a thermos.

"Wow, I'm impressed," Alice said.

"It's coffee."

"That was my second choice." She drank and waited for the sweet kick of caffeine to hit.

The sky got lighter the closer they got. A storm was brewing off to the west.

No one spoke. It was just as well. They were all huffing a little bit when the trail led them around a thick grove of trees and . . . to the water. Winter had obviously been light this year. Normally in April there'd still be large drifts of snow to wade through to get to the water's edge, and possibly still some ice covering the lake.

There was very little snow, and no ice. Just a cool, clear, glorious sunrise coming up in the east, the skies streaked with shades of purple and blue, while the tall pines swayed gently to a symphony of birds, insects, and the wind.

They stopped at the water's edge, side by side, silent. Alice sighed. "Let's just do this."

Knox looked at Lauren. "Do you have anything you want to say?"

Lauren shook her head.

"Okay, then—" Knox started to say, but Lauren spoke at the same time. "Actually—" She grimaced. "Sorry."

"Don't be." Knox removed the lid of the urn. "Say whatever you'd like."

Lauren drew a deep breath and looked skyward. "Grandma Ruth . . ." She paused. "Hi. I'm sorry I never got to know you." Her eyes got a little misty. "I really hope you're not here. I hope instead you're somewhere with a good book and a glass of wine, so that Eleanor can't yell at you."

After a moment, when it became clear she wasn't going to say anything else, Knox opened his mouth to speak, but once again Lauren went to say something at the same time.

"I'm sorry," she said. "Again."

Knox let out a very quiet laugh. "Get it all out, Pink. Take your time. Just tell us when you're done."

Lauren nodded, and drew another deep breath

before looking at the urn. "So, um, it's me, Lauren. Your grandniece. I'm really not sure why you left me a third of your estate, but I promise to try and live up to it." She paused. "I'm not going to pretend to understand what you were thinking. But that won't stop me from saying thank you for trusting me with what appears to have meant the most to you in life. I want you to know that in spite of everything, I'll do whatever is needed to fulfill your final wishes. In return, all I'm asking is that you please be nice to my grandma and my dad up there. And . . ." She closed her eyes. "Go in peace." She then nodded at Knox and took a step away. "That's all. I'm good now, thank you." She wiped a single delicate, perfect teardrop from her cheek.

And . . . Alice burst into messy tears. She felt both Lauren and Knox turn to her, but she shook her head vehemently. "Ignore . . . me," she managed to gasp between humiliating sobs.

Knox took a step toward her, his deep green eyes soft with concern. "Alice—"

"No, don't touch me! You'll only make it worse!" she cried, stepping back some more, panicked on top of being embarrassed.

"She's a sympathy crier," Lauren told Knox. "And she cries at all funerals. One time when we were in seventh grade, we went to a girlfriend's funeral for her goldfish. Alice cried so hard she got dehydrated and had to go to the hospital."

Alice had actually forgotten about that one. "Just . . . get . . . on . . . with . . . it," she hiccupped.

"You don't want to say anything?" Knox asked her.

All she could do was shake her head.

Knox held her gaze for a moment, then nodded. Crouching low at the water's edge, he slowly started to shake out the ashes. "We'll take care of your place, Eleanor. I promise. We've got you, so you can go do you."

His voice, low in timbre, solemn but true, blended in with the water gently lapping at the rocky shore, the rustling of the trees in the wind, and of course Alice's own desperate attempts to control her breathing. Looking out at the horizon rather than at what remained of the bigger-than-life woman she'd loved, Alice crouched next to Knox, putting a hand on his arm to stop him. Turned out, she did need to say something to Eleanor. "Thank you," she said, eyes closed, voice rough. "You were so much more than my dad's employer to me. You were a teacher, a mom, a grandma, a boss, a friend, and at times, my enforcer. I didn't want to, but somehow you conned me into growing up, while letting me think it was all my own idea. In spite of myself, you managed to turn a wild, feral, immature teenager into something resembling a person *almost* fit to face the world." She sucked in some air and then let it out slowly, releasing some of the pain with it. "I'll never forget what you did for me, what you continue to do for me by trusting me with your legacy, even though I'm not sure I deserve it."

A burst of lightning briefly lit up the morning like a disco ball, followed almost immediately by a ground-shaking clap of thunder.

"Okay, okay," she said on a gruff laugh, surprised that suddenly the threat of tears was gone, replaced by a sense of peace. "Enough reminiscing, I promise. You always did hate that." She swiped the tears off her face and turned to Knox and Lauren, who'd both risen to their feet at the thunder and lightning.

Lauren gave a single head nod and turned to start walking back.

Knox looked Alice over for a long moment, then reached out. And as if her hand were a part of someone else's body, it latched onto his.

He gave her a small but warm smile and a squeeze, and for a moment she held on. He didn't ask her if she was okay, for which she was grateful. Because she wasn't. Not even close.

But maybe she could get there.

Chapter 11

Dear Back-Stabbing Sister,

Have I ever told you about Alice? She was five when she innocently told her mom about the woman who'd been in bed with her daddy, and unintentionally blew up an already rocky marriage. Her mom bailed, but Paul stuck and tried to be a good dad. But if you ask me, he sucked at it. But he was a great mechanic, and knew his way around an engine, so I kept him on. He used to bring Alice and her brother along with him to work. I think Alice could wield a monkey wrench before she could use a pencil. The girl's all jagged edges and smart mouth, and I love it. But she actually believes she broke up her parents' marriage, that she disappoints the people she loves, that she ruins everything she touches, and for that I could murder both Paul and her mother—who never looked back, by the way—in their sleep.

Don't worry, I have no intention of going to jail, I look horrible in orange. But Alice is wrong about herself. She's a healer of hearts, she just doesn't know it yet. She hides behind a dogged scrappiness and fierce independence. In fact, she reminds me of . . . well, me.

I don't have many friends. Yeah, yeah, I know, you can stop laughing now. My point is that most people are happy to take my money for their causes, but would just as soon never see me. But Alice . . . she sees me as family. No-nonsense and brisk maybe, but she sees me. She knows she could come to me for anything. Granted, she'd sooner die than ask for help, something else we bond on, but she's smart as hell and, even better, has great instincts. She's going places. Or at least she will if she can get out of her own head and out of her own way. But she'll need a leg up, and that sure as hell won't be coming from her good-for-nothing parents. It'll come from me, happily.

Signed, The Only Good Graham Sister

A few days later in the late afternoon, Lauren stood on a ladder in the downstairs hallway, painting. She'd already worked all day at the library, a job she would no longer have in a matter of weeks, which she hadn't told a soul, much less dealt with that blow.

Nor the one staring her in the face.

Not literally but figuratively, because a few feet away, on the opposite wall, was Alice. Also painting.

They'd finished the upstairs hallway and would hopefully finish the downstairs hallway.

All while not having spoken a word to each other.

This suited Lauren just fine. Apparently she still had some resentment built up. And granted, they'd all sat around and read one of Eleanor's emails the night before, and it had been about Alice, about her past and why Eleanor had loved Alice so much, but . . .

But. It'd been touching. Seriously touching. Even Alice had tears in her eyes as Knox had read it.

Lauren too. But there'd been no mistaking that little seed of jealousy deep inside herself. Why had Eleanor believed her dad and stayed away from Lauren?

She should just let it go, but she couldn't, because Eleanor letting her dad dictate their relationship hurt. So did Alice leaving after Will's death and not looking back. She'd just left Lauren like she'd meant nothing.

And bingo, *there* it was. Her real problem. She was tired of begging people to love her. Her dad. Will. Alice. Her job. Oh, wait, none of those things were in her life anymore.

Her therapist would suggest she talk to Alice, but Lauren had zero intention of talking about any of this with her. Why should she share herself, especially the embarrassing things like losing her job, with someone she meant nothing to?

She had to give up the mental gymnastics in order to yawn so wide she nearly cracked open her jaw. God, she was tired. So effing tired. She'd been working on the inn's financials, keeping track of their expenditures, also making some contacts and plans for their big opening. Oh and writing Sunrise Cove's next monthly newsletter. All while also searching for other jobs. Unfortunately, the next closest librarian position was in south shore, an hour's drive from here. She was starting to think she might end up having to take a waitress job, which she'd done while in college, but damn. She'd miss being in a library so much she got teary every time she thought about it.

Another yawn, and this time her jaw cracked audibly. She knew she would have to get some sleep soon. When she was this exhausted and it was late—like now—she tended to say things she wouldn't say with a clearer mind. But she'd discovered the mechanical motion of painting was oddly soothing. Or at least it would be if she didn't have Alice in her peripheral, painting with lots of aggression. "You're doing it wrong."

Alice snorted. "Where have I heard that before?"

In spite of herself, Lauren smiled. One time in high school, their science teacher had taken them out on the lake in canoes to study the lake's unique ecosystem. Lauren, who'd never canoed before, had studied up on canoe techniques first. So when she'd been paired with Alice, Lauren had decided to take her under her wing. Only Alice had ignored all Lauren's attempts at small talk and had taken point on rowing.

Alice was laughing softly at the memory. "I'd been rowing all my life," she said. "You'd never gone out, not even once, and you still tried to tell me I was doing it wrong."

"Well, your technique didn't match my research," Lauren said in her own defense.

Alice snorted. "And the following year when we landed as science lab partners and you blew up our experiment and then tried to tell me *I'd* done it wrong?"

Lauren felt her face heat, but lifted her chin. "Well, you *had* done it wrong."

Alice rolled her eyes. "Tell me this—are you *ever* wrong?"

Yes. She'd been wrong to think that her friendship with Alice meant something, like *really* meant something. "Never," she said stubbornly. "And you're still painting wrong. I googled it. You're supposed to do it like this." And then, with a gentle but firm grip, she rolled up and down over the same area twice before shifting over to begin again.

"That's exactly what I'm doing," Alice said, rolling up and down, up and down, up and down. "I know how to paint, Lauren."

"You're piling the paint on too thick."

Alice sighed. "I told you I didn't need help doing this. You've already had a full day. I got this."

"I want to help."

"So go do another room, any other room. Preferably one where we won't be on top of each other."

Lauren had no idea why she'd thought this might be fun, a way to open up to each other.

Alice was looking at her with bafflement. "What do you want from me? I know it isn't my company."

She was wrong, but there was no way Lauren would admit that. "I want an honest conversation." There. She'd said it. "It's in our list of Ground Rules."

Alice's mouth was grim as she loaded her roller with more paint and went back to attacking the wall. "I'm not going to apologize for the accident that killed Will, so I really don't know what else there is for us to even talk about."

Lauren froze, then slowly turned to Alice in utter shock. "Is that what you think? That I want an apology?" Her heart sank and hit her toes. "I would never . . ." She had to stop and take a shaky breath. "*Never* ask you to apologize for Will's accident." She met Alice's gaze straight on. "I just needed someone to share the grief with. You were the only one who understood what losing Will felt like." She tried to swallow the lump of emotion in her throat, but failed. "Although, I wouldn't turn down an apology for brushing off my calls and texts."

"Not all of them."

"Fine," Lauren agreed. "Not all of them. But you let more and more time go by between answering until you just faded away. You couldn't even give me the respect a twenty-year friendship deserved to say more than hi, I'm busy, new job, can't talk . . . I felt like you abandoned me, A."

The old nickname slipped out unintended, and Alice reacted viscerally by taking a deep breath. "*I* abandoned *you*? Are you kidding me? Everyone thought I'd accidentally killed Will. Even you." At the word *you*, Alice pointed at her with her freshly loaded roller, causing paint to splatter the front of Lauren all the way down to her toes. "So excuse me if I only returned the occasional text. I was busy trying to bury my grief."

Lauren looked down at her now paint-splattered self. She blinked in disbelief. She swiped her face with her forearm and it came away covered in paint, causing a sudden rush of bottled-up resentment and anger. Helpless to hold it back, she said "And I *never* thought you killed him."

At Alice's long, pointed stare, Lauren closed her eyes. "Okay, so when I saw you at the hospital, I asked you about the car and if the accident had anything to do with the repairs you made earlier that day. We'd *just* found out he didn't make it. I was scared and sad and angry and emotional, and it probably came out wrong."

"You think?"

"I was lashing out." She opened her eyes. "I'm sorry you were the person I lashed out at. I would've said so, but you ran off and then stayed gone." Lauren emphasized the sentence with a jerk of *her* roller, and paint went flying.

It hit Alice square in the face. Slowly, she swiped at her cheek and looked at her fingers. Fingers that were now wet with paint. "I stayed gone, because it was *you* who put my brother between us, even though you'd promised you'd never do that, but you did."

"And how exactly did I do that?" Lauren demanded.

"When he died, you closed yourself off to me."

"No, the way I acted the night of his death doesn't count. I was . . ." She shook her head. "Lost. So please tell me besides that, how did I ever do anything other than accept the both of you, even with the Moore special brand of—"

"Don't you dare say *crazy*."

Lauren stopped and bit her tongue. "I was going to say . . ."

Alice gave a single crook of a brow, silently challenging her to finish that sentence.

Lauren blew out a regretful sigh and shut her mouth. No, she hadn't been going to say *crazy*, because it wasn't true. But her truth wouldn't be any easier to swallow. She'd already known for some time that Will was too much for her, that she couldn't have lasted with him. But she had no way to make that sound okay, so she searched for something, anything else. "Daring."

"Daring," Alice repeated dubiously.

"Yes, and . . . terrifying."

This clearly took Alice off guard. "Will scared you?"

Lauren nodded slowly, but Alice shook her head. "Will wouldn't have hurt a fly. He'd never have hurt you."

"Not physically. Never that. But emotionally . . . you both hurt me," she admitted.

Alice's expression was angered disbelief. "Not on purpose! There's a big difference! Here, now see *this* is on purpose—" And with that, she rolled paint down the front of Lauren's shirt.

"Wow." Fine. Fighting dirty it was, then, so Lauren very carefully and purposefully redipped her roller into the paint and then just as carefully and purposefully mimicked Alice and rolled it down *her* front.

Alice sucked in a breath, probably because the paint was soaking through her shirt and making her as cold as Lauren felt. In fact, Lauren was icy cold, with the exception of the hot tears pouring down her face.

"No!" Alice said, pointing at her. "No crying!" She stormed into the front room. Lauren followed in time to see Alice pick up the Sharpie and jab it at rule number one.

And though the paint covering them was the lovely, calming color of oak, Lauren saw red. "I'm not crying because I'm sad! I'm crying because I'm mad!"

They were painted-nose-to-painted-nose now, breathing heavily when Knox stuck his head into the room. "Hey," he said. "I just finished the—" He broke off, his eyes widening slightly. For him, this was tantamount to a huge surprise from the guy who was so chill Lauren had felt tempted on several occasions to make sure he was still breathing.

"Okay, first," he said calmly. "Paint is for walls only."

Lauren angrily swiped at her tears and her hand came away covered in paint. Perfect.

"And second," he went on. "Did it ever occur to either of you that Will was a grown-ass man? He *chose* to get into that car. He *chose* to race it. Those were *his* choices, not either of yours. So why are you mad at each other over his incredibly stupid and selfish decisions?"

Alice narrowed her eyes. "Don't talk about my brother that way."

Lauren, shoulder to shoulder with Alice now, nodded her agreement. "Seriously," she said. "He's *dead.*"

Knox stared at them both. "Okay, let me get this straight. You two can band together as long as it suits you?"

Lauren felt Alice look at her. Their gazes met and Alice nodded, and in unison they turned on Knox.

Lauren had to admit, he took it well, them both rolling him in paint. He barely raised a brow. "Really?" he asked. "What are we, children?"

"No, we're partners," Lauren said. "Which means when one of us is covered in paint, all of us are covered in paint." She pointed to Alice.

And with a nod, Alice moved to the rule wall and added rule 9:

We are in this shit together.

"Good to see you two still bonding over my misery" was all Knox said, but Lauren was pretty sure he was secretly pleased.

Knox left the living room, feeling several dollops of paint slide down his shirt and land on his boot. He passed the freshly painted hallway, noting that it was actually painted fairly well, and headed upstairs to his bathroom. There he kicked off his boots and socks and stripped out of his shirt. He'd just shucked his pants when Alice burst through the door.

Covered in paint.

Eyes locked on his, she stormed right up to him and poked him in the chest.

Paint came off her finger and stuck to his bare left pec.

"You shouldn't talk about things you don't know," she said.

"Then explain it to me."

Alice deflated a little bit at that, suddenly looking extremely young. And paint spattered. Her gaze ran over him. "You're . . . in just your undies."

"Yes, that's what happens when you don't knock." He paused, unable to stop himself from teasing her.

"Besides, wasn't this always your goal? To catch me without clothes?"

"When I was fourteen, yes. But I'm old now. I'm no longer run by my hormones." She gave him a long once-over. "Most of the time anyway. You grew up right nicely too, Knox."

Stepping closer, he swiped at a smudge of paint on her jaw with his thumb. "You okay?"

"Yeah."

"Rule number three," he invoked. "Honest conversations."

"That only applies to our partnership."

He just looked at her.

"Fine. I'm not okay. But it's not like I can do anything about it."

And suddenly he was looking at the Alice he'd seen only glimpses of, the vulnerable and endearingly unsure Alice. He thought about the previous night's reading of another Eleanor email, and what he'd learned about her parents' split. Alice blamed herself, which he hated for her.

"I guess I don't know how to stop being angry," she said quietly.

He put a hand on her arm, which was sticky with paint. He ran his fingers down to hers and entangled them in his. "It'd help to let it all out."

She squeezed his hand and dropped her head to his chest, leaving another imprint of paint on him. He didn't mind. Slowly, not wanting to spook her into running, he wrapped her up in his arms. When she didn't resist, instead took a deep breath and relaxed against him, he pressed his jaw to hers. "Talk to me."

"Just Google it like the rest of the world and you'll learn what everyone else thinks—that I screwed up the brakes on the car, which led to speculation that I caused his death. There was an investigation."

"And were you found to be responsible for screwing up the brakes?"

She tried to jerk free, but he held her until she looked up at him, eyes shooting fire.

"Were you?" he asked again.

"No." She closed her eyes, misery in every line of her long, willowy body. "*No*," she said much softer now.

He hugged her into him. "Then why do you act like you were?"

Slowly, she lifted her head. She still had paint on her face, and there were a few streaks in her hair as well. She smelled like acetone. And he thought she'd never looked more beautiful.

When she took a small step back, he let her, though he immediately missed the feel of her against him. She just stared up at him as he gently swiped his thumb over the smudge of paint on her jaw. "What?" he asked.

"You're the first person who's ever come right out and asked me if I was to blame. Everyone just assumes I screwed up because I was a Moore." There was something in her gaze now, something new in the way she looked at him. "Will was a wild, feral kid, and though I wasn't nearly as bad, the reputation was there." She shrugged like it didn't hurt, but it was there in her eyes and in her voice. "People like to believe the worst and were too chicken to come directly to me."

"Alice," he whispered, pained, aching for her.

She hesitated, very unlike her, then said, "*You're* not chicken. Never have been."

Knox gave a slow shake of his head. "Which got me into plenty of trouble in my own right."

"Because you're not afraid to ask anything or say anything."

"As long as it's the truth," he said. Truth had often been a rare commodity in his household, but he believed in taking responsibility for his own actions, at any cost. Unfortunately, he was often in the minority with that philosophy. "I've got a real thing for honesty."

"Because of your mom?" she asked.

This surprised him. "You know about her?"

"Of course. She worked here. She was lovely, and super sweet."

"And an alcoholic."

"And that," she said. "On the days she didn't come to work—"

"Because she was hungover . . ."

Her eyes held his, and he thought if she showed him even a flicker of pity, he wasn't going to be able to deal with it, but she just nodded. "Eleanor used to take great pleasure in giving me your mom's chores to do."

"What? *Why?*"

Alice's eyes held a self-deprecating humor. "Oh, because I'd mouthed off, or done something else equally stupid. She considered it penance."

He smiled. "*You* mouthy? I can't imagine."

She rolled her eyes and took another step back. She was going to leave him to his shower, and he needed to let her. But he wasn't ready. "So why are you in such a hurry to get out of Sunrise Cove?" he heard himself ask.

"I think maybe . . ." She looked down at her messy self. "I need a fresh start."

"You could have that right here."

She looked back up, clearly surprised. "You think so?"

"Maybe that's why Eleanor wanted you here."

"Or she wanted me here to put some work into this

place." She gave a small smile. "She *really* liked to make me work."

He had to laugh. "Yeah, she believed working me half to death would keep my demons at bay."

"Did it?"

He shrugged. "I think I just got good at hiding them."

"Eleanor caught me watching you once." She smiled at his surprise. "She told me I wasn't ready for the likes of you. And that you absolutely weren't ready for anyone. She said that while you were honest to a fault, and a great guy, you could hide your pain too well for a real relationship."

"True story." *Too* true. "And everyone hides something."

A wry smile curved her lips. "Including, apparently, Eleanor herself. I can't believe she thought that the three of us deserved this place. What is that?"

"Love," he said simply.

She looked away. "We both know that there was a lot about Eleanor to love. And yet she still died alone."

"Because she made mistakes. She'd be the first one to tell you that."

This brought her face back to his. "I don't want to be alone in the end."

The look in her eyes, the soft, mesmerizing mix of

vulnerability, pain, and stubbornness got him right in the heart. "So change the ending of your story."

She looked at him like he was crazy, and hell, maybe he was. "You make it sound so easy," she said.

This made him laugh roughly. "Nothing about love is easy." Which he knew firsthand. Yes, he'd had moments here and there of wanting someone special in his life, but he also knew it would be a disaster in the making. People didn't tend to stay in his life. "You gotta be brave." Look at him with the big talk. He was so full of shit.

But she appeared to give it some thought. "Brave, huh?"

"Yeah. You feeling brave, Alice?"

Their gazes met and held. And what he saw in hers made his pulse trip. She was looking at him like she looked at pizza. *Come on and take a bite, babe . . .*

"What I'm feeling," she said softly, "is easier to show than tell." Stepping back into him, she went up on tiptoe, pressed her paint-covered self to his, and kissed him. Her mouth on his tasted better than anything in his memory banks. Then their tongues touched and he couldn't access his memory at all.

When she pulled back, she had two large painted handprints on either side of her jaw—*his*—and he had two smaller handprints on his ass—*hers*—and a grin on his face.

"I don't know where that's going," she confessed, still looking at his mouth. "Maybe nowhere. I was just . . ."

He smiled. "Feeling brave?"

She smiled back, looking so . . . *sweet*. "Yeah."

Damn, he liked her. "You should feel free to be brave with me anytime you want."

She gave a slow nod of her head, another flash of a smile, and then he was alone. He turned to the shower just as Alice called through the door.

"Oh, and don't use all the hot water unless you want to die!"

Yep. Sweet as sin.

Chapter 12

THE GROUND RULES

1. No tears.
2. This is about Eleanor.
3. Open, honest conversations with actual words.
   DAILY—as long as it doesn't violate rule #1.
4. Do not kill your partners.
5. No nicknames.
6. No one sleeps with anyone.
7. No ties, emotional or physical, period.
8. Read Eleanor's emails together.
9. We are in this shit together.
10. Paint is for walls only.

When Alice's alarm went off at a wake-the-dead volume, she practically had to pry her fingernails out of the ceiling before she could turn it off.

At least she didn't impale herself on the moose head on the far wall.

Heart thumping hard in her chest, she sat up and looked around. On night one, she'd slipped into the first room she'd come to, which had turned out to be the trapper room. It was masculine and woodsy, but also actually very charming and quirky, with beadboard walls covered in antique tools of the trapper trade.

Knox had tried to convince her to trade rooms a hundred times. No way. It made her laugh every time she pictured him in the froufrou pink, lacy, silky room. And she needed the laughs.

She yawned, feeling exhausted. Last night she'd stayed up way past midnight, at the creek, just beyond the barn. She'd sat on the same large, flat rock that had seen her through way too many tough times to count; like the time her dad let Will drive one of the cars from the show but not Alice because she'd mouthed off to a teacher at school that day. She'd been so furious and so hurt, she'd extended her fury to her poor brother, who hadn't deserved it. He'd come out to the rock to try and talk to her. Too upset to be reasonable, she'd then stomped off and into the barn, and taken one of the cars, the 1964 Mustang that her dad loved more than his own children, out for a joy ride and had hit a rut in the road and ruined the suspension.

Will had come out and rescued her, no judgment as he'd helped her get the Mustang home and repaired. They'd had to stay up all night to do it too, and he'd done so without a single complaint.

God, she missed him.

Oh, and there had been the time she'd been cruelly dumped by her stupid prom date after spending every penny she had on a stupid dress. Eleanor had been her savior that time, hoofing it out to the creek, not to hug her or sympathize, but to tell her to suck it up because *anyone* of the male persuasion was stupid and she should've known better than to trust one.

True enough.

In any case, it was a good spot for reflection, and she'd stayed out there, watching the moon shadows on the surface of the water until her internal walls began to crumble, the stones around her heart shifting and drifting to the music of the water until she'd gotten cold. Then she'd hidden out in her room . . . knitting. Yes, hello, her name was Alice and knitting was her Xanax, thank you very much.

She'd already made two scarves and two beanies, which she'd hidden away, because while she could technically follow a pattern, nothing ever came out like it promised.

And now that morning had come all too soon, she

needed caffeine. She looked down at herself. She was in an oversize T-shirt and panties, so she added a flannel shirt and sweatpants, then shoved her feet into boots. She decided not to look at herself in the mirror, which solved the problem of what to do with her bedhead hair. If she couldn't see it, it didn't exist, right?

She did brush her teeth because she wasn't a complete heathen, then staggered toward the kitchen in search of coffee, but stopped short in the front room. There was a new rule on the board.

10. Paint is for walls only.

It was in Knox's messy half-cursive, half-print, barely legible man-scrawl, and it made her laugh out loud. It sounded a little rusty, even to her own ears. She should've been annoyed at him, but she wasn't.

Maybe it'd been the kiss . . .

Because good God, the kiss. Best not to think about it. She saw no sign of either of her partners, so with a shrug she headed into the kitchen, stopping to pull out her phone when it rang.

"Hey, Tumbleweed," her dad said.

His voice brought her back to another time, so much so that her own voice came out a little rough with emotion. "Hey, Dad."

"Didn't wake you up, did I? We all know how much you love that." He chuckled. "In the old days, I'd make Will get you up for school because you were mean as a hungry bear in the mornings."

"Still am."

"Good to know some things never change." He gave another chuckle, and then, as always, there came the awkward silence. Hers, because she desperately wanted to connect with him, but had no idea how. She was never sure what his silence was about. Probably, he was checking his social. Or he was trying to figure out how to get off the phone already. "What have you been doing?" he asked.

She hated that question. She never knew what to say. *I don't know, breathing. Probably getting mad at stuff more than I should. Sighing a lot. And so on . . .* "Not much," she finally settled on.

"I've got only a minute," he said.

Ding, ding, ding, door number two.

"Just wanted to make my monthly check-in as promised," he said. "Things are going great. How about there?"

He called only because she'd asked him to check in every month. She knew it, but it still felt shitty. She missed him. Missed having someone to belong to, missed having someone in her life she had a history with, even if it was obligatory—even if she told herself she didn't want or need ties.

But he wasn't coming back. She understood. He'd needed to get as far away from the tragedy that had taken his son, and he'd also needed a fresh start, as the subsequent lawsuit against the owner of the car Will had been driving—her dad's—had taken just about everything from him. He was currently residing in France, working as head mechanic for a street racing team, living life as he always had—wild and fast and free. No tethers, no ties.

Alice had always envied that. Tried to emulate it as well. And for a long time she'd done just that. But being back here, at the last real home she'd known, had something odd and unexpected happening to her. A shift in her thinking, along with a surprise envy of Lauren, who'd been able to put down roots and not let anything scare her off; not the loss of her parents or of Will, or anything.

"Tumbleweed? You still there? Do we have a bad connection? I know it's really early there . . ."

"I'm here." She cleared her throat and forced a smile so he'd hear it in her voice, because that's what he expected. He didn't need her problems. "Everything's good, Dad."

"I still can't believe the old broad left you one-third

of that place. I'm not sure I could be as courageous as you to go back. When can you get out of there?"

"Three more weeks or so." A few days ago, she'd have been able to tell him exactly how much longer, down to the minute. She wasn't sure when she'd quit keeping such close track, or why. She was still ready to go.

Wasn't she?

"I bet you're looking forward to it," her dad said. "Shoot me a text when you're free. Gotta go, kid."

"Bye, Dad. Love you—" But he was gone. She slipped her phone away and nodded to herself. It had been nice to hear from him, nice to know he was doing okay, but just the sound of his voice had given her an ache to have things back the way they were when she was a teenager. Working with her dad, Will alive . . . Funny how one never appreciated the good times while actually *in* those good times . . .

She bounced out of her reverie when she heard a car coming up the road. Moving to the window, she waited to see who it would be. In the meantime, her gaze snagged on Stella, just sitting there in the early morning sun, her two headlights and front bumper looking almost like a human face. A stern face that was judging her for not having filled up her tank or given her any of the maintenance and repairs she needed.

If anyone else had abused their classic like she had, she'd have words. A lot of words. It was painful to even think it, but she was a bad car mommy. A really bad one.

"I'm getting there," she told Stella through the window. "I just need you to be patient with me."

The car coming up the road appeared and parked out front. A man got out of the candy-apple-red 1972 Pontiac Firebird Trans Am that the old Alice would have drooled over.

Okay, so she drooled a little.

The driver stood on the driveway, hands on hips.

Nice car, but who the hell was he?

She moved to the front door and opened it, but remained in the doorway. She could see Knox's shiny new truck on the other side of the driveway, also judging poor Stella. But she had no idea where the man himself might be. Maybe Knox had done something crazy like run to the lake again. In any case, near as she could tell, she was possibly alone on the remote, isolated property, surrounded by a whole bunch of thick, remote woods, and since she'd seen every horror flick ever, she knew what that meant. "Can I help you?"

"You Alice?" he asked.

"Who's asking?"

"I'm here about the *AutoTrader* ad for the cars. I wanted to see what you have."

She blinked. "Ad? What ad?"

The guy pulled out his phone and showed her an online ad.

She stepped onto the porch and reached for the phone.

> Classic muscle cars in stock condition, all models and varieties, each looking for a good home and some tender loving care. Contact Alice for more information.

What the actual hell? She shook her head. "I didn't place this."

"You Alice or not?"

"*Not.* And I'm sorry, but you've wasted your time. You need to go. Now."

The guy looked vastly disappointed. "Yeah, I knew it was too good to be true. Hey, this is the place where those two shows were filmed, right? *Last Chance Racing?* And the western, too . . . *Last Chance Inn.* I used to watch the repeats with my dad when I was a kid." He pointed to a backdrop set, the interior of the show's saloon, leaning against the barn. "Man, that is so cool. Is the inn open?"

"No." Then she remembered she could be scaring away a future paying guest. "Not yet. Next month."

"Cool. Thanks." He paused. "You're *sure* about the cars?"

"Very."

With a disappointed nod, he got back in his Firebird and drove off, the car purring like she was well taken care of.

"Morning, Alice. Or should I say *Not Alice*."

She whirled around and found Knox on the porch behind her, Pickle at his side. Neither man nor dog looked like early mornings affected them one bit, especially the man, the sexy ass. He was in jeans torn at one knee, battered old work boots, and a T-shirt advertising some dive bar in Puerto Rico. His jaw still hadn't seen a razor, leaving a scruff that somehow highlighted his green eyes. Totally unfair. "Were you eavesdropping?"

"Not my thing."

She narrowed her gaze. "*You* placed the ad, didn't you."

"Nope. Haven't seen an *AutoTrader* magazine since I was a teenager and worked here."

"Then who? Who would've put the cars in the *Auto-Trader*?"

Knox rubbed the stubble on his jaw, and the sound scraped at parts of her that she'd almost forgotten about. "My best guess would be Eleanor. Or more likely, Eleanor's attorney, on her orders."

She was confused. "But why under my name?"

He shrugged. "She probably left instructions to wait until you were here. She knew you'd know exactly what was in the barn and what it was all worth."

Damn you, Eleanor, meddling with my life even from the grave . . . Needing a moment, she crouched low and gave Pickle a belly rub.

Knox vanished, then came back with two cups of steaming hot coffee, bless him. She took one with gratitude, at least until he spoke.

"What's so bad about showing the cars? It's a great idea, actually, and would add money to the till. You do remember that whatever's left over after we finish the renovations is ours, right? You could have that fresh start you mentioned."

Yes. But how ironic was it that in order to get her fresh start, she'd have to face her past?

"Even if you just show the inventory for fun, wouldn't you be into that?" he asked. "You used to love old cars." He eyed Stella. "Still do, apparently."

Her heart hitched. "Yeah. I *used* to love old cars." More accurately, she'd lived and died and breathed for them. It'd fueled those fantasies of someday owning her own women-run mechanics and renovation shop. How naive she'd been. "Things change."

"I used to see you working with your dad in that

barn. I could see the look in your eyes. It was never a passing interest for you, Alice. Renovating those cars, driving them, it was in your blood."

"I didn't drive them."

He gave her a get-real look.

"I was underage."

This earned her a second get-real look.

"Okay, so sometimes I got to drive them. Whatever." She'd never forgotten the few and far between times her dad had allowed her behind the wheel on the roads throughout the property. Or the times when she'd "borrowed" the cars without permission. She'd never felt so free in her life. Not before, and not since. "It was just a passing fantasy." She started to walk past him into the inn, but he caught her arm and gently but inexorably pulled her back around to face him. "What?" she asked.

He just held her gaze. "Maybe we should test the 'just a passing fantasy' theory."

Her heart kicked into high gear. "That's . . . dumb."

"Then why are you panicking?" he asked, lightly running his fingers over the pulse racing at the base of her throat.

She smacked his hand away, but only because she wanted him to hug her again. Talk about dumb . . . She didn't need anyone to hug her. She was absolutely fine.

Knox slid his hand down to hers and entangled their fingers before pulling her off the porch and toward the barn.

"*What are you doing?*"

"We've been here just over a week and we haven't even been inside the barn yet. You know what that makes us? Neglectful owners."

"That's dumb." She dug her heels into the dirt. "I can't, okay?"

He stopped and looked at her, his expression softening at whatever he saw on her face. Probably sheer dread. "You really don't even want to look at them?"

"Remember?" She tossed up her free hand. "I don't even want to be here."

"Alice . . ." He took a step toward her, his voice low, gentle. "I know you used to practically live in that barn. You must have lots of good memories there."

Oh great, she was already breathing funny, and her hands were sweating and . . . damn. She was shaking. Shaking in her boots. She yanked her hand free, set her coffee down, and hugged herself, attempting to hold herself together. "I vote that we just sell the cars."

"Sure." His eyes never left hers. "But do you really want to do that before spending any time with them? Maybe fixing one of them up for old times' sake?"

She crossed her arms. "If you know so much about everything, then *you* go in there and visit them."

He smiled at her. "You get this little furrow in your brow when you're pissed off at yourself."

"If I'm pissed, it's at you." But that wasn't true and he seemed to know it because he just stood there, quiet, calm, letting her think.

He was comfortable with silence in a way she'd never been able to manage. Especially with him. They had this weird chemistry thing going on, and she felt off her axis because of it, but clearly he did not. He was his usual impenetrable, imperturbable self. It drove her crazy, and somehow also calmed her at the same time.

But she hated that he was right. The inventory needed to be faced and deserved attention. She knew that selling now, from a monetary standpoint, was a stupid decision. The cars would be worth so much more if given even a little love. Could she provide that love? was the question. "I'd want them to go to a good home, to someone with a good history of car restorations, so I know they're safe."

"Alice, *you're* a good home, *you* have that history, and *you* already love them. If you want to keep them here and restore them yourself, they'll be safer than anywhere else on the planet."

His faith in her was staggering. "How do you know, when I don't know?" she asked.

Very slowly and gently, he slid his arms around her. "Because I at least know that much about you."

She found her hands fisted in his shirt, like he was her anchor in rough waters. "Okay. Maybe. But I'm still not ready to go inside the barn right now."

"Noted." Then he nuzzled his face in the crook of her neck, that delicious stubble scraping sexily over her skin.

She couldn't contain a shiver. It was much easier to resist him when he wasn't in front of her, looking like sin on a stick. It was so much harder to hold her ground when he was this close and seeming intent on getting even closer.

Harder still when her entire body agreed with his that this seemed like a great idea.

His hand shifted from where it was playing with her hair. A touch on her cheek turned her head to face him. His gaze searched hers, seeming to ask *Are you okay? Are we okay?* She gave him a small smile because oddly enough, she was, and they were.

Only then did he smile back. "You kissed me last night."

There was no denying that. "I did."

"And if I were to return the favor?" he asked, voice low and husky.

Her eyes locked on his mouth. "I mean, it'd be the polite thing to do."

He was still smiling when he kissed her, slow and smoldering. And it was a good thing there were several layers of clothing between them or she was certain they'd have been fused together, heated skin melded.

When they broke apart, his voice was a rough rumble in her ear. "Mmm. That's even better without the sticky, smelly paint."

She laughed softly and snuggled in. "Yeah."

He playfully tugged a strand of her hair. "You got this, Alice."

"This, as in . . . ?" She lifted her head. "Being here? Lauren? You? My life? You're going to have to be more specific."

He grinned. "All of it. You got all of it."

And damn, his belief in her was so strong, she almost . . . *almost* . . . believed in herself too.

Chapter 13

Dear Two-Timing Sister,

Regrets are a vicious thing. God knows, I did my best raising your baby, but I could've been more maternal. Instead, I blamed you for putting me in the position of having to be you. And to my shame, it wasn't until Evan graduated from high school that I realized you hadn't ruined my life at all. In fact, you'd given me the greatest gift. Being a mom.

But by then it was too late. I'd been too hard on Evan, expected too much, and I lost him and never got to have Lauren in my life. And that I do regret. I have to respect her wishes, but . . . I miss her. I don't even know her and I miss her. I think that's why I latched onto Knox. The kid was my chance at a do-over. He never once asked me for a thing. I know I didn't deserve him or Alice, but they each gave me back something I didn't realize I was missing. Humanity.

Forever Not Yours, Eleanor

For Knox, the days were a blur of retrofitting the plumbing in the bathrooms and kitchen, and replacing any galvanized pipes that had rusted out. He got up early and stayed up late to also give time to his construction company. He was exhausted.

Lauren came and went, putting in her hours at the library, then showing up to keep track of their expenses, work on their grand opening, and also handle whatever tasks she could help him and Alice with.

Alice worked every bit as hard as he did, if not more, while making sure to also stay as far away from him as possible. He got the message. What was happening between them, that odd chemistry and connection, scared her.

Ditto, babe.

They often ran into each other in the kitchen. Today, she was in jeans and a tank top. Hair back in a loose braid. Kickass boots on her feet. A little guarded. A lot beautiful.

"Hey." She grabbed a bag of chips and ran off before he could do something to take the wariness out of her eyes. Like kiss her. He really liked how she'd looked after he'd kissed her. Stunned. Discombobulated.

Aroused.

Shaking it off, he went back to work. After a full day in the downstairs bathroom setting the sink and toilet, he found himself alone and oddly restless. So he showered, then got into his truck and drove. It was there, on the narrow one-lane curvy road, driving around the lake, that he found his zone. He drove past his old high school and other places where he used to hang out, reacquainting himself with his past, with one stark exception—the small trailer park where he'd grown up. Nope, he still wasn't feeling prepared to face the avalanche of emotions going there would unbury.

It was a midweek night and traffic was nonexistent, so when he stopped at the local bar and grill, the place was only half full. Moving past the tables, he headed straight for the bar. He ordered a beer and then was stunned when Nikki sat on the barstool next to him.

She smiled. "Hey, stranger. So . . . did you order Sex in the Woods or a Blow Job?"

"Neither," the bartender said as he set a beer in front of Knox, then looked at Nikki for her order.

"Beer is boring," she said. "I'll have a Sex in the

Woods, please." She smiled at Knox. "In honor of that time we went to the woods to do it and you chickened out."

"I didn't chicken out," he said. "I just didn't want your first time to be in the woods."

Her eyes softened. "I forgot how sweet you could be. You didn't often show that side of you." The bartender brought Nikki's drink and she took a sip. "I saw you in *People* magazine's Favorite Earth-Friendly Companies issue a few years back. You left here a handyman, and now you build innovative, ecofriendly housing and have something like two hundred employees." Her eyes were bright with interest, and something else. Regret? "Impressive," she murmured. "You've made something of yourself. I knew you would."

When he didn't respond, her smile faded as she stared at him with that same sweet, girl-next-door look in her eyes, the one that once upon a time had drawn him like a moth to the flame.

"We were so young," she said softly. "And I was so very, *very* stupid. I know what I missed out on, Knox." She put her hand on his. "You were The One. Maybe you don't know this, but every girl has the one they wish had been their first. For me, that's you."

He shook his head. "This is all water under the bridge. We've both moved on."

"Have we?"

He looked into the eyes of the woman he'd once thought was his future, and nodded. "I'm just here for a drink, Nikki. I thought I'd be having it alone."

"That's the problem." She leaned in, her eyes sweet and warm. "You were so . . . self-sufficient." Her face was close to his now, her eyes still regretful but also . . . hurt? "I used to misread it as you not wanting to be with me," she murmured.

He shook his head. "You know that wasn't true."

"Did I?"

He looked at her, really looked at her, and waited for his heart to feel fileted. Didn't happen. "Nikki, you slept with someone else and got pregnant. You married him. This entire conversation is inappropriate."

"Inappropriate?" she asked on a laugh. "Nearly *everything* we did when we were alone together, which was all but the main event in case you need to be reminded, was inappropriate. Deliciously so."

He stood and pulled out some cash for the bartender.

"You're leaving?" she asked in surprise.

"Yes."

"Knox . . . don't be like that."

Her eyes were dark and hopeful. He had no idea what was going on with her and her marriage, but he found it a relief to realize he didn't care. "Have a good life, Nikki."

Thirty minutes later, he was at the inn again, even more restless than he'd been when he left. He parked in the back, since that's where he'd be working in the morning and it'd be easier to grab his tools from there. The lights were all off, and with a no-city-lights ordinance in Sunrise Cove, night was a whole new kind of dark. He walked around to the front of the inn, realizing someone was sitting on the porch.

Alice, with Pickle sleeping at her feet.

Her head was bent over whatever she was doing, brow furrowed in concentration. Her hands were moving, something in them glinting in the dark as she mumbled something that sounded like "In, wrap, pull out. In, wrap, pull out—*dammit!*" She paused, as if fixing her mistake, then went on. "In, wrap, pull out . . ."

She was knitting.

This rough-and-tumble woman who'd rather fight than admit she had emotions, who could take apart a car and put it back together again without blinking . . . could also knit. She was a paradox, an enigma, and he found himself moving closer, fascinated in spite of himself. "What're you making?"

She jumped, swore colorfully, then shoved her knitting behind her, scowling at Pickle. "Some watchdog you are." She looked up at Knox. "And you. You need to wear a bell."

"Was that a hat?"

"What's it to you?" She shoved her hair from her face. "And it's nothing that's ever going to see the light of day."

He smiled. "Then why are you making it?"

"It's a stress reliever." She scowled at him. "*Usually*. What are you doing up so late?"

"Why are *you* up so late?" he countered.

She lifted a bottle of beer. "Having a drink."

"I was trying to have a drink too. Was interrupted by my ex."

Alice raised her brows. "And how did that go?"

He walked up the porch stairs. "Learned something about myself."

She nudged the chair next to her with a booted foot in invitation. "And what was that?"

He sat and leaned back, closing his eyes, taking in the familiar, comforting night sounds of the wind rustling through the trees, insects humming, the occasional hoot of an owl. "I learned I know what I don't want in life."

"Which is?"

When he opened his eyes, she handed over her beer.

He took a swig and handed it back. "What I used to want."

She nodded and tilted the bottle to her lips. For some reason, sharing the bottle felt incredibly intimate, and he got momentarily distracted by her mouth being where his had just been.

"More words would be super helpful," she said.

He laughed roughly. "People using too many words annoys you."

She shrugged. "I'm a walking, talking contradiction." She handed him back the beer. "Let me guess. Nikki used a lot of words."

"Yep. She has . . . regrets."

"Don't we all," Alice said. "So . . . did you give her what she wanted? Did you sleep with her?"

He choked on his sip of beer, and after he'd coughed up a lung, he gave her a dirty look. "How did you know?"

"How did you *not* know?" She shook her head. "You've got a lot to learn about women."

"Are you offering to teach me?"

"God, no." She gave a rough laugh. "When it comes to matters of the heart, I'm the last person to teach anyone anything. I'm the don't-get-attached-to-me girl. Trust me, it's a public service I offer, remaining emotionally unavailable."

That this smart, resourceful, resilient, gorgeous woman actually believed she wasn't worthy of a commitment boggled his mind. "Alice, everyone deserves to find someone who loves them."

"True. I'd accept love from someone with soft brown eyes, messy hair, a cute button nose, and . . ."

"And?" Knox asked, wondering why he wished he had brown eyes.

"And four paws." She reached down to pet Pickle, who licked her hand.

Knox relaxed back, a smile on his face.

Until she asked her next question.

"Was Nikki that special someone for you?" she asked.

"I thought so when I was eighteen." He shook his head. "She was everything my life wasn't. Sweet. Kind. Warm."

"See, that also describes Pickle."

Pickle lifted his big, sleepy head long enough to see if there were treats, which yanked a laugh out of Knox. "For me," he said, "Nikki was the epitome of what I thought was missing from my life. She was way too good for me."

Alice frowned. "You've got that backward."

Not for the first time, Knox was struck by how with Alice, what you saw was what you got, flaws and imperfections and all. No hidden agenda. No secrets. No using emotions to manipulate. She was a real woman, smart-mouth, sassy, feisty . . . always battle ready to fight for what she believed in, always calling him on his shit, challenging him, pushing him.

"Have you been in a lot of relationships since Nikki?" she asked.

"A few. But nothing that worked out."

"Why?"

He shrugged. "Various reasons, mostly thanks to my self-defense mechanisms."

She waited, and when he didn't say more, she gave him the go-on gesture.

"I never went all in," he said. "Now you."

Her smile was almost embarrassed. "Same."

"Why?" he asked, really wanting to know.

"Because I'm a chickenshit. Attachments get you hurt, so I've developed an allergy to them."

He hated that that was what she'd learned about love. "Did you get hurt?"

She sighed. "I don't know. Yeah. Maybe a little. Early on, just after I left here, I was at a trade school, trying a few different things. I dated this guy from one of my classes a few times. I liked him, but he stopped asking me out. When I asked why, he said I was like one of the guys and he just didn't see me 'that way.'"

Knox shook his head, wondering if the asshole had decided that before or after he'd slept with her, wondering too why he wanted to go beat him up for being one of the people who'd taught her not to put her heart out there.

"He asked if we could still be friends," Alice said. "But I didn't want to be friends, I wanted to run him over with my car."

He laughed. God, he adored her.

She met his gaze. "You still haven't said what you *do* want."

Yeah, and wasn't that the question. "I guess I want . . ." He searched for the right words. "Something simple. Organic. No drama."

"Simple." Alice nodded. "I like it. If we had another beer, I'd toast to no strings."

He shook his head. "I didn't say no strings. And you deserve more than to be something easy, Alice."

"Oh, trust me, *nothing* about me is easy," she said on a laugh.

He smiled at that, but the thought of being with her appealed to him more than anything he could remember. "Alice?"

Her smile faded at the seriousness in his voice now. "Yeah?"

"I just realized there *is* something I'm looking for."

Her gaze turned wary. "What's that?"

"A certain beautiful brunette with a ponytail, sexy tattoos, long legs that make my mouth water, and a major attitude problem."

Her gaze dropped to his mouth, making him realize that he'd leaned in and so had she, and they were sharing air. He took the now empty bottle from her hand and set it on the floor. "Shame you're in such a hurry to get out of here."

She looked away. "Share one beer and a man thinks he knows her."

She was wily and tricky, but he *was* getting to know her. And as a result, a part of him had been feeling like the worst kind of dick for not offering to buy her out like she'd wanted. Because he could have.

But Eleanor had left her one-third of this place for a reason, and while she hadn't figured it out yet, he had. Problem was, she seemed to think the only way to get over her brother's death was to leave town and stay gone. Except the one thing Knox did know was that you had to face your past head-on.

Says the guy who's avoided his own childhood home since he's been back . . .

"Knox?"

"Yeah?"

"There's one thing I'm *not* allergic to," she murmured.

Their gazes met and held, and the chill in the air evaporated, replaced by a heat he absolutely knew what to do with. He reached for her at the same time she reached for him, and in the next beat he had her out of her chair and into his lap.

Kissing Alice was an experience, the very best kind of experience. She kissed like she did everything else, with her entire heart and soul. She'd deny it, of course, but fact was fact. She tasted like forgotten hopes and dreams, and he completely lost himself in her.

When she pulled back, he had one hand cupping the nape of her neck, the other at the small of her back, holding her close, even knowing it was too good to be true.

"For clarity's sake," she said softly. "This is just for the night, yes?"

He had to make a surprisingly Herculean effort not to take the scraps she was offering. "I'm not a one-night sort of guy." This wasn't strictly true. He'd been exactly that, for a long time. But he didn't want just one night anymore, not with Alice.

She blinked. "But what if we have no chemistry? Or you're bad in the sack?"

"We do and I'm not." He grinned. "Try me."

She bit her lower lip, looking adorably intrigued. "It sounds suspiciously like a string."

"Does it?"

She narrowed her eyes. "*Yes.*" She cocked her head and studied him some more. "You're big on rules," she finally said. "Maybe we should lay out some ground rules for this thing."

"Like a safe word?"

She laughed. "Number one—we start with just the one night."

"Rule number two," he said. "Honesty."

"This is starting to sound familiar," she said dryly. "*And* you sound like the chick."

"Maybe I'm just enlightened."

She snorted, then shifted her position so she was straddling him. She made a little rocking motion with her hips that had his eyes crossing with lust. Thoroughly rendered stupid, he watched through heavy-lidded eyes as she slid her hands beneath his shirt, seeking—and finding—bare skin. When she leaned over him and kissed the secret sweet spot right beneath his ear, he tightened his grip on her rocking hips and groaned.

There could be no doubt in either of them that he wanted her, and he knew she wanted him too. But if he rushed this, chances were that she'd run scared in the morning, and that would be that. Knowing there was only one right thing to do here, he drew a deep breath. He needed to go to bed—alone. It nearly killed him to do so, but he pulled back and cupped her face until she looked at him. "Rule number three," he said, his voice husky thick to his own ears. "If you're only giving me one night, I want a *full* night. And this one's already half over. So I'm going to take a rain check."

Her mouth fell open. "Are you serious?"

"Very." He gently shut her mouth, then lifted her off of him. "'Night, Alice."

"I hate you."

"I can work with that." And then, in spite of what his body wanted, he nudged Pickle, then took himself and his dog inside the inn, where he headed for a very cold shower.

Chapter 14

Dear Rude Sister,

When Knox left town after his mom died, I got it. I mean, it nearly killed me, but I understood. I told him he'd better make something of himself or else. He smiled, hugged me, and left, uttering no promises. That's Knox's way. He only promises what he can deliver. No lies, no misleading, no pretense. He worked hard, so hard, to make something of himself. I'd like to think he got that from me. It would mean I wasn't a total failure as a pseudo parent.

Signed, The Not Rude Sister

———

I t was late when Lauren found herself tossing and turning, unable to sleep. She finally glanced at the clock—4:00 a.m.—and had to revise. It wasn't late. It was early. Too early. She was tired, but she needed to shake her melancholy more than she needed sleep.

Her usual mantra was an automatic "I'm fine," but she could pretend all she wanted, the truth was that deep down she *wasn't* fine and she wasn't living her best life.

In fact, she was lonely, and she hadn't realized it until they'd read Eleanor's letter and had heard a matching loneliness in her great-aunt's tone.

Giving up on sleep, she showered and went to work. She needed to put some time into her new secret project, and for that she needed access to the records she hoped to find in the library.

Like she needed a new, nonpaying project, but she loved history, always had. It was her inner-nosy-body. Diving into the past was fascinating. So was writing about Sunrise Cove for the town's monthly newsletter. It'd given her such a rush to find people truly interested in what she wrote, so it seemed like a natural transition to now dive deep into the Last Chance Inn and write about that as well. Her hope was to combine her writings about the town and the inn into an actual book. If nothing else, she could self-publish it and maybe their guests would get a kick out of it.

Only, as she'd discovered, she couldn't do that without learning far more than she'd ever been told about her great-aunt Eleanor. She had no idea how the woman would have taken to the thought of Lauren writing about her life and the inn, but Lauren suspected—more like hoped—she'd have been pleased. In any case, Lauren planned to write an honest account, no matter what she found.

Two hours later, she sat back. What Eleanor had hinted at in her letter was true—she truly had been a closeted philanthropist, and thanks to a healthy trust fund and a successful run at acting, a huge one. The town of Sunrise Cove could thank her for the boost in tourism going back as far as the 1960s. On top of that, she'd funded the hospital, the rec center, the children's museum, and many, many more places, including the biggest surprise of all . . . the library.

Where Lauren had discovered herself.

It was getting harder and harder to reconcile the Eleanor her dad had told stories about with the Eleanor she was learning about from her research and the woman's own emails.

When it was time, she shifted from personal research into work mode, readying for her shift. Knowing her remaining time here at the library was coming to an end soon felt bittersweet to say the least. Vowing to enjoy every minute, she reminded herself to stay present and enjoy everything: putting the books back on the shelves, helping people find what they needed, ordering new books, talking to the patrons as they checked out, and Story Time—which by far was her favorite.

Today she was Little Red Riding Hood, simply because it was just a hooded red cape over her regular clothes, which would come in handy later when she headed from here to the inn.

She was halfway through reading a book to the kids when Hope called out, "Tommy and Mateo are fighting again!"

Lauren separated the boys.

"My grandma thsays fighting iths unbecoming," Hope said. "But my daddy thsays it's okay to fight if it's to protect yourself." She pointed at Tommy. "He pushed Mateo and called him a bad word."

Lauren marveled at the little girl's bravery and willingness to stand up for someone else. It was humbling, honestly, because Lauren herself had never been all that brave. In the past, she'd let Will and Alice be her brave. And in the time she'd been without them and on her own, she hadn't stepped up, not to be brave, or to make a life for herself.

It was time. Past time.

When her shift was over, she thought about heading home to go to bed, but her FOMO ran deep, so she drove to the inn. Alice was still painting, and knowing how much Alice hated the chore, she picked up a roller to assist. "We going to have another paint fight?"

Alice slid her a look. "I'm tempted, just to break one of our Ground Rules so I can see what happens."

"That always was one of your favorite things to do." Lauren smiled. "Remember when we were high school seniors and the principal forbid our entire senior class from pulling a school prank?"

"Yeah." Alice smirked. "He promised if we did, he'd find the culprit and prosecute that person to the fullest extent of the law."

"Uh-huh, so what did you do? You organized a coup." Lauren couldn't help but laugh at the memory. "You told every single senior to meet you at the school at midnight with a screwdriver. We got in through an open window and went through the school, unscrewing everything nonessential we could, and then left the buckets of screws in front of the principal's office."

"Yeah." Alice shook her head. "But I got us all

caught. I forgot about the school cameras, remember? Rookie mistake."

"True, but because every single one of us was involved, he had to drop the threat of prosecution. It was epic." She laughed. "I still laugh every time I think about it."

Alice smiled and set down her roller. "We need another can of paint. I've got them stacked in the living room, hold on a second."

A few beats went by, then Lauren heard Alice give a sudden, shocked gasp. Lauren went running, finding Alice on her knees in the far corner, peering under a sofa.

"I can't believe it! It's Minnie!" Alice cried. She came out from under the table with a small cage, and one mouse in it. "This is all Knox's doing!"

"How do you know it's Minnie?"

They both eyed the quarter-size black field mouse sitting daintily on her haunches, eating the cheese that had been left for her. She was perfectly unharmed, black eyes shiny and happy, nose and whiskers vibrating as she ate. "It's *totally* Minnie," Alice said. "*In a cage.* Mice are people too!" she yelled, clearly for Knox, but there was no sign of him.

"It's a humane cage," Lauren said. "She doesn't appear to be hurt."

"But what if she's got a family, and needs to bring that cheese back to them?"

"Knox promised to relocate whatever mice he found," Lauren reminded her, standing back a few feet. She wasn't exactly afraid of mice like she was . . . well, everything else, but she wasn't a huge fan either.

Alice opened the cage and slid her hand in.

Lauren gaped at her. "What if she gets free? What if she bites—"

"Ouch! Sonofabitch!" Alice yanked her hand back and stared at her finger.

Minnie took the opportunity to make a break for it. She jumped out of the cage and hit the ground running. She was down the hall and out of sight in two seconds flat.

Lauren turned back to Alice. "Are you okay?"

"Yeah." Alice shook it off. "It was my own fault, I scared her." She went after the mouse, and Lauren went after Alice, finding her in the office, butt up, head down, searching under all the furniture.

"Are you bleeding?" Lauren asked.

Alice straightened. "Do you think she got outside?"

Lauren grabbed Alice's hand to check for blood.

"She didn't break skin." Alice pulled free and headed for the kitchen, stopping short because the back door was open. "What if she got out?"

"Um . . ." Lauren hustled after Alice down the back steps. "Wasn't that what you wanted?"

"Yes . . . Maybe." Alice was eyeing the woods at the edge of the property. "It's cold today. Going to be even colder tonight."

"You know what? No more painting for you. You've clearly inhaled enough fumes for today." Lauren squeezed her hand. "And I'm sure she didn't get outside, okay? She's smart, she stayed inside. And I bet you by nightfall, she's moved her entire family in."

Alice stared at her, eyes narrowed. Then she sighed, shook her head, and gave a little laugh. "I'm being ridiculous, and you're lying through your teeth."

"I've never lied to you." Omitted, yes. Lied, no.

Alice didn't say anything to this. Just bent over her phone, her fingers a blur as she texted.

"What are you doing?"

"Telling Knox."

ALICE: Warning—sleep with one eye open tonight.

> KNOX: Sorry, can't hear you. We've
> got a bad connection.

ALICE: THAT DOESN'T WORK WITH TEXTS!

Lauren let out a horrified laugh and covered her mouth. "You like poking at the bear?"

"*I'm* the bear. He's poking at me." She turned on a heel and went back to painting.

Lauren sighed and did the same until Alice's phone buzzed an incoming text. They looked at each other, and then Alice read it and went back to rolling paint on the beadboard.

"Hello?" Lauren said with a dramatic hand wave. "What did he say?"

"Why? You writing a book?"

"Actually, yes." Whoops. She hadn't meant to say that out loud.

Alice stopped painting and stared at her. "What?"

"You first," Lauren said.

"Knox sent me a fake auto response that he hasn't and won't be reading texts. I think it brings him great joy to mess with me. Now you." Alice pointed at her with her roller. "You're writing a book? For real?"

Lauren sighed. "Yeah. It's on the history of Sunrise Cove, and there's going to be several chapters about the inn. And Eleanor." She paused. "You got a problem with that?"

"Will it be factually accurate?"

"Yes."

"Then no, I don't have a problem with it. I think it's . . ."

"Stupid? A waste of time?" Lauren asked, braced for criticism.

"Awesome," Alice said simply.

Undone, Lauren just stood there.

Alice gave her a long look. "You're not going to cry, are you?"

Lauren sighed and went back to painting. An hour later, they ran out of paint for the downstairs powder room.

"Nose goes," Alice said, touching her finger to the tip of her nose.

"What does that even mean?"

"It means *you* have to make the store run."

"Seriously?" Lauren asked.

"Hey, I promised to create an inventory of the barn. I've got to get on that."

"You've been avoiding the barn like the plague." Lauren paused, wanting to tread lightly. "You haven't been out there yet."

"Exactly, so I need to get started."

Lauren sighed. "You're impossible."

"So I've heard."

Lauren went outside. Knox was putting up new

window shutters. "Those look great," she said. "I'm going into town for more paint. Need anything?"

"Food that I don't have to make." He picked up a stick and tossed it. Pickle went from zero to hero, leaping up in the air to try and catch it.

He missed, then scooped it up from the ground before turning to grin with sheer doggy joy at Knox, not at all embarrassed or worried because he hadn't caught the stick, instead just thrilled he had the stick.

Schooled in life-ing skills by a dog. Lauren laughed, but it backed up in her throat when Pickle caught sight of her and headed her way, making her squeak.

"Pickle," Knox said. "Stop."

Pickle stopped about ten feet from Lauren.

"Sit."

Pickle sat.

Lauren took a shaky breath.

"You okay?" Knox asked.

Pickle was smiling, his tongue lolling, still looking a lot like a bear. Like a teddy bear. "I mean, he's kind of cute, right? In an overgrown sort of way."

"He has his moments." Knox brushed off his hands on his jeans and came toward her. "I'll drive."

"Is that a guy thing?"

"No, it's a survival thing. The roads are wet and probably a little icy, and you have shitty tires."

They took Knox's truck. "I'm starving," he said as they pulled out. "Let's eat first. Text Alice. See if she wants us to bring her back anything."

"You should probably text her yourself."

He slid her a look.

"Fine, but don't be surprised if she doesn't answer just to spite me."

LAUREN: Going to the hardware store with Knox, stopping for food first. Want anything?

                                   ALICE: Yes.

LAUREN: Okay . . . and your order would be?

                  ALICE: One of everything.

Lauren rolled her eyes. "She says one of everything."

She didn't know what she expected, but it wasn't for Knox to laugh in genuine amusement.

"How is that funny?" she asked.

"You're as bad as she is, holding on to the past like it was a security blanket."

Since this was mostly true, she got defensive. "And you don't?"

"No," he said flatly.

"Right." She rolled her eyes. "That's why you stood in the aisle at the hardware store mooning after your ex."

"I've never mooned."

She laughed. "You so mooned."

"How did you know she was an ex?"

Oops. She turned to look out the window. "How about this weather, huh?"

"Alice told you," he guessed.

"Maybe a little birdie told me."

He gave her the Knox-patented spill-your-shit look, and she caved like a cheap suitcase. "All right, so maybe Alice mentioned when we were watching Nikki fall all over you that she was your ex."

Knox looked annoyed. Interesting, because Lauren was pretty sure she'd detected a new and odd chemistry whenever Knox and Alice were in the same room, but she couldn't be sure, because the only person more closed off about her emotions than Alice was . . . Knox. She decided to test the waters. "Are you annoyed at Nikki, or at Alice for thinking you were after Nikki?"

"Neither."

Okay, well, that cleared everything up. *Not.*

Knox pulled into the diner's lot and parked before

turning to look at Lauren. "Trust me on this. The past is always best left behind."

"You think Alice and I should get over ourselves."

"Not for me to say."

"But you think it," she pressed.

"What I think is that life's too damn short. You and Alice, you two were once important to each other. And we both know that no one gets to know you as well or better than the kind of friends you make when you're young. So why would you turn your back on that?"

Feeling defensive, she lifted her chin. "Because one of us is too stubborn to apologize."

"After all this time, does that matter?" he asked.

Did it? Maybe not. And if *that* was true, did she make the first move? She'd have to, because there was no way Alice would.

Food for thought, she supposed.

Chapter 15

Dear Ungrateful Sister,

As I sit here all alone in this big old place, I think of Grandma Alda. She always had something to say that I didn't appreciate. Her kernels of knowledge and her words keep coming back to me. "Sometimes all you can do is be happy in the little moments," she'd say. "Like making someone laugh at work, or a smile from a loved one." I know now that she meant enjoy yourself between all that life flings at you. Live for those moments. I wish I'd done that more.

Signed, The Sister Who Wishes She'd
Chosen Happy

Lauren followed Knox into the diner, thinking about what he'd said. *Life's too damn short.* It actually felt the opposite to her. She was twenty-eight years old and already burnt out on life.

They were seated right away. Knox knew the hostess, apparently from high school. He laughed when she made a joke about how old and decrepit he looked, probably because he wasn't anything close to old or decrepit. In fact, he stood out in a crowd in the best of ways, which surely he knew. But it wasn't just that he was easy on the eyes. It was that his smile could draw you in, that he had a way of holding eye contact—not in a creepy way, but as if he was truly interested in what you had to say. He was laid-back, and his easygoing charisma was devastatingly charming.

"Why are you single?" she asked.

He eyed her over his menu. "Excuse me?"

She felt herself flush. "I just mean that you could probably have any woman you want. So . . . why don't you?"

"I'm not exactly a monk."

Which wasn't an answer, and they both knew it.

"And I could ask you the same thing," he said.

She shrugged that off. "It's hard to meet someone at the library. It's usually younger kids, or the over-sixty set."

"Do you like the job?"

She'd actually forgotten she hadn't told anyone about being let go. It was too humiliating. "I *love* the job." God's honest truth.

"Are you planning to stay there for a while?"

She froze. "Why? What've you heard?"

At her defensive tone, he cocked his head. "Nothing. It's just a question. Like hi, how are you, great weather, how's the job?"

"Oh." She grimaced. "Sorry."

He went brows up, and when Knox went brows up, he was asking a question.

"It's nothing," she said. "I'm handling it."

"Handling what?"

Well, hell. "Work."

He looked at her for a long beat. "You know if you were having trouble, you could tell me about it, right?"

"Sure." Like maybe when hell froze over would she admit she was so pathetic that she'd been fired while wearing a Mother Goose costume.

Thankfully, their waitress came over. Her name was Kelly, which Lauren knew because it said so on her little badge, and plus Lauren ate here a lot and Kelly was almost always working.

Kelly smiled at Knox. "What'll it be, handsome?"

"I'll take the three-egg scramble with hash browns,

sausage, and sourdough toast," he said. "And if you could double that and box the second order up to go, please."

"Sure thing," Kelly said and smiled at Lauren before turning to walk off.

"Wait," he said. "You didn't get Lauren's order."

Kelly turned back. "Oh, I already know it. It never changes. It's Will's favorite—tofu scramble with a short stack of pancakes on the side, no butter."

Knox blinked, then opened his mouth to say something, but Lauren shook her head. "Just let it happen." She waited until Kelly was gone to speak again. "The town thinks Will and I are still dating."

"But he's dead."

"Yeah, well, tell them that."

Someone walked by their table and stopped short. It was Ben, the cute guy from the hardware store.

"Knox," he said with a nod and then turned to Lauren, a warm smile curving his mouth. "Hey there, remember me?"

Did she remember the first guy to approach her after four years? Who also happened to be the guy who'd given her a stunningly erotic dream the other night? Yes. *Very much* she remembered him. "Of course. You helped me pick out a plant." Which was dying, by the way, not that she was about to admit it.

Huh. Guess there were a lot of things she wasn't admitting lately.

"The garden supplies and decor you ordered come in tomorrow," Ben said.

She could feel Knox give her a look. She met it evenly. "I know, you wanted to wait, but the patio and yard need a pick-me-up. Curb appeal, Knox. It's something I can do when you and Alice are doing stuff I'm not skilled enough for."

"I could deliver, if you'd like," Ben said. "I'm eating three tables down with a few coworkers. Just let me know either way before you leave."

"That's so sweet," Lauren said. "Delivery would be *great*, thank you."

"But not necessary," Knox said. "I usually end up at the store almost every day anyway. We'll pick up the order and save you the trouble."

"Oh. Okay then," Ben said, with a flash of disappointment. "If anything changes, let me know."

Lauren glared at Knox, which was wasted because he'd turned his fat head away.

"Have a great breakfast," Ben said, his smile slightly less bright. And then he pivoted and walked off.

Right into a beam.

"Oh my God," Lauren gasped, jumping to her feet. "Are you—"

"Yep!" Ben gave a wry smile and rubbed his forehead. "I'm fine." And then he turned away again and this time walked very carefully around the pole and back to his table.

Lauren sank back to her seat, shooting eye daggers at Knox, who was shoving in the food that had come. "That was mean."

"I didn't do anything."

Lauren rolled her eyes and then craned her neck to look at Ben's table, but his back was to her now. "You think he's okay?"

"I think he'd rather run into another pole than admit he's not."

"He's such a nice guy," she said. And not her usual type, which had always been fast, not particularly kind, self-focused, and . . . full of shit. Ben seemed anything but. "And talk about customer service," she said. "He was going to deliver for us."

Knox gave a low laugh. "First of all, no guys are nice. And second, which also proves point one, *you're* what he wants to service."

Her pulse gave a little leap. She almost didn't recognize the feeling. "Right. There's not a man within these city limits looking to date Will's girlfriend."

This had Knox stopping with his fork halfway to his mouth. "That's ridiculous."

"And yet true." She poured nearly the entire pitcher of syrup over her gluten-free, dairy-free, sugar-free pancakes.

"Having a little pancakes with your syrup?" he asked.

"Don't judge me, you've got more cholesterol on your plate than I've had in my entire life. How in the hell do you stay in shape?"

He shrugged. "Work, and sometimes I run."

"I bet it's because you have a penis."

He choked.

"Are you really choking on your own sausage right now?" Lauren asked on a laugh, reaching over to pat him on the back.

"Believe me," he finally managed, "the irony isn't escaping me." He took a drink of water. "So what you're telling me is that the town won't let you move on."

"That's what I'm telling you. I'm clearly going to die a renewed virgin."

He grimaced. "Okay, now I'm sorry I scared Ben off. If he doesn't have a concussion from the face-plant into that beam, I can talk to him and—"

"Don't you dare! You're intimidating enough just sitting there." She poured more syrup over her pancakes. When in doubt, sugar up. "Everyone was all so devastated when Will died. They still miss him. It's like they're in perpetual mourning."

"And you?" he asked. "Seems to me, it should be about you, not them. What do you want?"

Lauren sighed. "I want him to be not dead. But . . . would we still be together? No." Crap. She hadn't meant to say that. She jabbed her fork at him. "Do *not* tell Alice that part. She wouldn't understand."

"It's your choice, Lauren. You do realize that, right? You can let them win and die a"—he grimaced— "renewed virgin. Or—"

"Or what? Leave town and start over somewhere? I don't want to do that."

"I was going to say you could take the reins. Go out on a date and show everyone you're moving on. And I'm betting that Ben's up for the challenge."

"Flirting doesn't mean he wants to date me."

Knox laughed. "Oh, he wants to do a whole lot more than that."

Again came that leap of her pulse. *Excitement*, she realized, an almost alien feeling. "How do you know?" she asked with pathetic hope in her voice.

"How do you *not* know?" He shook his head on another low laugh. "Lauren, the guy just walked right into a beam watching you. You need to just go for it."

"Is the guy who just had drinks with his cray cray ex giving me dating advice?"

He grimaced. "Did Alice tell you that too?"

"Nope. One of the guys who works at the library in maintenance was at the bar last night too. He posted a selfie and you were in the background with Nikki, all cozy and chatting away."

Knox looked like he wanted to bang his forehead on the table. "I forgot we lived in Mayberry," he muttered.

"Where?"

"Never mind. And there was nothing cozy about it, and she was the only one chatting. Trust me, she was more concerned about missing out on reaping the rewards from my company. She read about me in an article in *People* magazine."

"*People*?" She gaped at him. "Are you famous?"

"No." He looked uncomfortable. "It was just their favorite eco-friendly-companies issue."

She knew this meant his company had to be a huge success. "Oh my God."

He frowned. "What?"

"You're rich. *And* famous." She gasped. "Which means you probably could've bought Alice out of the inn. But you didn't, because . . ." She stared at him, trying to read his thoughts. "Because you wanted her to stay . . . because you wanted her to suffer?" She searched his gaze. "No. No, that's not it." Then it hit her, the real reason, and she laughed and leaned back. "You like her. As in you *like her* like her."

This got her another grimace. "I just want her to slow down and stop running," he said. "I want her to take the month here and remember how much she loved Sunrise Cove, remember that she could be happy again, in a way I don't think she's been since she left."

Good answer, and her amusement at his expense faded. "Trust me, I want to see her happy again too. But you do get that she's *not* going to stick, right? No matter what timeline we have for the inn, she can't wait to get out of here."

"Yeah, she made that very clear last night."

Lauren took in his unmistakable disappointment. "What happened last night?"

Knox turned his attention back to his food. "Nothing. We shared a beer."

Lauren wondered what else they'd shared. Then she took in his tense shoulders, and the carefully blank expression on his face. The kind of expression a person used when they didn't want to reveal their feelings. She should know, she was most excellent at the blank face these days as well. "Listen," she said gently. "You gave me some advice, so I'm going to return the favor. Tread lightly and cautiously, because the more she likes you, the faster she'll run."

"Speaking from experience?"

She sighed. "We have unresolved issues."

"No kidding." He looked at her for a moment. "How did you guys become friends?"

Lauren smiled. "You mean unlikely friends, right?" She never talked about this, but suddenly she was tired of holding it all in. "We met our freshman year of high school. I got really good grades and liked my teachers, which meant school was hell for me. The other kids thought I was a suck-up, when really, I was just a shy wallflower with so few friends, I was able to spend all of my time on my schoolwork. Then one day this stupid guy wanted me to do his homework for him. I didn't want to, but he . . ." She paused, hating the memory. "Scared me. So I did the stupid homework for him. And then he wanted me to keep doing it."

"Ah, Lauren," Knox said, voice low. "I'm sorry."

She shook her head. "It was a long time ago. I was just mad at myself because I was too afraid to say no to him. One day Alice came along when I was handing over the homework. I didn't know anything about her except she was always in jeans and a ponytail, played ball with the boys at every break, and could swear like a sailor. She made an impression."

Knox smiled, like he felt the same. "What happened?"

"She told that guy that he was *never* to ask me to do his schoolwork again. That, in fact, he wasn't so much as to look at me, or she and her brother would beat him up."

Knox didn't look surprised, but he seemed both a little amused and a lot impressed. "And the guy left you alone?"

"Yep, and as opposite as we were, and even with next to nothing in common, Alice and I became the unlikely best friends." She smiled at the memories, then sighed because that's all they were now. Memories.

"And you eventually got engaged to her brother."

"Not engaged." She wasn't about to go into all that had happened. How she and Will had been fighting for months. How she'd planned on breaking it off, but he'd shocked her half to death by pulling out a diamond ring—his grandma's—which had been passed down to him from his dad. How she'd frozen in place, because while she'd cared about him, she hadn't quite been *in love* with him, and even back then she'd known the difference. She'd needed time, and well . . . *more*. She'd needed him to grow up.

But he'd never gotten to do that.

"Not engaged," she repeated softly. "But we were close. It's hard to resist a Moore." She smiled. "As I think you're starting to get."

If he had thoughts on that matter, he kept them to himself. Thirty minutes later, they were at the hardware store, and to her huge disappointment, Ben wasn't there.

Just as well. Her life was in flux. It was a terrible time to be thinking about a potential date when she didn't even know where she'd be working next month.

But a part of her didn't want to accept this. That same part decided she could be in flux and *still* have a life, and that she deserved one. All she had to do was reach out and touch it.

Chapter 16

Need
Alice—A new life.
Lauren—I second that, preferably in Bali.
Lauren—mousetraps (the traps are gone, don't
even bother trying to find them—Alice, in
case you didn't know)
Lauren—Dark chocolate with sea salt, pronto.
Lauren—for Alice to stop being mean.
Alice—I'm not mean! Just honest!
Knox—this is for WORK-RELATED NEEDS
ONLY, LADIES!

The next day Alice stood on the porch, watching a truck drive away from the inn. Lauren and Knox stood on either side of her, silent and unmoving. Well,

Knox was silent and unmoving. Lauren was practically jumping up and down.

The truck belonged to the hardware store, which turned out to be owned by Ben. He'd personally just delivered live greenery for the inn's back deck, along with patio furniture.

Hence Lauren grinning from ear to ear, the sort of grin a woman gets when she's been struck by Cupid's arrow, and she was excitedly poking Knox, demanding. "How? What? When? Why?"

Alice had no idea what she was talking about, but apparently Knox did because he shrugged. "I might've called and asked him to deliver after all."

Lauren threw herself at him and hugged him tight, leaving Alice surprised and . . . jealous? Lauren hadn't hugged Alice like that since . . . well, since Alice had left Sunrise Cove.

Yeah, and whose fault was that? She went hands on hips. "Okay, what am I missing?"

"Ben's got a thing for Lauren," Knox said. "And likely also a concussion."

Alice looked at Lauren for an explanation that made sense.

Lauren grinned. "It's true. It happened at the diner. He walked right into a beam when he was looking back at me. Do you know what that means? It means that someone has a crush on me and he's not eighty."

Alice hadn't seen that look of happiness on Lauren's face since the old days. Since before everything had gotten screwed up. Maybe Alice had no clue about how to breach the huge crevasse between them, but she knew Lauren was a good person, one of the best, actually, and this town had held her back for too long.

Knox turned to the two pallets of stuff that Ben had dropped off, and Alice joined him. Patio furniture—not assembled—plants, pretty pots, dirt, lights, and yard decorations.

"I might've gone slightly overboard," Lauren admitted.

Alice snorted. "You should've just slept with him. You didn't have to warm him up with this huge order. I mean, since he already walked into a beam for you."

"I didn't order this stuff to catch his attention," Lauren said. "We've talked about the back covered deck, how it's just a pad of concrete, cold and uninviting, remember? I said we should fix it up, make it so people want to gather there and socialize."

"And who's the 'we' in this equation?" Alice asked. "Because those cute little baby spruces need to be potted, as do the other plants you bought. The furniture has to be put together, and all those strings of fairy lights hung."

"Oh good," Lauren said, looking at her watch, moving toward her car. "I knew you'd know what to do. I've got a shift at the library. I'll be back later."

"Hey, new Ground Rule," Alice said. "Whoever orders the stuff without consulting the other two partners has to be prepared to handle the stuff without the other partners."

"Sure," Lauren said. "Starting next time."

"You Mother Goose again today?" Knox asked.

She smiled. "Clifford the Big Red Dog."

He laughed, and Alice stared at him as the sound woke some girlie parts deep inside her that she'd been neglecting. Annoying. "Are you really leaving Knox to plant all this stuff?" she asked Lauren's back.

Knox went brows up. "You mean Knox . . . *and Alice.*"

"I really don't."

"I'll bring a pizza for dinner after my shift," Lauren called out, moving quickly to her car, as if to avoid further argument.

"Large *nonvegan* pizzas," Alice yelled after her. "*Plural*—with the works. Specifically, pepperoni is a requirement. Invite Ben."

Lauren tripped over her own two feet, then turned back. "I . . . couldn't do that."

"Why?" Alice asked. "If you need an excuse, it's to thank him for the delivery. He seems like a good guy."

Something crossed Lauren's gaze. Frustration, maybe. Annoyance at Alice, certainly. "He is." She tossed up her hands. "But I don't remember how to do this."

"Be a friend?" Alice asked.

"No, that's *you*. *You* don't remember how to be a friend. *I* don't remember how to date."

Alice tried to duck the barb, but it nailed its intended target—her heart. Trying to shake it off, she said, "Maybe it's like getting back onto a bike."

Lauren looked hopeful. "You think?"

"I mean . . . maybe," she said, squirming, all too aware that Knox was watching this interchange with interest.

"Are you saying you haven't 'gotten on a bike' in a while?" Lauren asked, using finger quotes. "Like how long a while?"

How had she gotten herself into this conversation? "I haven't dated since . . . I don't remember exactly. Probably since Kevin."

Lauren looked surprised. "Kevin, Will's racing friend from France Kevin? The one who dated you for a year and then decided he missed his ex and went back to France? That Kevin? Because that was *five* years ago." She stared at Alice. "Oh my God. I'm not the only renewed virgin in the house!"

"I didn't say I hadn't *slept* with anyone," Alice said. "I said I hadn't *dated*."

Both Knox and Lauren went brows up at this.

"Get over it," Alice snapped. "I have needs."

"Like . . . lipstick vibrator needs?" Lauren asked.

"Hey," Alice said. "At least she was taking care of herself. Nothing wrong with that." Alice caught Knox looking amused and glared at him.

He just gave her a slow, more-than-slightly danger-ous smile that unexpectedly sent heat spiraling through her. She pointed at him. "Knock that off."

Knox gave her an innocent look. *As if.*

"What did he do?" Lauren asked.

Knox's amusement kicked up when Alice tried and failed to come up with an answer. "Never mind!" she said.

Lauren started to open the car door, but hesitated. "So . . . I've sorta got a serious question. About, um . . . those needs."

Shit. No way was Alice going to admit that she wanted to break rule number six with Knox—*no one sleeps with anyone*—bad. Like really, *really* bad. "Uh—"

"How does it actually work?" Lauren asked.

"They have books on that," Alice said. "Right there in your library probably."

"Okay, funny, ha ha. I'm talking about the . . ." Lauren tossed up her hands. "Whole casual sex thing. Because I'm not sure I'm cut out for physical contact without an emotional attachment."

"You mean, like I am?" Alice asked with what she thought was remarkable calm.

"Hey, it's a *compliment*," Lauren stressed. "I *want* to be more like you. Tough. Courageous. Resilient. Take-what-you-want. Tell me your secret to staying emotionally unattached."

Alice let out a slow, deep breath. Of all the veiled barbs, this one hit home the hardest. "Look, this isn't about me. It's about you and Beam Ben."

"Once upon a time you'd have talked to me about this. You know. Before you stopped talking to me."

"Really?" Alice asked. "You really want to do this here? Now?"

"Yes."

Still painfully aware of Knox watching them, Alice tried to swallow past a ball of emotion stuck in her throat. "Well, I don't."

"Then when? Name the time and place."

"Never works best for me." Alice was pretty sure

she didn't actually mean that, but oh how she hated being backed into a corner.

"Fine," Lauren said. "Message received." And she stormed off.

Pickle, sensitive to moods, let out a whine.

Alice sighed. "It's not you, buddy." Unable to stand Knox's silence, she glanced his way. "*What?*"

This got her an almost smile. "You've got a certain way with people, I'll give you that."

His amusement didn't improve her mood any. "God-given talent."

He smiled and shook his head. "Come on. It's fix-all-the-railings day. We're going to need some stuff from the shed."

As they headed that way, Alice glanced over at the old red barn, sitting there surrounded by several massive pine trees, looking like a postcard.

"Been in there yet?" he asked casually.

No, which his nosy ass damn well knew. Inside that barn sat her past, and for all her big fancy talk of leaving said past in the past, she hadn't been all that successful at it.

"It's just a barn, Alice. No ghosts."

Oh, but he was wrong. So very wrong, because *all* her ghosts were in there. Every last one of them . . .

"Are we getting stuff or not?"

Hours later, they'd filled old wine barrels they'd found stacked in the shed with the baby spruces, had strung the lights, built a small gas firepit, and put together the table and chairs.

It was getting dark, so she flicked on the newly hung twinkle lights, then stood there, stunned. The deck had been transformed into something that belonged on a Pinterest board.

They had one more tree to plant. Knox was on his knees in front of the last wine barrel. He had his ball cap on backward, his mirrored sunglasses shielding his eyes from the slanting sun. His jeans and long-sleeved Henley were smudged with dirt, as was every inch of her, and yet somehow it only served to make him look even hotter. Despite the cool air, they'd been moving big heavy pots and mounds of dirt, and they both glowed with a fine sheen of sweat in the last dying rays of daylight.

Didn't stop her from thinking about how it might feel to get rid of their dirty clothes and rub their overheated bodies together.

"You going to help me with this last tree or just keep staring at my ass?" he asked.

She moved to his side and dropped to her knees. "It's a good thing you've got a nice one."

He flashed her a smile. "And it's not even my best part."

Note to self: Not ready for prime time with Knox Rawlings.

She held back the dirt while he muscled the four-foot tree into the barrel in an impressive display of strength and agility. They were all up in each other's personal space, and somehow, in spite of the day they'd had, he still smelled good.

"You okay?" he asked.

"Yes." She narrowed her eyes suspiciously. "Why?"

"You just moaned."

She refused to blush. "Did not."

"You did." His grin widened, his teeth white against his dirty face. "You like me."

"Shut up."

"It's okay." He nudged her shoulder with his and leaned in to brush his mouth across her temple. "I like you too."

"Why?"

"Why do I like you?"

She crossed her arms and gave him a dark look.

He smiled and counted off the reasons on his fingers. "You're smart, snarky, you default to edgy when backed into a corner, and you're not afraid to come out swinging no matter what you're up against. Truth is, I've never met a woman quite like you."

She snorted. "I'm not sure any of that is a compliment."

"It is from me," he said, and they stared at each other across the wine barrel. "This is actually the most fun I've had in a while."

This got a full laugh from her. "You need to get out more."

"No doubt. Come here, Alice."

"Why?"

"Just lean in a little bit more, Ms. Suspicious."

She gave another inch or so, aware of how sweaty and dirty she was. "*What?*"

"This," Knox said. And then he kissed her.

Her moan was entirely involuntary, and when she heard herself let it out, she jerked back with a startled laugh. "I'm all dirty and sweaty and icky."

"I know." His voice was rough and husky. "I like it."

She ignored the warm fluttery feeling that gave her. Spending time with Knox had always made her feel warm. Hot, even. But the fluttery thing was new. And scary. She was treading on thin ice here, and she needed to walk carefully or that ice would break beneath her.

His mouth slid along her jaw. "The dirtier and sweatier the better."

"You're a very sick man."

He stood up and pulled her to her feet as well, then backed her against a post and cradled her face in his hands. "No doubt," he said.

She bit her lower lip, but a laugh escaped. "You're also ridiculous." And way too close, because suddenly she was remembering just how long it'd been since she'd slept with anyone. She talked a big game, but it'd been months. She glanced at him, marveling that he seemed to accept her as is, even enjoying the rough-and-tumble side of her, along with the fact that she wasn't afraid to get dirty or work hard. Because neither was he.

And damn, she was in over her head, because if he had a hold of her heart—which was likely, the sneaky bastard—she wasn't entirely convinced he'd be careful with it.

Watching her think too hard, he smiled. "You promised me a night," he reminded her, and though the words made her quiver from the inside out, she managed a wobbly nod.

He studied her for another beat. "Do you have regrets? You can take it back."

"I know."

"Which doesn't answer the question," he said.

Right. Because she didn't know how to answer. She hadn't changed her mind. She wanted him. But he seemed more like one of those ideas that sounded really good in the moment but had the potential to turn out spectacularly bad. Like when she opened a family-size bag of those little candy bars and then ate the whole thing. "I don't have regrets. And I don't want to take it back." She sighed, then admitted her truth. "I think maybe I've just been waiting for you to bring it up."

He looked surprised. "Why?"

"Maybe a woman can sometimes still want a guy to make the first move."

His lips curved, and then his mouth slanted over hers, making her actually gasp at the unexpected pleasure of it. He seemed all too pleased to take advantage of her parted lips, and when their tongues touched, she could've sworn her bones dissolved. He cupped the back of her head, his other hand sliding down her throat, her arm, along her hip, then around to press on her lower back, urging her even closer to him. She went eagerly, their kiss not gentle but rough and deep and hot as hell, and she loved it. It felt inevitable. Essential . . . like breathing.

When they finally broke apart, she almost whimpered at the loss.

"Consider that my first move," he murmured, brushing his lips to hers one more time. "Your turn."

Oh, boy. But then, to her disappointment, he pulled back and answered his suddenly ringing phone. "Hey. Yeah," he said. "Two minutes." He looked at Alice. "Let's go."

"Where to?"

"We've got a date with a couple of pizzas and Lauren. She's just driving up."

At the word *pizza*, Pickle—who'd fallen asleep at their feet—came immediately wide awake. He lifted his big head, hopeful.

Knox was herding them toward the inn's back door at a good clip.

"Looks like Pickle isn't the only one eager for pizza," she said.

"You know how Lauren gets when someone's late. Plus she hates cold pizza."

"How do you know?"

"Because I listen."

This was true. He did listen. And though they hadn't spent a lifetime both together and apart, like she and Lauren had, he'd made it his business to get to know them. Like they mattered. Like *she* mattered.

It was nearly dark now, and the inn lights were on. The place seemed to glow with warmth and personality.

Same as the man next to her. "Knox?"

"Yeah?"

She reached for his hand, smiling when he looked over at her in surprise. Holding eye contact, she squeezed his hand. "Consider *this* my next move."

Chapter 17

THE GROUND RULES

1. No tears.
2. This is about Eleanor.
3. Open, honest conversations with actual words. DAILY—as long as it doesn't violate rule #1.
4. Do not kill your partners.
5. No nicknames.
6. No one sleeps with anyone.
7. No ties, emotional or physical, period.
8. Read Eleanor's emails together.
9. We are in this shit together.
10. Paint is for walls only.
11. When someone orders stuff without the partners, they have to handle the stuff without the partners.

Alice inhaled three pieces of pizza before she could talk. Landscaping was effing exhausting. Apparently so was kissing, at least at the level Knox did it. He really was a world-class kisser, and even just thinking it made her hot all over again. She reached for her water and downed the whole glass. When she glanced over at him, he gave a little smirk.

The ass. "Where's Ben?" she asked Lauren.

Lauren flushed. "It's complicated."

"Or you're chicken," Alice said.

"Or that." Lauren was nibbling at her salad and looking at the To-do List on the wall. "We can cross off painting the downstairs hallway. And the planting and deck, too."

"Subtle subject change, and the hallway and planting weren't even on our list," Alice pointed out, moving over to the wall and grabbing the Sharpie to update the board.

Lauren sent her a look. "While you're at it, add that we need to figure out what we're doing with the cars."

Alice dropped the pen. It was stupid, and uncomfortably revealing, as was the awkward silence behind her.

Lauren sighed. "I'm sorry. That was thoughtless of me," she said genuinely. "But you bring out the worst in me."

Alice shrugged. "It's a special talent I offer."

"If it's too hard for you," Lauren began, "we can figure something else out—"

"I said I'll get to it, and I will." She picked up the pen, hating the weighted silence from her partners. But she'd learned some new dirty tricks working with all guys this past year. They always, without fail, assigned blame. "I just haven't had time," she said lightly. "I've been busy planting, since *one* of us doesn't like to get her hands dirty."

"I could've handled the deck and planting by myself," Knox said. "If you wanted to get to the barn."

Alice swiveled a long gaze on him next. "You sure you want to keep talking, because I can promise you, it's going to mess up your plans for tonight."

He grinned. And God help her, she melted a little bit.

"Wait, what's happening tonight?" Lauren's eyes narrowed as she divided a look between them. "Oh no. No, no, no. We have a rule, remember? Business partners don't sleep together."

"Oh, there will be no sleeping," Alice said.

Knox's smile widened.

"Okay," Lauren said, standing up, looking every bit the bossy librarian as she eyed them both. "I just want to put this out there to make sure you both think this through. Because one of you is emotionally bankrupt, and the other's emotionally unavailable."

Alice looked at Knox. "Who's who?"

"Haven't the foggiest," Knox admitted.

Lauren tossed up her hands. "See, if you don't even know which one you are, you have no business . . . *fornicating!*"

"Please *never* say *fornicating* again," Alice said.

Lauren walked to the board and pointed to the rules.

"Are you talking about the Do Not Kill Your Partners, or the No One Sleeps with Anyone part?" Alice asked.

Lauren jabbed the Sharpie at her. "Both."

"Don't worry," Alice said. "We've talked about this. We've got our own set of rules to make sure everyone walks away happy. Right, Knox?"

"Right," Knox said. "And I can guarantee you, Alice is going to walk away happy."

Alice blushed. *Dammit.*

"Ohmigod," Lauren moaned. "You're so going to mess this up. And then our trio's going to be screwed."

"We're not a trio," Alice said, and then felt like a jerk when Lauren flinched like she'd slapped her.

"Is anyone ever going to tell me what your problem with each other is?" Knox asked.

Alice and Lauren said "no" in sync.

Knox sighed.

"And we *are* a trio, whether you like it or not,"

Lauren said and pointed to Knox. "One." She pointed to Alice. "Two . . ." She pointed to herself. "Three. See? A threesome—"

Knox choked on a soda.

"*Not that kind of threesome!*" Lauren turned back to the rules and wrote rule number twelve, all in caps:

NO FALLING IN LOVE!

Alice lifted her hands. "Something we can all agree on." She went back to eating.

Lauren too.

Knox watched for a moment. "Okay, well, since two of the three of us are already annoyed, I've got a couple of things. We still have a ton of shit to do, so we're going to get up an hour earlier each morning. And while we're all here, we might as well read another of Eleanor's emails."

"See." Lauren looked triumphantly at Alice. "Even Knox thinks we're a trio."

"Whatever." Alice pulled the iPad from the small desk in the corner and came back, feeling a sense of dread she hadn't expected. Mostly these days she tried to feel nothing at all, but her blessed numbness had ceased and desisted the moment she'd stepped foot back in Sunrise Cove.

Correction. She'd been fine until she'd seen Lauren again.

And then Knox. That'd been when the floodgates to her emotions had let loose, and she was *not* a fan.

Knox vanished into the kitchen and came back with the bottle of whiskey, a bag of chips, a gallon of cookie dough ice cream, and a wooden spoon.

He handed Lauren the chips and Alice the ice cream and spoon. And if she'd been looking for a keeper, she'd have fallen in love with him right then and there. Good thing she *wasn't* looking. "Thanks," she said softly and took three fortifying bites before turning on the iPad. "The subject of the next email is Knox." She looked up at him. "Do you want to read it?"

He shook his head. "You do it."

"Okay . . ." She looked at them both. "Ready?"

"No," Lauren said. "But don't let that stop you."

She drew a deep breath and began to read out loud:

Dear Dead-To-Me Sister,

Have I told you that Knox's mother works for me? She's . . . well, to be honest, she's a mess. But she's sweet and kind, and can clean a house like no other. Problem is, she's been pickling her liver for years now, leaving poor Knox to raise himself. Let's just say that thanks to our own good ol' dad, I recognized his need for direction and guidance, so I put him to work. Yeah, yeah, child labor laws, blah blah blah, but there's something to be said for having a purpose, for learning to direct your anger into something productive. You, Ruth, could've used more of a firm hand in that department and you know it. Too bad you always did look for the easy way out.

Not Knox. He's learned so much and come so far. He's smart as hell, resilient, and he never gives up. I admire that, and him. That all said, I always knew I'd lose him to the world one day, and that was fine with me. It was all I wanted for him. Enter Nikki Waters. You remember her grandmother, right? That girl could make you think you were her best friend and then stab you in the back. Well, let's just say the apple didn't fall far from the tree. Knox was goners for Nikki though, and no amount of reason could get him to see she wasn't right for him.

So I did a thing. I sent him out of town on loan to go work at the Nash Ranch, the place Daddy always sent us for the summer. Remember? I'd work and you'd pretend to be sick? Anyway, Knox worked hard and earned a bunch of money.

And yes, okay, when he came back, Nikki was pregnant by someone else.

Sound familiar?

I can practically hear you yelling at me to get to the point, so I will. It's this: I know I made mistakes in my life, too many to count, but what was I supposed to do, just stand by and watch Knox give his heart to a woman who was going to break it into a million pieces? Yes, I should've told him, but it wouldn't have changed anything. The deed had been done, their relationship effectively ruined. Whatever they'd had could be no more. Same with us . . .

Signed,
Your better half

The words were so Eleanor, it was as if she stood right there in the room with them. Hell, knowing Eleanor, she *was* right there in the room with them, a feisty, spirited ghost from hell. Alice could hear her own pulse in her ears. With every passing second that Knox didn't speak, head bowed, staring at his hands resting on his thighs, her heart squeezed harder for him. "Knox—"

"I need a minute."

Understanding, she offered him the ice cream.

Shaking his head, he grabbed the whiskey bottle instead, stood, and strode from the room.

Alice had loved Eleanor. Still did. But she didn't understand what the woman had been thinking to interfere in Knox's life the way she had.

"You're going after him, right?" Lauren asked.

"He wants to be alone."

"So did you. But he went after you anyway. You didn't need to be alone then, and neither does he."

Alice wanted to go after him, but she'd seen the flash of betrayal and hurt in his eyes as he grabbed the whiskey. She was pretty sure it didn't have anything to do with wishing he was still with Nikki and everything to do with Eleanor pulling strings that had affected his life. He'd hate that. And he would hate that she'd seen that flash of vulnerability on his face. "I'm not sure me going after him right now is a good idea."

"Why not? You're the one who wants to fornicate with him."

"What did I say about using that word?"

Lauren didn't give up. "*Someone's* got to go. And let's be honest, out of the two of us, you two are closer. You've become real friends. And friends are there for each other, to talk when one of them needs that."

Maybe, but their plans for the night hadn't involved talking or being friends. She wasn't sure she even knew how to do that. "You're the one who put up that rule about not falling in love."

Lauren blinked. Opened her mouth, and then shut it. "Who said anything about falling in love?"

Alice felt the heat flood her cheeks and, horrified at herself, she stood and headed toward the door.

"You're going after him, right?"

She didn't answer because she didn't know *what* she was doing. But when she walked outside, she was hugely relieved to see Knox's truck still in the driveway.

Okay, so if she were Knox with a bottle of whiskey, where would she go? Her eyes locked on the shadow of the barn in the dark. *Damn . . .*

Reeling from all that Eleanor's letter had revealed, Knox strode right out of the inn and kept walking, Pickle at his side. He'd have gotten in his truck and gone as far as a tank of gas could take him, but he didn't have his keys on him.

He'd left them back inside, with a good chunk of his heart and soul.

So he kept walking. The shed didn't hold any interest, but he stopped at the barn. Once upon a time, when this place had been an actual working ranch, long before the first TV show, the building had been filled with horses and gear.

No longer. He opened the double doors. The space was large, with windows high up on the walls, allowing the bright moonlight to filter in. There had to be twenty cars neatly parked, some covered, some not. In the back was a small tack room turned office. The walls were lined with shelves that were filled with tools. A mechanic's heaven.

He moved closer to the cars and slid behind the wheel of the first one—an army-green 1970 Land Rover Defender that had been used in the opening sequence of every episode of the *Last Chance Racing* show. He leaned his head back, took a swig of whiskey, and closed his eyes.

Before his mom's death, the biggest event to shake his life had been the girl he'd loved leaving him, and it all might've turned out very differently had the *one* woman he'd trusted given him a heads-up.

At the sound of the barn door squeaking open, then soft footsteps heading his way, he stilled. He strained to hear more, but the footsteps stopped, then began retreating . . .

Then stopped again.

He knew from the barrage of emotions hitting his

chest that it was Alice. He remained where he was, eyes closed, waiting. *What's it going to be, babe?*

He took a second swig of the whiskey before those footsteps began moving again, heading his way. So she'd made a decision, she'd come after him, even though it'd meant stepping foot inside the barn. Unintentional as it'd been, he'd forced her into the space of her own nightmares. When the footsteps stopped at the front of the Land Rover, he drew a breath. "I'm sorry."

"Minnie? Is that you?"

He snorted and opened his eyes to take her in. She met his gaze through the windshield, her skin glowing under the golden glow of the light bulbs hanging above from the rafters.

He got out and met her at the front of the car, leaning back against it.

Mirroring his pose at his side, she rested her perfect ass on the bumper before taking the bottle of whiskey— the one he'd forgotten he was holding—from his hand. She knocked back a good swig of her own, winced as it went down, then let out a heavy breath as she set it down on the ground.

"Wasn't sure if you were in or out," he said.

"Of the barn?" Her mouth curved very slightly. "Neither was I."

"Actually, I meant in or out . . . of us."

She turned her head to meet his gaze, her own hooded and troubled. "There's an 'us'?"

"You were there when we kissed, right?"

"Yeah. It was . . ." She paused. "Good."

As the guy who'd been knocked flat by the explosive chemistry between them, he had to laugh. "*Good?*"

She bit her lower lip. "Okay, so maybe it was a little better than good."

He shook his head and she let out a small smile. "Like you need your ego stroked," she murmured, squirming a little, which was interesting. She was about to say something she wasn't sure she wanted to say. He waited her out.

"Fine. It was heart stopping," she admitted. "Better?"

"*Much.*"

She rolled her eyes. "So . . . we're not going to talk about it then?"

"You mean how when we kiss we could provide electricity to the entire state of California?"

She gave him a get-real look. "Eleanor's email."

No. He was tired of thinking about the past that'd never done him any favors.

When he didn't speak, Alice nudged her shoulder to his. He turned his head her way and found her looking at him with worry. "I'm fine," he said.

"It's okay to be not fine."

Odd, how that one line loosened the knot in his chest very slightly. "Okay, so I'm not fine."

Her eyes softened. "I'm so sorry Eleanor blew things up with you and Nikki."

Is that what she thought he was upset about? "Nikki did that all on her own." He shook his head. "I just hate that Eleanor didn't trust me with the truth. That she didn't think I could handle it. But in the end, she really did me a favor."

"You mean you never dreamed about owning your own jogger stroller and walking through the hardware store to avoid the humidity for your hair?"

He found a laugh. "Smart-ass."

"You like my smart ass."

"I do. I like that you're smart, and I like your ass."

She laughed too, and warmed from just her presence, he reached for her hand. "Let's go back to the question you haven't answered."

She grimaced. "Fine. Yes, I know there's an 'us.'"

"But?"

"But . . ." Her gaze skittered away. "I don't know anything more than that. I don't know about tomorrow, or the next day. Or the day after that." She looked at him beseechingly, as if trying to will him to understand. "I'm not built for this, Knox. I literally live one moment to the next, and have ever since . . ."

"Will died? Since your dad moved to Europe to mechanic on the racing circuits there? Since you and Lauren have been on the outs?"

"Yes. All of that," she agreed, waving a hand as if to encompass everything. "It was easy to tell myself I could forget everything when I was in Arizona. It was like I had a clean slate because no one knew me. And I still haven't let anyone know me, not really." Her voice wobbled like she was starting to get emotional, but she pressed her lips tight together, clearly intending to hold it all in.

He hated that she'd been taught to do that. "Hey," he said softly, squeezing her hand. "Alice, look at me."

She did, and yeah, he nearly drowned in the surprising amount of emotion he saw there. Passion and hunger, which was gratifying, but far more so was the affection, reluctant as it was, affection for *him*. "You're not alone anymore, Alice. Not unless you want to be."

She drew a deep breath. "I don't want to be. At least not right now . . ."

He knew she was asking if he was really okay with her philosophy of taking just this one moment in time, with no promises for more. If he thought about it too hard, he absolutely wouldn't be okay with it. He'd have that pesky fear of not being enough rearing its ugly head. But she'd been burned just as bad as he had in the past, and who was he to rush her journey? In the end, all he had was his truth, and he'd let her decide. "I want you, Alice. Very much. And I'd really like to be able to say I'll take whatever crumbs you've got for me, but I want more than that." He gave that a beat to sink in. "If any of that scares you, you should leave now, because I'm done begging people to have feelings for me, or to accept me as is."

Turning to him, she cupped his face. "I like you just as you are, Knox. You don't have to beg me for anything. I mean . . ." She smiled. "Unless we're in bed . . ."

That tugged a smile from him. "Now you're just teasing me to distract me."

"Is it working?"

He looked into her pretty eyes, finding both comfort and an easy warmth that he hadn't seen aimed his way before. Sliding a hand to the nape of her neck, he drew her closer, then closer still, because he'd take this kind of distraction any day of the week. "*Yeah*," he murmured against her mouth. "It's working." And then he kissed her.

Chapter 18

THE GROUND RULES

1. No tears.
2. This is about Eleanor.
3. Open, honest conversations with actual words. DAILY—as long as it doesn't violate rule #1.
4. Do not kill your partners.
5. No nicknames.
6. No one sleeps with anyone.
7. No ties, emotional or physical, period.
8. Read Eleanor's emails together.
9. We are in this shit together.
10. Paint is for walls only.
11. When someone orders stuff without the partners, they have to handle the stuff without the partners.
12. NO FALLING IN LOVE!

A s always when Knox put his mouth on Alice's, her brain derailed. She'd started the playful shenanigans to distract him, but now she was the one distracted by the way he pulled her into him, his hands in her hair, the way he tasted, the scent of his soap . . .

She had no idea what was happening between them, but it was like being on one of those roller coasters where you drop three hundred feet without warning and your stomach lands in your throat. She'd started this, which meant she was asking to get hurt.

At her hesitation, he lifted his head and studied her face. "You've changed your mind."

"It's been a long time," she blurted out, feeling awkward. "I think my body's forgotten what it's supposed to do. I can't remember any of my good moves."

"Alice, you don't need moves, not with me." He smiled, eyes warm and sexy, and surprisingly affectionate. "I've got you, I promise."

And there went the bones in her knees.

He kissed her softly, sweetly, an appetizer off the varied menu of Knox's kisses. It wasn't often she allowed herself the luxury of wanting something, much less someone. The few and far between times she'd allowed it to happen, she'd looked at it as quenching a thirst.

But deep down inside, where she allowed her hopes

and dreams to live, she knew it wouldn't be like that with Knox. If she slept with him, it'd be the equivalent of a bag of potato chips—she wouldn't be able to eat just one, much less stop at the ridiculously small serving size recommendation.

He was leaning back against the Land Rover, with her pressed to his front. He was stealthily gorgeous and patient as ever as he waited for her to decide. Except she knew he couldn't be *quite* as calm as he looked because she could feel him hard against her.

Everywhere.

But she knew he was trying not to influence her decision. He assumed she was an adult and, as such, capable of making up her own mind. Which meant she needed to be that adult. She took a glance over her shoulder at the barn door, which she'd closed behind her when she'd entered. Then she looked back at Knox and caught his unguarded expression—a longing that stole her breath. "What time is it?" she asked.

He seemed surprised at the question, but pulled his phone from his pocket. "Seven thirty."

She tapped her chin, like she was thinking. Truth was, she'd given up thinking the moment he'd looked at her like she meant something to him, something precious. "Seven thirty p.m. to seven thirty a.m. would just about give us a full night," she said.

He gave her a purely carnal smile. "Not nearly enough time, but I can work with that. This is your show, Tumbleweed. Tell me where to start."

"Um . . ." So many choices, all of them good . . .

"How about here," he suggested and kissed her lips. "Or maybe . . ." He brushed his mouth along her neck. "Here?" When she moaned, his hands slid to her waist, lifting her onto the hood. Then he bent his head to her breast through her tee. "Or *here* . . ."

Already panting, she gave him a push so she could sit up and take off her shirt. She wasn't wearing a bra. She watched his eyes darken. "Start anywhere you like," she said. "Just don't stop."

He boosted her higher onto the hood with an effortless strength so that she was spread out on the smooth surface of the car, then nudged her legs apart so he could stand between them. "You and this car belong on the cover of a magazine," he murmured huskily. He leaned over her, but then hesitated, meeting her gaze. "I need you to know that it wasn't my plan to lure you out here for this."

"It wasn't my plan either." She slid her fingers into his hair and met his searing gaze. "But what others might call just a car, I call an aphrodisiac."

Apparently not at all threatened that she might have found the car even sexier than him, he laughed low in his throat, and she realized that while the car *was* incredibly sexy, he was even more so. Especially as he looked at her, eyes dark with desire. He was a man who could deviate from a plan, and she appreciated that. Plus, the thought of what he was going to do to her right here on the Land Rover made her pulse race. "Knox?"

"Yeah?"

"*Hurry.*"

With a slow shake of his head, he said, "I'd do just about anything for you, Alice. Except that." He was smiling when he kissed her, shifting to pull off her boots. They hit the floor with twin dull thuds as he turned his attention to her jeans. They were tight, and in fact had taken her five good long minutes to shoehorn herself into, so she understood him giving this some thought. She reached down to help him, but he wrapped his fingers around her wrists and set them at her sides, his eyes suddenly serious. Very serious. "I know you don't want to think beyond this minute," he said. "But I can't help but do exactly that. You need to know, Alice, I still want more than tonight."

She struggled to think beyond her pulsing, needy body. "You mean like tomorrow night too?"

"For starters."

She stared at him for the longest beat, but she was

tired of having her head and body at war. "I'm pretty sure I'm going to want to do this tomorrow night too."

He smiled that smile of his, the one that was both very bad and very good, and kissed her, not pushing for more promises than that.

Because he understands you . . .

"I'm going to unwrap you like a present," came his roughly uttered words, muffled a little because he had his mouth pressed to the soft skin of her belly, moving southward as he worked her jeans down her legs and off, *not* needing a shoehorn.

Then he stopped and she realized she'd not given a single thought to her undies that morning. "If you laugh, I'll kick you," she said, meaning it.

She could tell it took a lot to control himself, and for a moment she wished he hadn't removed her boots yet, because then she *could* kick him.

"'Kiss This,'" he read, his voice full of amusement and a whole bunch of other things as he ran a finger over the two words embroidered in red on the tiny scrap of black satin masquerading as panties. "It will be my pleasure," he murmured and bent to do just that.

What could've been a minute or an hour later, she was still completely outside her own body when he raised his head from between her thighs. He smiled as he helped her climb into the roomy back of the open Land Rover. He came up with a moving blanket from somewhere to cushion the truck bed beneath them. She tugged his shirt until he pulled it over his head and tossed it behind him. His skin gleamed in the moonlight slanting in through the high windows as he stripped. He looked as beautiful and powerful as the vehicle beneath her when he entered her, and she was *still* outside her own body when she came again.

And then again.

In fact, her body didn't reconnect with her soul until she felt his arms, still quivering slightly as he lifted his weight off her. She was still breathing heavy, her body nothing but Jell-O. She couldn't have moved to save her life when her phone began to vibrate from her jeans, which were on the floor.

Knox pulled back. "You need to get that?"

"No."

"You sure? Your phone doesn't ring often, but when it does . . ."

Yeah. Shit. He was right. She fished the offending phone from her pocket, giving Knox quite the show to do it too, at least given his heartfelt groan. That's when she saw Lauren's name flashing on the screen. "You better be bleeding," she answered. "Like an arterial bleed."

"Did you find him? Are you guys doing it? Did you guys talk?"

Yeah, they'd talked. If words like *oh God,* and *right there,* and *harder* counted. She disconnected and Knox took her phone, setting it aside before leaning over her for a gentle kiss. "What did she want?"

"To know if we'd talked."

"That would be nice," he said, kissing the sweet spot behind her ear.

"We don't have anything to talk about."

"I can think of a bunch of things," he said, lifting his head to look into her eyes.

"Like?"

"Like . . . what do you dream about? Do you want help fixing up Stella? What happened between you and Lauren all those years ago?"

She froze, but he didn't. His mouth toured southbound along her throat, and her body was arching into his. Sliding her hands into his hair, she tightened her fingers and pulled his head up to hers. "Are you serious right now? I'm lying in the bed of the car that was infamously used in the opening sequence of every episode of *Last Chance Racing,* and you want to talk about my issues? I'm every red-blooded man's fantasy right now."

"Don't I know it." His voice was like rough gravel

as he slowly took her in. "But it's *also* my fantasy to lie here with you and hold you while you tell me what's going on in that incredible brain of yours."

As he was saying this, his hands never left her, caressing and reigniting . . . basically slowly driving her crazy. "If you want me to talk," she said shakily, "you're going to have to stop distracting me."

"Oh, I've already learned that lesson," he said, a smile in his voice. "If I stop distracting you, you won't talk at all." When he lifted his head, she almost whimpered at the loss of his mouth on her skin. "Knox . . ." She closed her eyes. "I can't . . . I can't talk about it."

His voice was gentle. "Why?"

"Because I'll violate Ground Rule number one."

With a very male sound of empathy, he pulled her into him. "We're not in the house. The rules don't apply out here in the barn."

After that, he didn't say anything, just kept his hands on her, soothing, comforting, quiet and calm . . . patiently waiting for her. And maybe because of that, she found she could talk after all. "What do you already know?" she asked.

He held her gaze, letting her see that he wasn't hiding a thing. "I know that when Lauren lost Will, she somehow also lost you."

"And I lost her, but it was my doing." She swallowed

hard. "You know the story of Will's accident. It . . . messed me up." She dropped her forehead to his chest. "Even though officially, it wasn't my fault. Knowing it and believing are two very different things."

"No one forced him behind the wheel," Knox said, leaving his hands on her. "An unnamed witness came forward and claimed Will was driving recklessly at high speeds, and that he often drove like that late at night."

"Yeah." And she blamed that unnamed witness for the in-depth investigation that had blown up her family. She closed her eyes. She could see her brother exactly how he'd looked that day: a tall string bean with a mop of curly brown hair that stuck up on his head like an explosion in a mattress factory. How when they'd finished working on the car, he'd slid out from beneath it and grinned up at her. "Tonight's going to be epic," he'd said.

And it had been epic. An epic nightmare. She drew a deep breath. "After I finished working on the car, he vanished for a while. When he got back, he was clearly upset, but he wouldn't tell me what was wrong, only that I couldn't tell Dad or Lauren where he was going. He said he needed to blow off steam and think. He seemed so . . . I don't know. *Desperate*," she added softly. "I should've stopped him, but he was my big brother. He always looked out for me, and for the first time he was asking me to look out for him." At the memory, she sighed. "He and my dad both always got that same look in their eyes when they were in a dangerous mood and needed to test the limits. I figured it wasn't worth the fight to try and stop him. But it'd rained earlier. The first rain of the season. The roads were slick, and oil sat on top of the pooling water. I should've known what would happen."

Knox cupped her face. "Just like you couldn't control the fact that it rained that day, you couldn't control what he was going to do. He should never have asked you to lie to the two closest people in your life. Is that what happened between you and Lauren? She got mad about you covering for him?"

"She says she's mad that I left town, but yeah, I think it's because when she called me looking for Will, right after he'd taken off, saying she needed to talk to him, I told her I hadn't seen him." She'd out-and-out lied to her best friend.

"And yet you still don't work on cars, ever, even though it's your passion."

Used to be her passion. Big difference. But instead of even attempting to explain, she gave another shrug. It was all she had. She shifted away from him then, overwhelmed by the emotions she'd gone through in the past hour. First, the best car sex she'd ever had.

Okay, maybe the *best* sex she'd ever had period. And now reliving the worst night of her life, and how the loss had created a huge hole in her heart that went far beyond Will.

And now Eleanor was gone too. If she thought about it too hard, how alone she really was, how alone she felt all the time, she'd definitely lose it. Not an option. Not in front of this man, one of the strongest men she'd ever known.

He tipped her head up to his. "These cars didn't hurt you or disappoint you, Alice. People did."

Suddenly, she didn't want to do this, not with him. With him it was supposed to be just hot mindless sex and a few laughs. Nothing serious. Nothing that hurt.

And then there was the look in his eyes. Worry.

She refused to be anyone's burden. So she slid out of the Land Rover and shut the tailgate before he could get out as well. She heard his muffled curse as she grabbed the rest of her clothes from the hood and barn floor, then strode toward the double barn doors.

He caught her before she got outside, turning her to face him. He'd slipped his jeans back on, though they weren't fastened, and he was sans shirt and barefoot.

"I'm done talking," she said, pulling on her jeans. This took an embarrassingly long time. Her shirt was easier, but she pulled it on inside out, swore, then decided to leave it. Finally, she met his gaze, and caught the emotions flickering over his face. Frustration. Concern. But also understanding. Drawing her in, he rested his face against her hair, taking a deep breath of her. Fair, as she'd done the same with him more than once. Letting herself get lost in the sensation of him for this last minute, she molded her body to the length of his.

"I understand you're done talking," he murmured. "But I've got something to say, if that's okay."

She nodded.

He nodded back, his expression soft, affectionate. "I'm sorry I pushed you to talk before you were ready. I shouldn't have done that. I won't do it again. But I hate to see you turn your back on something you love so much. I mean, look around you. You're in your own personal car heaven, and most of these babies bear the stamp of your loving work."

"You want me to deal with the cars for the good of the property."

"No." His voice was firm on that. "It's *not* about the money it'd bring in. It's about *you*, Alice. About giving yourself your life back. Will you at least think about it?"

She looked into his quietly serious face, utterly trained on her. She believed him that this had nothing to do with the inn and everything to do with her. Once again, she was struck by the fact that she couldn't remember the last time someone had given a shit. She could feel the barn doors at her back, and the warm, hard Knox at her front, both the barn and man a lure she hadn't felt in years, each equally hard to resist. "I'll think about it," she promised softly.

She'd never had anyone look at her the way he did, like he was proud of her. Another alien feeling. "If it's okay with you," she said quietly, "right now I'd rather think about something else." She'd gone a long time without being intimate, truly intimate, with anyone, and now she couldn't seem to get enough. So she slid her mouth up the side of his neck until her lips rested just beneath his ear. Slowly, she brushed them back and forth, smiling when he let out a rough groan. "I mean . . . unless you really want to use the rest of our night to talk some more . . ."

He lifted her up so she could wrap her legs around him, supporting her with his hands on her ass, his body pressing hers to the wood doors. "Sometimes," he said roughly, "talking's overrated . . ."

Chapter 19

Dear Mean Sister,

I always told myself to live with no regrets. But I'm starting to think that's impossible. Wonder if you would have felt the same if you hadn't gotten yourself killed.

Signed, Eleanor

A few days later, Lauren sat in the front room of the inn, in front of the big windows that looked over the land, working on the inn's bookkeeping and the grand opening reception. She didn't have to be at the library until noon today, and she felt a twinge of sadness at her dwindling shifts there.

It was unseasonably warm for April and she had

the windows open. The sky was a sharp blue, dotted with white puffy clouds that seemed close enough to touch. The land was green and vibrant from the recent weather, making the barn look like something right out of a book on the wild, Wild West.

Which, of course, it was. *Her* book.

The thought made her smile. As did the fact that the barn doors were open. Because something was going on that she'd begun to fear never would.

Stella was parked in front of the barn, top off and Alice's head buried under the hood. Lauren was so shocked at the sight that she texted Knox, who was upstairs hanging new doors. It was a bitch of a job, which she knew because she could hear him muttering about it under his breath.

One minute after her text, he appeared at her side, tool belt low on his hips, his UNDER CONSTRUCTION ball cap on his head. His eyes locked on Alice through the window. "I saw her go out there," he said. "I felt like a proud parent watching their kindergartner go off to school for the first time. I had to hold myself back from following and hovering."

She grinned. "You really do like her."

"Yes," he said with zero hesitation, gaze still locked on Alice out the window, and Lauren realized it was probably a lot more than "like."

"I got a call from the management firm," he said. "We've got to decide if we're hiring them. They'd like to know by next week."

She'd read their proposal. They seemed great, but something was holding her back, and she was starting to understand what it was. "What do you think?"

Knox eyed the front room closet's doorjamb and blew out a sigh. Then he vanished for a minute and came back with a door like it weighed nothing. Setting it down, he pulled a bag of hardware from his tool belt. "I mean, it would be one huge headache off our plate," he said.

"Yes." But . . . well, so many buts, starting with how much she'd miss this. Before she could dwell on that, her phone buzzed with a text from Naleen canceling her shift. Ignoring the pang that gave her, she shrugged it off and went back to the bookkeeping—which she wouldn't be doing for much longer if they hired the hotel management company. Soon the three of them would go back to their own lives.

She wasn't ready. "We should go on rotation," she said. "One of us checking in with the firm weekly to make sure everything's going okay."

"Monthly is probably easier for all of us."

"But weekly is better," Lauren said. "I could do it, for the three of us." Just the words gave her an unexpected smidgeon of excitement. "I mean, I'm the one who lives in town, right? I could do whatever's needed . . ." She trailed off, because suddenly she knew the truth. She wanted to do more than check in on the place. She wanted to be the one to manage it. No one would work harder than her.

She understood this sounded absurd. After all, she'd worked at a B and B for exactly two weeks one holiday season in high school. But she'd taken business courses in college, and she was a quick learner. Her doing this would mean that when Alice went back to . . . well, wherever she wanted, and Knox back to his life and business in Seattle, Lauren would also have something. Yes, Eleanor had ignored her all her life, and her dad had wanted nothing to do with this place.

But this wasn't about Eleanor, or her dad. It also wasn't *for* them.

It was for herself.

She'd spent her whole life giving other people the power to control her destiny and future, and then living up to everyone else's expectations. It was about time she made herself happy and lived up to her own expectations. She was *more* than a damn widow. Hell, she wasn't even technically a widow at all.

The front door opened and Alice came in wearing some grease on her jaw and down the front of her tee.

She looked even more dumbstruck at Knox in the tool belt than Lauren had, which gave her a feeling of superiority. So Alice *did* have a weakness. Good to know.

Knox caught them both staring. He lowered his arms from where he'd been hammering at the doorjamb above his head and gave a slight chin jerk.

Male speak for "what's up?"

Alice snorted and pushed past them both, heading for the kitchen. Interesting. There was no outward sign between the two of them that they were sleeping together, and it was really none of Lauren's business, but . . . she'd really love to see Alice open her heart. If she wouldn't, or couldn't, do it for Lauren and let her back in, then she hoped she'd do it for Knox.

"Hold up," he said to Alice's back. "I need someone to go into town. I've got two lists, one for the hardware store, one for the lumberyard."

"Nose goes," Alice said, quickly touching her nose at the exact same time as Lauren.

Knox divided a look between them. "Since you've just jinxed each other, you *both* can go. I'll take a breakfast sandwich and coffee in a cup so big it needs its own zip code."

Alice narrowed her eyes at him.

Knox held her gaze, reading her oh-hell-no quite clearly because he smiled. The man must have a death wish. "Please and thank you," he added.

Alice paused, then looked at Lauren. "Wow. A please *and* a thank-you. Did you feel the world tilt on its axis?"

Lauren covered her mouth to hide her shocked laugh.

Alice did an about-face and headed toward the front door.

"Don't doctor it up like you do yours," he called after her. "I'm not interested in dying young. Feel free to try it my way, you might sleep better."

Was that confirmation that they were sleeping together?

"It's not my coffee keeping me up," Alice said. "It's the sex fiend in my bed."

Lauren almost swallowed her tongue.

Knox just grinned at Alice.

Lauren sucked in a breath because it was a shame Alice was going to kill the man. He'd been extremely handy to have around.

But Alice just grinned back at him and reached for the door.

Knox went back to his work.

"I'll just . . . stay here and help," Lauren said.

"Great," Knox said. "Someone's got to clean out the squirrel and rat nests in the cellar entrance."

"On second thought . . ." Lauren pivoted toward the front door. "Alice needs me."

"No, she doesn't," Alice said.

"Try to both come back alive," Knox said.

Alice snorted and headed for Stella. Lauren headed for her own car. They both stopped and stared at each other.

"Stella's lonely," Alice said. "She needs a drive."

"You've got the top off," Lauren said. "It'll be too cold."

"I'll crank the heat."

"Do you even have gas?" Lauren asked.

"Of course I do. Come on, Stella's a better ride than the Nissan."

"Not for the environment she isn't."

Alice eyed Lauren's car. "Look, good for your girl here on being electric and all, but there's barely enough room in there for you and your suitcase of a purse, much less me and all the stuff we need to get."

Okay, that was probably true. Plus, she knew she needed to get into town to charge her car before they could go far, so . . . they got into Stella.

Alice cranked the engine over and revved the gas a

few times. It sounded like they were in a rocket ship heading for Mars. When Alice pulled out of the driveway and hit the gas, they accelerated with a rush that sent something through Lauren she hadn't felt in a long time.

Adrenaline.

One of the things she'd enjoyed about being with Will had been taking drives with him. He'd loved to go fast, and Lauren had discovered a secret, deeply buried desire to do the same.

Alice, a Moore through and through, handled her car like a pro. Lauren held on to the oh-shit bar mounted above the passenger door, grinning over the thrill.

Alice glanced over. Raised a brow. "Are you . . . *enjoying* yourself?"

"Absolutely not. You drive like a bat out of hell on crack."

Alice looked back to the road. "Yeah, well, tree . . . apple. And don't you have to be at work at noon today, right? We should divide and conquer."

She opened her mouth, and then shut it. Her stupid pride, of course. She still didn't want to admit her shift had been canceled, much less that she'd been fired.

Just the reminder had the now-familiar panic bubbling in her gut.

"What's the matter?" Alice asked.

"Nothing."

This got her another quick glance from Alice. "Your voice goes up four octaves when you lie. Figured that out in high school. So I'm going to ask you again. What's wrong?"

"I'm fine!" she said, irritation bubbling up into her humiliation. "Jeez, since when do you want to talk about emotions and feelings anyway?"

"You're right. Forget I asked." Alice pulled into the hardware store parking lot, right up in front of the store, engine running. She looked expectantly at Lauren. "You need me to hold your hand, or can you do this on your own while I go get the lumber we need?"

Lauren ground her teeth at her tone as she eyed the list. She didn't even know what one of the items was, but, not about to admit it, she shoved the list in her pocket anyway. "Just make sure to come back for me." Then she slammed out of the car.

"Hey, be gentle with my baby!" Alice said and then chirped her tires pulling out of the lot.

Gentle her ass. Alice would bite the head off anyone who dared to be gentle around her. On edge, Lauren headed into the store. She knew part of it was the nerves and dignity loss from being let go. But it was also about what she was holding back from telling Alice. She'd reasoned with herself that since it affected only her, it was no harm, no foul.

It was also about Will, which meant Alice deserved to know. By keeping it to herself, she'd violated their friendship, maybe even more than Alice had. Taking a deep breath, she grabbed a basket and wandered the aisles, staring at the list. "Okay, so if I were a window zipper, where would I be?" She walked up and down the aisles. "And what the heck is a window zipper anyway?" Thinking maybe she'd missed it, she turned and bumped into someone.

Ben.

"It's a tool used to break a painted seal between window sashes," he said, without an ounce of that annoying I-know-things-you-don't vibe she sometimes got from Alice and Knox. "Need an assist?"

What she needed was a lobotomy for wishing she and Alice could be close again. "I'm fine."

"You're definitely fine," he said on a smile. "Very fine. But I'm happy to help."

She met his gaze, having to ignore how mesmerizing his hazel eyes were, and how when he smiled, he flashed a sexy dimple in his left cheek, because suddenly she felt suspicious. "Let me guess," she said flatly. "Alice told you I needed help, right?" She craned her neck.

"She's watching me walk around like an idiot, I bet. Where is she?"

"Who's Alice?"

She turned back to him, but he looked genuine. "One of my business partners," she said slowly. "She was there when you dropped our stuff off, and also that time I was in the store before."

"Oh, right," he said, nodding. His dark hair was finger tousled, his eyes lit with genuine warmth and curiosity. He wore black cargoes and the store's signature blue polo shirt with the apron in place. And a smile that seemed just for her. "Haven't seen her. Just you, wandering the aisles talking to yourself. I thought maybe I could save a pretty lady some time and offer an assist."

She hesitated.

His smile widened. "Think about it. Let me know. The window zippers are in aisle ten A. I could help you decide on one."

"I wouldn't want to take up your time."

He leaned in a little bit and lowered his voice to a husky whisper. "It's actually my job to help you."

Horrified embarrassment filled her. "Oh. Of course. I—" She started to back up.

"Lauren." His eyes softened as he caught her hand before she ran off. "I'm teasing you. And I'm doing that because I'm an awkward idiot who likes you and can't figure out a better way to make that clear. You know, because of the awkward idiot part."

"Really?"

"Really." He smiled, that twinkle of fun in his eyes shining bright as he leaned in a little more. "So maybe you can help me look good for my boss . . ."

"But you're the boss."

"Yeah," he said. "But I do have a review with myself coming up, so . . ."

She laughed. *Laughed* . . . She was starting to realize he was so much more than just . . . Cute Guy. Not to say he wasn't cute, he was. He really, *really* was, but he was also funny, and . . . maybe interested in her. "Tell the boss he's got a winner."

He flashed that smile, dimple included, and it *wasn't* a wild bad boy smile filled with trouble. It was open and real and . . . hopeful. "Maybe you could tell him in person sometime," he suggested. "Over dinner?"

Okay, so possibly the most shocking thing wasn't that he seemed interested in her. It was that *she* was interested right back. But enough to go out with him? Yes. Which had panic filling her. She'd been wanting her life back, but she also felt so rusty that she wasn't sure she actually could.

"Lauren?"

"I'm . . ." She closed her eyes, feeling defeated. "I'm working on being ready."

He studied her a moment, then nodded like he understood, maybe more than he wanted to. "How about this. You just tell me when."

She must've looked at him stricken because he squeezed her hand, his big, warm, and slightly calloused. "It's okay, Lauren."

"No, it isn't. I *want* to be ready."

He smiled, warm and genuine. "Well, that's half the battle. No rush though. Not with me, not ever."

She wanted to hug him for that, but she was frozen.

"What do you still need?" he asked quietly.

"Kindness," she said without thinking. "Genuine affection. I mean, also physical attraction, but I need to really *like* the guy I'm with."

He blinked, and her heart stopped. Oh, God . . . "You meant what do I still need from this store . . ."

"Yes," he said on a smile. "But I like this list better. What else is on it?"

A huge hole to gobble her up when she needed one . . . "A man who won't laugh at me."

His smile faded. "I'd never laugh at you, Lauren. Honestly, I just feel so stupidly attracted to you, I think it's making me a little slow on the uptake." He gently took the list from her fingers and her still empty basket. "Please let me help?"

If it would get her out of the store faster . . . She nodded, and they walked the aisles, getting every item on the list. The basket he held was completely full and certainly heavy, but he never said a word about how she should've thought to get a cart instead. Not that he had any trouble carrying it. She knew because she kept looking to make sure. Or maybe she kept looking because she liked the way his shirt stretched taut over his shoulders and chest.

And then they were suddenly at the checkout line and he was ringing her up. She had no idea if they'd checked everything off her list or not, and didn't look either because she was too busy listening to him talk in that husky voice.

"So what do you do when you're not at the library?" he asked.

"You know I work at the library? I've never seen you there."

He slapped a hand to his heart and said "*oof,*" but recovered with an easy smile. "My daughter goes to Story Time."

He had a daughter . . . Dear God. *Was he married?*

"Normally, my mom takes her because I'm working,"

he said. "But the other day she had a dentist appointment, so I took the time off. You were reading *Captain Underpants* and wearing a red cape and a big diaper over leggings."

Seriously. Where was that big hole?

"No, you were amazing," he said. "You had every single one of those kids leaning in, hanging on your every word. You *became* those characters, brought them to life. I mean, *that's* how you hook kids on reading. It was incredible to watch."

"Oh. Well . . ." She felt herself flush, from pleasure this time. "Thanks." As always when she was flustered, her eyes wandered. Behind him was a wall of pictures from over the years, starting decades ago, or so it seemed, given the change in hair and clothing styles. Her eyes scanned straight to the present, and she caught sight of Ben with . . . "Hope? Your daughter is Hope?" she asked, stunned.

He smiled, and she realized he and Hope had the same warm, kind, caring eyes, with a hint of the promise of fun. "Yeah," he said. "She's pretty great, isn't she?"

"She's the sweetest thing, Ben. Truly." Her smile faded when she realized the implications of Hope being his daughter. Hope had told her that her mom was in heaven. Which meant that Ben's wife had died.

How had she not known that? Probably because she'd holed herself up these past few years. "Oh, I'm so sorry," she said softly. "I . . ." She trailed off, at a loss for words.

He shook his head. "It's okay, Lauren. I'm . . . okay."

He had no way of knowing how much she understood the sentiment. She knew *exactly*, and she had to look away from the sudden intensity in his gaze, the one that was trying to tell her it really was all right, that *he* was all right.

Needing a moment, her gaze drifted back to the wall of pictures, and she realized with a shock that she recognized someone else.

A little boy around eight, whom she'd seen before. In the family photo album. It was her dad, standing next to . . . Eleanor . . . holding up a birdhouse that they'd clearly made together. Both were smiling. And Eleanor didn't just have her arm around him, she had *both* arms around him, looking so proud it almost hurt to see it. Her dad was positively beaming. She'd never seen a smile on him like that. In fact, she'd rarely seen a smile on him at all. And then she realized she also recognized the birdhouse because it was hanging on the patio at the inn this very moment. "What are these pictures from?" she heard herself ask, as if from a great distance.

"My grandpa started up this store. Back in the day, he did workshops for local kids. They made Soap Box Derby cars, birdhouses, stuff like that. We still do them sometimes."

She scanned the other photos, noting that only a very few had adults in them. "Is it normal for the parents to come?"

"Every once in a while you get dedicated parents who want to do the craft with their kid, but most take the opportunity to have an hour or two to themselves alone." He looked at the picture she was fixated on. "You knew them?"

"That's my dad."

"Eleanor Graham was your grandmother?" he asked, clearly surprised.

"My great-aunt. Did you know my dad?"

"No, but Eleanor used to talk about him all the time."

It was still a shock to her system that her dad's stories didn't match up with anything she now knew about Eleanor. Everything he'd ever said about her had been so negative. Had there really been bad times, or had her dad's bitterness colored everything he'd remembered?

Ben unpinned the picture from the wall and handed it to her. "You should have this."

"Thank you." The love in Eleanor's eyes couldn't be misread. It was as real and genuine as she'd ever seen. Granted, she hadn't seen much in the real and genuine love department, but that didn't mean she couldn't recognize it.

"Lauren? Are you okay?"

She met his concerned gaze. "Actually, yes." She carefully slid the photo into her purse, knowing she'd hang it in a place of honor at the inn. "I think I'm better than okay." She looked up as he came around the counter and handed over her receipt. "Thank you," she said quietly, going up on tiptoe to brush a kiss to his cheek. "Like really . . . thank you."

Once again he slid his hand over hers and met her gaze. "Anytime." He'd swapped her out from a basket to a cart. "Can I help you out to the car?"

"I've got it." She channeled her inner Alice, who always knew what to do. "Do you still want to do dinner sometime?"

He took the receipt back from her fingers and wrote something on it. His phone number. "Whenever you're ready."

The words *I'm ready right now* nearly popped right out of her, but she smiled and somehow walked away from him, knowing she needed to think things through and be sure. She hoped she seemed mysterious and spontaneous, and not the huge dork she felt like. Pushing the cart out into the bright sun, she shaded her eyes, looking for Alice.

A horn honked off to her right. Alice got out to open the back. She eyed Lauren. "Why are you glowing?"

She slapped her hands to her cheeks. "It was just a kiss to the cheek!"

Alice's brows vanished into her hairline. "Cute Guy kissed you?"

"His name is *Ben*," she said. "And I kissed him. Are you going to help me unload or what?"

Alice reached into the cart and Lauren got into the Blazer, leaving it all for Alice to unload. She could hear some swearing but ignored it as she pulled out the photo of her dad and Eleanor again. Yep. They still looked happy. So happy it brought tears to her eyes.

When Alice opened the driver's door, Lauren turned her face to the window.

Alice turned the key and then glanced over and froze. "What are you doing?"

"Nothing!"

"So you're not crying?"

"No! But if I was—*which I'm not*—we're not inside the inn. It's not against the rules in the car."

Alice had gone still. "Did that jerk say something to you?"

"No, and he's not a jerk. In fact, he's a really great guy." She welled up some more. "And kind." And then she burst into tears.

Looking pained, Alice turned off the Blazer. She hunted up some napkins and shoved them at Lauren.

She blew her nose and twisted in the seat to face Alice. "Did you know that my dad made the birdhouse hanging off the porch at the inn?"

"No. But I really like that birdhouse." Alice paused. "Is it . . . nice to have something of his there?" she asked carefully.

"He made it with Eleanor when he was like eight years old. And she kept it all these years. Why did my dad ask her to stay away from me? And why would she listen?"

Alice shook her head. "You're asking the wrong person for family advice, but I'd imagine the only reason she would've stayed away was out of respect for your grandma and dad, no matter what her relationships with them were." She eyed the picture. "It seems like that was a happy day for them."

"He's smiling." Lauren jabbed a finger at the photo. "My dad was smiling and they were hugging each other. Do you know what this means?"

Alice met her gaze. "That Eleanor wasn't the monster you wanted her to be?"

"The emails already told me that. But it means my dad was a liar. Why would he lie?"

Alice shrugged. "Who knows why males do half the shit that males do. But one thing I do know is that there are several sides to every story. In this case, there're three—his side, Eleanor's side, and then there's the truth."

Lauren stared at Alice, who once upon a time was the only person in her life she could trust. And damn, no matter that they were barely speaking, Alice was still one of the very few she trusted implicitly. "What do *you* think is the truth?"

Alice drew a deep breath. "I can tell you that Eleanor was one of the hardest, toughest women I've ever met. But she also had the biggest heart in town. Ask anyone."

"I'm asking you."

"Okay . . . Well, to be honest, the picture doesn't surprise me in the least." She hesitated. "You've never wanted to talk about this with me, but I was being serious about asking anyone in town."

"After seeing this picture, I don't have to."

Alice shocked her by reaching out to take Lauren's hand in hers. "Are you okay?"

With a sigh, Lauren scooted closer and set her head on Alice's shoulder, like she used to do.

And like *she* used to do, Alice wrapped her arm around her, resting her hand on Lauren's head.

There was a long beat of silence before Alice broke it. "Even through everything," she said very softly, "and realizing we're still not one hundred percent . . . I love you, Lauren. Please don't cry."

Like she could stop the tears that streamed down her face now. "I love you back, Alice."

After another long silence, this one more comfortable than any moment they'd had in years, Lauren lifted her head from Alice's shoulder. "If you tell Knox I broke the cardinal rule, I'll tell him you cried too."

Alice swiped her face on her sleeve. "You always were such a tattletale." And with that, she started Stella up again and headed back to the inn.

Halfway there, the car sputtered and slowed to a stop.

"Oh my God." Lauren looked at her. "Don't tell me. We're out of gas."

Alice hopped out, grabbed the gallon gas can from the backseat, and started to walk off.

"What's happening?" Lauren called after her.

"You just asked me not to tell you."

Lauren gaped as she watched Alice continue down the road, the gas can swinging at her side.

Lauren looked around. Surrounded by woods. No

other car in sight. Dammit, she *knew* she shouldn't have stayed up late watching those British crime shows last night. With a sigh, she grabbed her purse and one other thing before getting out of the car. "Wait up!"

Alice smirked at her. "You were watching those scary mysteries again last night, weren't you?"

"Maybe I just need a snack from the convenience store."

"*Liar.*"

"Fine." Lauren tried to catch her breath as they walked at a good clip down the road side by side. "I inhaled a whole season. You've got *no* idea of the things that lurk in the woods."

"Sure I do. I watched too. It's why I keep a tire iron handy on the backseat."

Lauren lifted the hand she'd had at her side, the one holding said tire iron.

Alice smiled. "Proud of you." And then, with those three shocking words, just kept walking.

Lauren's feet had stumbled to a halt and she stared after Alice, feeling a warmth spread through her, dissipating the chill. "Don't be too proud. I've considered using it on your fat head more than once or twice."

Alice's laughter drifted back to her. "Ditto. And hurry up."

Lauren rolled her eyes and ran after her.

Chapter 20

Need
Alice: gas, and to replace Lauren's not-so-
secret stash of cookies before she realizes
they're gone.
Lauren: You do realize I can read this, yeah?
It's a SHARED NOTE.

A week later, Alice stood inside the barn, looking at the two rows of cars, quiet and peaceful in the predawn light. The vehicles, relics of the past, seemed to glow in the purple light slanting in through the high-cut windows on the walls.

They weren't the only things glowing. She knew from her own mirror that she also had a certain . . . air about her, though not from the coming dawn. Nope, it came courtesy of one Knox Rawlings, and the long nights they'd been spending in the dark of the night turning each other into puddles of sated goo.

And that wasn't the only thing. She was making up with Lauren in spite of herself, and that felt good. *She* felt good.

When was the last time that had happened?

She eyed the cars, reasoning with herself that she'd survived working on Stella, so she could survive this too. Fixing the Blazer had been for herself. But now she needed, wanted, to do something for her partners.

She walked to the 1970 Land Rover. If she could have an orgasm—or three—in it, certainly she could give the car some badly needed TLC.

Right?

Right.

But it went deeper than that. If one old photo pinned to the hardware store's wall could change Lauren's entire view on life, then Alice could certainly admit being back here in Sunrise Cove was doing the same for her.

And if *that* was the case, then there really was nothing to stop her from doing the sort of work that she'd secretly missed more than life itself.

Working on cars.

She'd already done the work Stella needed. Changed the throw-out bearing, fixed her reverse gear, and tuned her up so that she'd be able to make the trip back to Arizona without any problem. Which she'd be free to do in a little over a week.

Not ready to face her feelings about that, she slowly walked around the Land Rover. Maybe she could come back and forth now and then, fixing up one car at a time. The thought gave her more than a little thrill, especially now that she and Lauren were going to be okay. And maybe Knox would meet up with her here too, from wherever his next job took him.

She was smiling as she began taking inventory of what needed to be done. A complete tune-up at the bare minimum. That wasn't a big deal. But she'd need to do a lot more as well. Maybe even replace the brakes, and just thinking about it had her palms sweaty, and yet she also felt cold to the bone.

You got this. Remember that time you were in Mexico with the guys, and their girlfriends all insisted on a spa day? You wanted to go scuba diving with the guys, but the girls insisted you join them. Sure, you nearly died when they all got naked in the mud bath and expected you to join, but you lived through it. She even nodded to further convince herself. Yep, this would be like that mud bath—no problem at all. She looked into the back of the Land Rover and got a memory flash of entangled limbs, mouths fused, Knox's eyes locked on hers as he'd taken her apart and put her back together again.

Look at that, she was no longer chilled, but fighting a sudden urge to go find Knox and lock them both in a closet for an hour. Wait, who was she kidding? She didn't need a whole hour, not with Fort Knox, who could lock the outside world away with one touch, so that all she could see and feel and think about was him.

Oh boy. She took a lap around the barn, which brought another set of memories, entirely different. Like hooky bobbing with Will—which was the very *not* smart winter adventure of one person driving as crazy as they could, trying to dislodge the person stupid enough to be snowboarding off the back bumper on rural country roads at excessive speeds.

And then there'd been learning to drive at age thirteen with her dad in the passenger seat, laughing his fool head off as she tried to handle a manual transmission for the first time, giving them both whiplash.

She let herself into the tiny office at the back of the barn. Sure enough, the coveralls she used to wear still hung on a hook on the wall, right next to her dad's.

Her brother's were gone.

He'd been wearing them the night he died, so . . .

"*Stay on track,*" she whispered to herself as she shucked her jeans and pulled on the coveralls. Grabbing a dolly, she slid under the Land Rover to see what she was dealing with. Twenty minutes later, she was pleasantly dirty, her knuckles were nicked and bloody, and she was smiling, wondering why it'd taken her so long to do this. She'd never felt more connected to her past, to her dad, to her brother, than she did right now, and it felt good. Really good.

Armed with a list of what she needed, she drove Stella to the local auto parts store, loaded up, and went to work. She had no idea how much time had gone by when she reached out from beneath the Land Rover to grab a wrench and someone set it in her hand.

And then that same someone wrapped his fingers around her ankle and tugged her out from beneath the car.

From flat on her back, she peered up at Knox smiling down at her, looking better than any man had a right to in worn jeans, beat-up work boots, and a long-sleeved T-shirt with his company logo on a pec. There was the skittering of electricity along her entire body that always accompanied his presence, and more—the tiniest seed of burgeoning joy.

"You know I love it when you're dirty," he said.

"Then you're going to love this." Standing up, she pressed herself up against him and his clean clothes.

"Mmmm," he said and wrapped her up tight in his arms, burying his face in the crook of her neck to take a deep inhale of her. "Grease and oil and gasoline. My favorite perfume."

Damn. He always called her bluff. Instead of moaning in pleasure and wrapping her legs around his waist like she wanted to, she gave a wry laugh and pushed him away. "What are you doing out here?"

"I woke up and my warm blanket was gone before dawn." His green eyes met hers with warm curiosity. "Since you're not a morning person, I figured I should make sure you weren't kidnapped."

"Ha ha. And trust me, I'm *still* not a morning person, but grumpy or not, I had stuff I wanted to do."

"If you stayed in bed with me, early mornings wouldn't make you grumpy." He flashed a smile full of wicked promise that she knew he could deliver on.

"Stop smiling at me like that. It makes my knees vanish."

He laughed softly, but his eyes were serious as he reached out and ran a finger along her temple. "You're working on the Land Rover."

"Yeah." She paused. "I wasn't sure I could."

"I'm pretty sure you can do anything you set your mind to." He looked her over, his eyes heated and sexy.

"What? Do I have something in my teeth? On my face?"

"No. Well, yes." He ran his thumb over her jaw,

presumably rubbing off a dirt smudge. "You look like how you did when I had you in the back of this baby," he murmured. "*Satisfied.*"

"I feel satisfied." She smiled. "Your considerable skills have some serious competition now."

"Are you saying that working on the Land Rover is better than being inside it, with me inside you?"

She pretended to give serious consideration to the question. "Maybe."

Not looking concerned, he gave a slow, lazy, confident smile, making all her good parts quiver, and she had to laugh. "Okay, so we both know that working on the car is second to being with you," she admitted. "But it's a *close* second." This was a complete lie. The next best thing to being with him in the Land Rover was being in bed with him. Or being in the shower with him, and she could do this all day long, so she slid her hand to the nape of his neck and into his soft, perpetually tousled hair. When he practically purred at the touch, she fisted her fingers, tugging a rough, low growl from his chest.

"You could've woken me up to come out here with you," he said into the crook of her neck just before he took a nibble of her.

It made her shiver in the best of ways. "I didn't want either of us getting confused by what this"—she gestured between them—"is."

He lifted his head. "There's no confusion about what this is." He lifted his head. "Not on my end anyway."

She stared at him, feeling her heart kick into gear at his confidence in her. "And if I'm still confused?"

"Then I trust you to let me know if you need me to clear anything up for you. Otherwise, take your time. I'm not going anywhere, Alice."

Her heart tugged. "Well, at least not for a week or so anyway."

His eyes never wavered. "Whatever happens can be adjusted to suit us, if you want it bad enough."

Wanting wasn't the problem. Getting over her fear of being vulnerable or getting hurt was the problem. But it didn't have to be *today's* problem. "Knox?"

"Yeah?"

"The Land Rover wants to take you for a ride."

"And what does Alice want?"

She just smiled.

He returned it. "I'm all yours."

Knox figured he'd probably go anywhere Alice asked, so she encountered no resistance from him when she took his hand and tugged him to the little office at the back of the barn. There, she shoved the top of her coveralls down to her hips, leaving her torso covered in just a white tank top, looking like a tall, leanly toned drink of water.

And he was suddenly parched. "I like where this is going."

She smiled and kicked the coveralls the rest of the way off, making him groan at the sight of her tank and matching undies. He was still trying to access brain cells when she pulled on her jeans, then extracted a set of keys and swung them around her finger. "Let's go."

He shook his head, trying to clear it. "That was just mean."

"I know." She took his hand again. "It was also fun. Nice to know I can render you stupid."

"It's the blood loss," he said in his defense. "It all drained out of my head for parts south."

She laughed and tugged him along. "Hurry."

"What have I told you about hurrying?"

She snorted but led him to the passenger side of the Land Rover. "Get in."

"Want me to drive?"

"I let you drive last night in bed."

He laughed and buckled in. "Babe, you can drive me anytime, in bed or out."

She flashed him a smile, and five minutes later they were out on Old Highway 40 going up, up, up. The historic narrow, winding, heart-palpitation-inducing road went as far back as the 1800s, when it'd been the only trail west through the Sierras. And at well over seven thousand feet altitude, it was like climbing to the top of the world. "Are you taking me to some nefarious place to have your wild and merry way with me?" he asked hopefully.

She laughed. "In your dreams." At the summit, she turned onto a side road, which turned into a dirt road, which turned into . . . nothing when the road ended. She parked the car and got out, leaning back against the hood.

He got out and joined her, smiling. He knew exactly where they were. Up near Rainbow Bridge, overlooking Donner Lake about a thousand feet below, a gorgeous alpine-blue lake made entirely of snowmelt and surrounded by 360 degrees of tall mountains.

Of which they were on top of one.

He'd come up here when he was a teenager, many times. The railroad had long tunnels cut into the mountains here, through which trains had passed for over a century, bringing supplies to the remote Wild West. The tunnels were no longer used. Well, except by teenagers who wanted to walk the tracks, get high, have sex . . .

Alice pointed to the east, and the farthest point of the lake far below. "Look."

A dot of bright yellow appeared, and in the next blink, it was a curved strip.

Sunrise.

From this high up, it was breathtaking. The slice of sun was a golden glowing orb tipped with orange flame, leaving the sky awash in mingling shades of blue and purple to the west, tapering to a fiery red in the east.

Where they sat was an area that attracted rock climbers from all over the country. Off to the left in a sweep as far as the eye could see, from the edge of the cliff down, were stacks upon stacks of massive house-size boulders that had tumbled free back in the Ice Age.

A rock climber's dream.

It was so beautiful, it almost took his breath. Turning, he looked at the woman at his side, even more beautiful than the view, which *did* take his breath.

She was still eyeing their view as she spoke. "I'm toying with the idea of staying here all day and just watching this view."

"And I'm toying with the idea of staying in Sunrise Cove."

She whipped her head to his. "What?"

He smiled. "I miss it here. Don't you, even a little?"

Her eyes were wide, her mouth hanging open, and he gently closed it with a finger under her chin. "It's just a possibility right now, but I wanted you to know."

She drew a shaky breath and nodded. "Okay. Now I know."

"And you?" he asked carefully, wanting to know what she was thinking but not wanting to push her. "What do you plan to do when we're done here?"

"My boss wants me back, like yesterday," she said.

"And what do *you* want?"

She drew a deep breath. "I'm not sure."

Whether that was true or she just didn't want to say was anyone's guess. If he could choose a superpower, it would be reading minds so he could know what she was thinking. The only time he could read her at all was when they were wrapped around each other skin to skin, mouths fused. "All these years," he said, "I let the idea of Sunrise Cove hold a lot of painful memories for me, memories I haven't been ready to face. But since I've been back, I've realized something."

"What?"

"That in order to be at peace, they *need* to be faced."

"That feels . . . brave," she said.

He gently slid a hand along the waistband of her jeans, his fingers slipping beneath the denim and tracing over the delicate tattoo script he'd memorized. "You're braver than you think. It even says so right here."

She laughed but was clearly still stunned by his admission. "You really going to stay?"

He shrugged. "Construction's booming in Tahoe. My partners and I think we could make a satellite office work here, and build eco-friendly homes in and around Sunrise Cove."

"But your overseas trips . . ."

"I would still do those. But this would be my home base."

She let out a long exhale. "I didn't see that coming, but I should have. You love it here. You love the inn."

"I do. And I know we've got Lauren as our boots on the ground watching over the management firm, but having two of us around to keep an eye on everything wouldn't be a bad thing."

"No," she agreed and seemed to pull into herself. She bent her knees, wrapped her arms around them, and went back to staring at the sunrise.

"Alice."

"Hmm?"

He waited until she looked at him. "Talk to me."

"What do you want to hear?" she asked. "That I'm not good at this? That I don't think I'm made for it?"

"*This?*" he asked carefully. "It?"

Instead of answering, she asked her own question. "Did you know I've never managed to stay in a relationship? Not once?"

He shocked the hell out of himself by saying, "It only takes the right one."

She closed her eyes and dropped her head to her knees.

"What?" he asked softly, running a hand up and down her back.

"Sometimes I think about it," she said to her knees. "With you. The truth is my heart and my brain are at war."

He let that soak in. "And your gut? What does it say?"

"I don't know. I've never given it a say."

"Because I've found that my gut is almost always right," he said.

"My gut's almost always right too. Which is why I haven't asked it." She grimaced. "I don't want to ruin . . . us."

He ached for her because he understood. More than he wanted to. "You're superstitious."

"About anything good in my life staying good?" she asked with a rough laugh. "Yes."

Okay, so at least she was counting him as something good in her life. He reached for her hand at the same moment she reached for his. He brought her hand to his mouth and had just brushed a kiss over her palm when they heard a scream.

"The cliffs," Alice gasped.

Yep. He was already up and running, and Alice was right on his tail. He wasn't surprised in the least. She'd always been the sort of person to run toward someone needing help, not away.

They skidded to a stop at the climbing staging area, a small dirt clearing where climbers could climb up a sheer rock face, or down massive Ice Age boulders. He couldn't see any climbers on the rocks, but a backpack lay way too close to the thousand-foot drop-off.

"Help! Someone help me!" cried a female voice, sounding shrill and panicked.

Knox dropped to his knees and peered over the edge. "Call 911," he said to Alice without taking his eyes off the woman, maybe twenty years old, hanging on to a narrow ledge a good ten feet beneath him, her body swinging free, nothing but air below her.

"I slipped!" she said, terror in her eyes. "I don't think I can hold on . . ."

Hearing Alice on the phone with emergency services behind him, he lay flat on his stomach on the edge, but there was no way in hell he'd reach her from here. He was going to have to climb down to the ledge that she was clinging to. Problem was, that edge was *maybe* a foot wide. "What's your name?"

"S—S—Summer."

"Summer, I'm Knox. I'm going to come to you. All you've got to do is hold on."

"I'm trying, but my hands are slipping!"

"Where's your gear? Your ropes?"

"I was going to free climb. My boyfriend said I couldn't, so I wanted to prove him wrong . . ." She started to cry. "Hurry! Please hurry! I can't die and let him know he was right!"

Alice was on her knees by Knox's side. "Help's on the way, but . . ."

But they wouldn't get here in time. Knox started to climb over the edge, but Alice put her arm out, blocking him. "*What are you doing?*" she hissed.

"I'm going to drop onto the ledge and get a hold of her. If I can give her a boost up, you can pull from the top. If that doesn't work, I'll hold on to her until help shows up with ropes."

"No," Alice said. "Hell no. You could slip over the ledge, as she clearly did. It's a foot wide at the *most*."

He looked her in her stormy eyes. "I'm going to be okay."

Clearly realizing, as he already had, that if they did nothing, the girl was toast, she shook her head, mouth grim as she dropped her arm. "Okay, but if you die in front of me, I swear I'll jump off after you just to haunt your ass for the rest of eternity."

"Noted." He gave her a fast kiss and carefully climbed over the side of the cliff, slowly lowering himself to a few feet above Summer. Waiting until his momentum slowed and the length of his body hugged up against the rock, he gingerly let himself drop onto the ledge, quickly digging his fingers into the wall of rock to hold on. A few loose rocks fell free with his movement, tumbling down from above both him and the woman below him. One got him in the face, leaving a sharp stinging sensation above his eye.

Summer's face was sheer horror, but blood free, thankfully. *"Oh my God! Are you okay?"*

"Yes." He lowered himself to a crouch, holding on to the rock with one hand, the other reaching down to grab her wrist. "I've got you." He could feel his other hand slipping off the rock above his head, but he never took his eyes away from Summer's as he pulled her up enough that she could get her feet curled against the rock for balance.

"Breathe," he said, and once she'd drawn air into her lungs, he pulled and she crab-crawled upward until they were both on the ledge and he could steady them. He looked up and found Alice lying flat, watching with eyes wide as she reached her arms down. "Boost her up to me."

He wanted to say hell no, back up and stay safe, but

that would've made him the biggest hypocrite on the planet, so he nodded and looked at Summer.

She peered over her shoulder at the unsurvivable fall waiting for her and whimpered.

"Don't look down," Alice said. "Focus. You got this."

The girl nodded. "I got this," she whispered back.

Knox hugged the side of the rock and stuck his knee out to the side so she could use it as a step. "Raise your foot up and brace yourself on my knee. I'll boost you up so you can reach Alice at the top."

Summer's entire body trembled, but she didn't hesitate as she placed her right foot on his knee, then immediately cried out and recoiled. "My ankle!"

Knox grabbed her by the belt loops and hoisted her up, taking her weight off her ankle.

Alice grabbed Summer's hands, and with her pulling while Summer toed her way up the side of the rock with her one good foot, they got her to the top, where they then vanished.

A few seconds later Alice's and Summer's faces appeared above him, both creased in worry.

"What do you want me to do?" Alice asked.

"I'm okay. I'm going to climb back up."

"*How?*"

One of his favorite escapes when he'd been younger

had been rock climbing out here in this very area. He'd done far more dangerous climbs than this with his eyes closed. He grinned. "Watch me."

He found a toehold between the rocks and scaled up with his fingertips and toes. He pulled himself over the edge and landed on his ass beside Alice. "You okay?" he asked Summer.

She nodded shakily. "Other than my ankle, yes, thanks to you."

But she was trembling, so Knox gave Summer his sweatshirt and checked out her ankle.

"It's broken," she said shakily.

He was pretty sure she was right. "Rescue is on their way." He turned to Alice. "Some sunrise."

She leaped at him and he fell backward from the impact, wrapping his arms around her, trying to absorb the aftershocks of her post-adrenaline high. Holding her close, he gently caressed her back as her body stopped vibrating.

"*Watch me*?" she finally repeated, her voice an octave higher than normal. "Were you *having fun*?"

"Of course not."

"I have to second that," Summer said. "It wasn't fun at all."

Alice snorted and lifted her head to meet Knox's gaze. Then she quickly cupped his jaw, her smile gone.

"You're bleeding above your right eyebrow from a two-inch gash."

"I'm okay—"

"You need stitches," she said, just as a Cal Fire rescue truck pulled into the staging area and a team of firefighter paramedics piled out. They took Summer out by stretcher, but while Knox accepted gauze and an ice pack, he refused an evac.

Alice drove down the mountain with white knuckles, flicking him a glance every two seconds. "Are you really okay?"

"I promise."

She let out a shaky breath. "This is all my fault."

"How in the world is this your fault?"

"I dragged you up there."

"Yeah, I really had to be dragged," he said, teasing her. "Please stop worrying and trust me when I say I've had worse."

"You need to be checked out."

"I can take care of myself."

"Well, of course you can," she muttered. "You're a red-blooded male, aren't you? Look, we're going to the ER so you can get looked at by a professional, and I'm going to hover and probably bug the shit out of you. Just know that now." Reaching out, she took his hand. "You do know it's okay to accept a little help once in a while."

"Maybe. But I won't." That had been all he'd intended to say, but she was craning her neck every few seconds to look at him, so he gave her more. "I don't like letting people help me. Even Eleanor had to trick me into it, making me think I was doing a job for her, when the truth was, she was teaching me life skills I sorely lacked so that I'd be okay on my own."

"Wait," she said. "Are you saying that you don't ever let anyone help you?"

He didn't answer.

"Never?" she asked in disbelief, voice quiet and . . . dammit. Kind. Sympathetic. Great, and now she felt sorry for him.

There was little he hated more. "Are you having trouble with the definition of *never*?"

She narrowed her eyes at his tone but didn't call him out on it. "No," she said calmly. "I'm actually quite familiar with the word."

Feeling like an asshole, he opened his mouth to apologize, but she shook her head. "Don't."

"Alice, you don't know what I was going to say. I—"

"You were going to say you're sorry for snapping at me, but I'm perverse. I like to know what a person's like when they're pissy, in pain, or just generally over life."

He stared at her and finally gave a rough laugh. "I did not see you coming, Alice Moore."

"Ditto. And something else." She looked at him. "I understand you." On that remarkable and surprising statement, she parked at the ER.

"Really. Just a tube of superglue," he said.

Ignoring that, she came around and yanked him until he got out. "Come on, tough guy, I'll even hold your hand."

Suddenly a little sympathy wasn't looking so bad when its name was Alice. "What else will you hold?"

"Whatever you want," she promised, keeping a hold of his hand as she steered him to the ER entrance.

"You're also going to kiss it better, right?"

That finally eased the tension in her shoulders and the worry in her eyes. "If sex is what's on your mind, I'm going to assume you're not dying."

"Good assumption."

She gave him a small smile. "And the answer is yes. I'm going to kiss it all better."

It took twelve stitches, a tetanus shot, and a script for antibiotics before he saw daylight again.

"Are you always this difficult?" Alice asked as they walked through the lot to the car.

He looked at her in surprise. His head pounded and his eye throbbed with every beat of his heart, but he'd deny that to his deathbed. "What are you talking about? I didn't say a word."

"Oh, not difficult on others," she said. "On yourself. You refused the numbing shot. You refused the pain meds. And we both know you're going to want to go right back to work."

"And?"

She smiled at his testy tone, and he found himself with a reluctant smile. "You're a sick woman," he said.

"I meant what I said before. I like knowing how someone is at their worst. I don't enjoy surprises." She unlocked the car and opened the door for him.

When he sank into the passenger seat, she crouched at his side, eyes softened as she fastened his seat belt. She kept her hands on him as she met his gaze. "Will you please be nicer to yourself? If you can't, I'm happy to do it for you."

"I hope that's going to be as naughty as it sounds."

She laughed, and he smiled, but it faded quickly. "I'm not into being babied or coddled."

"God forbid," she said and kissed him gently. "Can I at least feed you?"

"Sustenance isn't first on my list at the moment."

She smiled. "I really like men with massive, throbbing . . . vocabularies."

That got a snort out of him.

She shut his door and came around to slide behind the wheel. "You are the most stoic person I know, Fort

Knox, but I think I detected some discomfort back there. On a scale of one to losing your beloved 1970 Dodge truck, how bad is it really?"

"*Nothing* compares to the pain of losing that Dodge. But it's fine. I'm fine." He leaned his head back and closed his eyes. "I'm just . . ."

"Not a good patient?"

"Actually, I've never been the patient."

She glanced over at him as she drove them out of the lot. "There's a scar on your chin—"

"Milling incident in South America. Also handled by superglue."

"And the scar on your shoulder?" she asked.

"Bar fight. But don't worry, I hardly ever get in those anymore."

That made her laugh. "You're pulling my leg now. You're too mellow to get in a bar fight. Hell, I've been tempted to check you for a pulse plenty of times. Well, except when we're in bed." She smirked. "I know how to get your heart going when we're there."

Yeah, she did.

"Seriously, though, Knox. What about when you were a kid, like when you fell down and scraped your knee?"

"I'd pick myself up and slap a Band-Aid on it."

She hesitated. "You don't say much about your growing-up years."

Since that wasn't a question, he didn't respond.

"Have you been by your old place?"

"No."

She glanced at him, her eyes warm, caring, and he blew out a breath. "I haven't been there since my mom died."

She met his gaze. "Why?"

"I failed her."

She gaped at him. "You didn't fail her. You couldn't have even if you'd tried. You're not wired that way."

Her blind belief in him was staggering, leaving him completely undone. "I knew that I needed to get her into rehab, but she kept saying she wasn't ready, so I let it go. Then it was too late and she was gone."

"That's not on you," she said fiercely, surprising him into meeting her gaze. "I knew her, Knox. She was the kindest, sweetest, most loyal soul I knew. She raised you. She knew you loved her." She paused. "Have you thought about going back and asking whoever lives there now if you could have a moment inside? It might give you some closure."

He closed his eyes, concentrating on the physical pain rather than on the emotional one. "No one's living there."

"How do you know?"

"Because when my company had its first big year,

we all got bonuses. I bought the trailer through a Realtor friend, who had it cleaned out for me. It's empty. It's been empty all this time. I don't even know why I kept it."

"Maybe because you need to say goodbye for the closure."

He took in her warm voice, the one that held affection and worry, for him, and felt a catch in his throat. "Maybe."

"Growing up like that must've been really hard on you."

"It was harder for my mom. She wanted to stop drinking, but couldn't."

Alice shook her head as she drove, eyes harder now, mouth grim. "Her demons had a hold on her. But you should've come first. A kid should always come first. Having one should've been enough to keep her sober."

He let out a mirthless laugh. "Yeah, well, I've always had a hard time being enough for the women in my life."

"Clearly, you've been hanging out with the wrong women."

He turned to look at her. "Are you saying you're the right kind of woman?"

"You certainly thought so last night."

She said this so casually, he burst out laughing.

She glanced over at him again, her eyes reluctantly amused. "Is there anything else I can do?"

"Keep your promise to kiss it and make it better when we get home." *Home.* The word had never meant anything close to the traditional sense of the word, mostly because he'd never really had a home. Still didn't.

He was starting to think that maybe the word wasn't a place at all, but a person. The thought wasn't as scary as it should have been.

"We need a shower," she said. "I'll have to help you, of course. But then you're going to rest and not work, at least for the rest of the day. Lauren and I can keep things moving." She flashed him a quick smile. "I got you, Knox."

Too moved to smile back, he took her hand in his and held on tight. Because when had anyone said that to him, ever? He thought maybe she was the most surprising, most amazing woman he'd ever met. Tough, determined, and beneath her armored exterior hid that secret soft sweet side . . .

"Shit," she said suddenly, slowing for a sudden traffic jam because of road work. "Damn. Hell. *Fuck.*"

He grinned. Okay so her secret soft sweet side was deeply, *deeply* buried, but he liked that too.

Chapter 21

Dear Sister Who Shall Not Be Named,

I've learned a lot over the years about men. Dad was alpha. Walter was alpha. And while I loved them both, I always knew in my heart that I was missing something. I told myself that when I loved again, it would be a different man altogether from those I knew in my past.

But I'm pretty sure that man does not exist. At least not for me.

That isn't to say I no longer hate you. Because I still do.

Signed, The Sister Who Can Still Hold Her Head High

L auren swiped the sweat off her brow. She abso-lutely hated to sweat. The only time sweating was even mildly acceptable was during sex, and even then, it'd been so long she might be remembering it wrong.

Since that thought was depressing, she put her entire concentration into removing the wallpaper in the inn's kitchen. It'd been there since circa 1984, when country blue and roosters had been the decorations of choice. Alice had said she'd do it, but if Lauren helped, she figured she wouldn't have to face the fact that she was bored with herself.

You could've called Ben.

And she nearly had a bunch of times, but something kept stopping her. She was out of practice, for one thing. At peopling and at life. Somehow she'd become this wallflower who'd forgotten how to open her heart.

It was fear, plain and simple. When people had hopes and dreams, they got hurt. Look at Eleanor. She'd tried to follow her dream of love, and had lost the guy she wanted to marry *and* her sister. Lauren's dad had gone for his dreams as well, and they'd ruined him. Okay, so greed had ruined him, but still. And then there'd been Will, who'd dreamed big and had paid the ultimate price for those dreams.

So Lauren had said no thank you to doing the same.

Behind her, she could hear Alice swearing under her breath. She'd already stripped three walls to Lauren's one and had moved on to cleaning out cabinets and drawers to get rid of "the old shit for the new shit." Lauren tried to feel bad about being slow at the physical work but failed, because frankly, Alice was good at everything. Lauren had envied that back in the day, and as it turned out, she still envied it.

She also envied Alice's easy confidence. A few hours ago, Alice had received a FaceTime call from the guys she worked with. They'd been at a bar and wanted her to know they'd created a countdown calendar. She had six days left until her month was up. Bottom line—she was clearly missed.

Lauren hadn't been missed a day in her life.

It was midnight and she should just go home and get some sleep. But she wasn't tired, she was . . . well, the very opposite of tired. Somehow, working on the inn had given her a sense of ownership that actually becoming a one-third owner hadn't. She felt invested, and more than that, she felt at home.

It was surprising, since she'd grown up thinking she didn't belong here. She'd spent the time since Eleanor's death feeling more than a little uncomfortable at being left part of the legacy, feeling like a fraud. Was it silly to let one single photograph change all that for her? Probably. But that was exactly what had happened.

The inn *was* a part of her legacy now. She *did* belong here. And whether Alice truly accepted it yet or not, they belonged together too.

She turned and looked at her old BFF, who was still going through the cabinets, silently. It wasn't in Alice's blood to make small talk or to chatter on, like it was in Lauren's. Lauren liked to fill a silence.

Silence gave Alice peace. Or at least it used to. But tonight, there was something in her expression that didn't look peaceful. She seemed . . . melancholy. "What's wrong?"

Alice just lifted a shoulder.

No shock there. Lauren used to have to poke at her, irritate her, to get her to talk. Easy enough to do. "Eleanor was such a pack rat. This might take us longer than planned."

"We don't have longer," Alice said in a tone that suggested anxiety was on the loose in her head.

It'd been a few days since she and Knox had rescued that climber. Ever since, Lauren had sensed an even closer bond between Alice and Knox, so she wasn't sure why Alice was still rushing out the door.

"We've got new kitchen stuff coming tomorrow,"

Alice said, "and we still have to paint the cabinets. Let me show you how to deal with a pack rat." She scooped up an armful of crap on the countertop and dumped everything into the big trash can they'd dragged inside from the barn.

Lauren gasped in horror, her hand going to her heart. "You can't do that! What if you throw away something important?" She dove into the bag and pulled out a ratty-looking notebook. "Like this."

"Come on, that's clearly trash."

The irony of having Alice, who'd loved and adored Eleanor, trying to rush through this, and it being *Lauren* who wanted to take her time and look at everything didn't escape her. Opening the notebook to a random page, she pulled out a picture, then stared at it in shock.

"What?" Alice asked impatiently.

"It's . . . us," she said. "You and me." They'd been sophomores in high school and dressed up for Halloween. Lauren was Clifford the Big Red Dog. Alice had gone as Hermione Granger.

Alice took the pic. "Wow. You look the same. Well, except for the boobs." She looked over at Lauren. Specifically, her chest. "Remember how you used to pray to the boob gods to bring you a set of D's?"

"Ha ha," Lauren muttered, but it was true. "And they didn't give me D's. I only got C's."

"But really nice C's. I'd be ecstatic with C's." She looked at her own *maybe* B's with what could only be annoyance.

Lauren grinned.

"Seriously?" Alice asked. "Me being jealous makes you happy?"

"More than you could imagine. I've *always* been jealous of you."

"What? Why? My boobs stopped growing when I was twelve."

"It's not just your boobs," Lauren said. "It's that you're tall and toned, even though you hate exercise. You're smart as hell, and on top of all that, beautiful. It's not fair. You've even got your life all figured out."

Alice looked incredulous. "Are you kidding me? I've got *nothing* figured out. Not my job. Not my personal life. *Nothing.*"

"You've got a job in Arizona with a bunch of hot guys who all love you. You're able to . . . um, engage in physical affairs with an even hotter guy named Knox in spite of it being against the Ground Rules—which means you're still a rule breaker, and that just makes you *cool* on top of everything else."

Alice was brows up. "*Engage in physical affairs?*"

"You know what I mean."

"Assume I don't."

Lauren sighed. "Sex. Okay? You get to have sex."

Alice blinked. "You do realize you're not an actual virgin, right? You're of age and don't answer to anyone but yourself. You don't have to live like a nun."

Lauren sagged and leaned back against the fridge. "I know. But I forgot how to be me. I don't even know who I am anymore."

Alice looked like she was biting her tongue and Lauren braced herself for sarcasm. "Just spit it out."

"I don't know who I am either," Alice finally said quietly.

"Uh-huh." Lauren crossed her arms. "I bet all the good sex helps though."

"How do you know it's good?"

"You know I can hear you guys, right?" Knox called out from somewhere else in the house.

Alice grimaced. "We should have reinsulated." She raised her voice a little, eyes lit with humor that she sent Lauren's way as she said, "I mean, the sex was okay . . ."

"I'm going to make you take that back later!"

Lauren rolled her eyes, even as she loved their easy comradery because it suited Alice perfectly. "Great, you're jealous of my boobs and I'm jealous of your sex life."

"*Call Ben*," Alice said.

"A man isn't going to solve my problems."

"Of course not. But he could take your mind off them for four minutes or so."

"*Wow*," they heard Knox say.

Alice snorted and went back to scooping things into the trash.

Lauren thought that was that, but after a few minutes, Alice asked quietly, "So what would make you feel like you again?"

"I don't even know." She stared at the pic of her and Alice some more. "Being with people who know me, who like me."

"I'm a people who knows and likes you."

Lauren felt herself well up and Alice pointed at her. "Don't you dare, or I'll take it back!"

This made Lauren laugh on top of crying. "Thanks," she whispered.

"For what?"

"For still being willing to be with me."

Alice's vague amusement faded and her expression went very serious. "No, you've got that backward. Thank *you* for being willing to be with *me*."

They stared at each other, Lauren unbearably moved, and she thought maybe Alice was too.

"I'd like to remind you we're out of tissues," Knox called out. "Also . . . *Ground Rule number one!*"

"Hate to break it to you," Alice yelled back, "but between the three of us, we've broken most of the rules."

"Why did Eleanor have this?" Lauren asked about the photo.

"It was mine." Alice dragged the trash can to the back door and dusted off her hands. "She's got a bunch, actually. She gave me a photo album to keep my pictures in. I was putting it together at this kitchen table and she asked if she could have some of you."

Lauren felt an odd sensation in her chest. Emotion, a good one for a change. "That's . . . sweet."

Alice craned her neck to eye Lauren. "Did you just say something nice about Eleanor?"

"Hey, I never got to see that side of her, okay? Or *any* side of her. But knowing she held on to this picture tells me that at some level deep down it did exist."

"And her leaving you one-third of everything she owned didn't?" Alice asked dryly.

"Of course it did. But that could've been her sense of responsibility to her sister, to my dad. The picture, though . . . *that's* sentiment," she said.

"I've been telling you, Lor. And not everyone's an open book."

"I know," she admitted. "But some people don't

understand that, when they're young and dumb. Sometimes certain people have to grow up first. I'm working on it."

Alice looked at her for a long beat, then nodded. And that was it. The same thing she'd always gotten from Alice.

Acceptance. "I missed this, Alice," she said softly. "I can't tell you how much it means to me to feel like I'm part of a family unit again."

Alice's expression was the one she gave every time someone said something that made her feel. Pained. But then she took the picture from Lauren and gave it a closer look. "That's the same costume you were wearing just the other day when you came here straight from work."

"Yes. I worked in it. And then I got fired in it. No, wait. I got fired in the Mother Goose costume."

"What?" Alice lifted her head. "You got fired?"

Damn. "I hadn't planned on blurting it out this way, but yeah, I got fired." And it felt . . . right to finally let it out.

"That's bullshit." Alice's brow was furrowed, the way it got when she was angry. "You're the best librarian ever."

Lauren snorted. "And you know that how?"

"Because you're the most anal, overly organized person on the planet. You even have an organizer in your purse for your pencils, pens, and Chapsticks."

"Well, that's just good sense."

"You know every book under the sun," Alice went on. "You were *born* for that job. Are you okay?"

Touched, Lauren managed a smile. "Working on it."

"What are you going to do?"

"Honestly, I'm not sure." Lauren shrugged. "Ever since Will's death, I allowed the library job to become . . . well, me. I need to find a job fast, but it's not that easy. At least not something that I actually want to do."

"What can I do to help?"

Lauren's chest got warm at the offer. "A hug would be nice."

To Alice's credit, she allowed the hug, even squeezed Lauren back.

"Is there food?" Knox asked, coming into the room, bandage still over his right eyebrow covering his stitches. He moved straight to the sink to wash his hands. "I'm so hungry my stomach is eating itself—" Hands cleaned, he turned and looked at them, eyes widening slightly when he found them hugging. "Who died?"

"No one," Alice said. "Lauren lost her job."

"Are you serious?" Knox looked at Lauren. "You're great at what you do."

With his blind faith added onto Alice's, Lauren had to pretend to sneeze a few times to hide the tears that escaped.

Pickle got up and slunk out of the room, making her feel like the worst jerk on the planet.

"I'm sorry about the job," Knox said. "Do you need anything?"

"Pizza," Lauren decided.

Knox smiled. "You're my very favorite partner."

Alice rolled her eyes, but said, "Pepperoni."

Lauren shuddered as she pulled up the app.

Knox was moving through the kitchen, taking in everything they'd done. "Looking good."

It *was*, Lauren realized. They were nearly done too. The place was starting to look rustic, and not the old crappy "rustic" either, but a real warm, welcoming cabin-y-like rustic that looked and felt intimate and inviting. "We're really going to pull this thing off."

"Knock on wood," Alice said, ever the skeptical one.

"We are," Knox said. "And for the record, I'd hire you two in a hot minute. Lauren, keep that in mind if you're in for a career change. There wouldn't be any costumes required."

Lauren gave him her most genuine smile for that offer, which she suspected would consist of hard physical labor and no doubt dirt—of which she still wasn't a fan—but thought it was incredibly kind of him to offer.

Alice turned to him. "Okay, who are you and what have you done with Mr. There's a Ton of Shit Left to Do?"

"I like to give credit where it's due," he said.

Alice looked like she had no idea how to take a compliment from him, and it was actually endearingly cute. At first, Lauren hadn't been at all certain that the two of them wouldn't kill each other, but she had to admit, Knox was good for Alice. His patience seemed infinite, and he'd never felt the need to be competitive or prove to either of them his obvious strength. Instead, he'd clearly taken pleasure in their hard work and growing skills.

"You know what comes after the pizza, right?" he asked. "Eleanor Email Time."

Lauren's stomach sank. "But I was just starting to like her."

Thirty minutes later, the pizza was gone and they were looking at the iPad like it was a locked and loaded rattlesnake. They'd read both good ones and hard ones, so it was a crapshoot on what they'd get tonight.

Alice grabbed the bottle of whiskey and they all turned to sit at the kitchen table. Knox flipped his chair backward and straddled it. Alice didn't grab a chair at all, she simply perched a hip against the table, as if wanting to be able to escape at a moment's notice.

Lauren sat in a chair the correct way. Alice smirked until Knox said, "The subject line says 'Alice.'"

Alice leaned over his shoulder and paled.

"What?" he asked.

"It's dated the night of the accident." Alice seemed to pull into herself as she shoved her hands into her pockets, looking physically ill.

"Let me read it," Lauren offered softly, adding a small smile and a hopefully reassuring nod to Alice as she pulled the iPad to her. "I've got this. I've got you."

Alice closed her eyes.

Knox reached over and took one of her hands in his as Lauren began to read out loud.

Dear Despicable Sister,

I saw something horrific tonight and I can't get past it. Every time I close my eyes I see it all over again. My mechanic's son is feral, always revs his engine at three in the morning and wakes up the dog. Well, tonight he was driving by like a bat out of hell, racing down our road, and then suddenly I heard a huge crash. By the time I got to the site, he was on his way to the hospital. He didn't make it.

Lauren stopped reading to swallow the ball of anxiety and grief blocking her throat. She glanced at Alice, who still stood there, way too pale, eyes burning bright, mouth tight with anger, but stoically silent. Lauren shut down the iPad. "I think we get the gist."

"No." Alice shook her head. "I want to hear the rest of it."

Lauren looked to Knox.

He squeezed Alice's hand. "Babe—"

"Read the rest of the damn letter," Alice bit out.

Lauren read ahead, and swallowed hard. "Alice, trust me. You don't need to hear—"

Alice grabbed the iPad, read to herself, then carefully set the iPad down in the center of the table and walked out of the room.

Leaving a thundering silence.

Knox stood to go after her.

"Knox. You need to hear the rest of it first," Lauren said quietly.

"How bad is it?"

Lauren drew a breath. "Bad."

"Read it."

Lauren picked up where she'd left off.

The kid had driven right through a fence and the barn of our nearest neighbor. A senseless tragedy, but I'm far more worried about his sister. Will meant everything to Alice. Their mom reminds me of you, Sister, because she also ran out on her responsibilities. That big stupid brother of hers was one of the few good things in her life, and he had to go and do something selfish like this and get himself killed. And that's just what I told the cops, when I went down to the station to give them my account. That he'd undoubtedly been drinking and illegally racing as usual. They needed to know, otherwise they were never going to take my complaints seriously and get people to stop doing that on my road.

Awful, awful business, all of it. But done now. The police were grateful for my insight and will look into it, and that will be that. Oh, and I heard through the grapevine that you're in the Bahamas on a cruise. I hope you get sunburned and/or catch a tropical disease.

The Only Decent Graham Sister

Shaken, Lauren pushed away the iPad. "Will did have alcohol in his system. Not over the legal limit, but she was right. He drove through a fence and into a barn. Thankfully no one was in it." She closed her eyes. "I don't know if you know, but the whole reason Alice's dad had to leave town and take that job overseas was because the owner of the barn sued. Her dad lost everything."

"Because Will wasn't racing his own car, he was racing his dad's," Knox said. At her surprise, he lifted a shoulder. "The story was big. It wasn't hard to hear the details."

"People love a juicy story," she said bitterly. "After Alice's dad lost his house and business, he took off."

"Leaving Alice behind to face the fallout."

Lauren acknowledged that with a pinch to her chest, because even though Alice had been the one to physically leave, Lauren had deserted her emotionally to face the fallout.

Alone.

"I'm going to go find her," Knox said.

She nodded. "Seems like it's a rite of passage. Read Eleanor's email and one of us walks out."

"She's hurting," he said. "She tends to run to ground when she's hurting."

"And you're afraid she'll run now?"

"Aren't you?" he asked.

"Trying not to be," she said candidly. "You really do care about her."

He tweaked a strand of her hair. "I care about you

too, Pink." He pulled her out of the chair and hugged her, and it felt so comforting, she clung for a moment. Finally, she patted him on the back and pulled free. "You know she only acts like a tough girl, right? That she's really got a soft center? That just because she doesn't show how she feels to the world, doesn't mean she doesn't feel? In fact, with Alice, it's the opposite. The more she hides from you, the more she feels."

"I'm not going to hurt her. Ever."

"You promise?"

Knox let out a low laugh. "I can promise you that if anyone's going to get hurt, it'll be me."

On that surprising reveal, he was gone.

Chapter 22

It was a dark, starless, moonless night, but Alice didn't need light to find her way across the backyard, past the barn, to the same place she always went when her world had been rocked—the creek. She'd been walking this path for years. When she got to the big, flat rock that she considered hers, she sat heavily.

This was the last spot she'd seen Eleanor, who as usual had come out to find Alice alone. She'd been grieving Will, and the loss of her life as she'd known it.

Eleanor had sat and given Alice a rare hug, promising her things would be okay.

The only promise Eleanor had ever broken.

Alice felt the sorrow like lead in her heart, but sucked it up. So what if the woman she'd thought of as her own grandmother had hated her brother? That wasn't exactly news. But that she'd gone out of her way to try and raise trouble in the investigation . . . that *was* news, at least to her.

Will had been no innocent, but he had been her brother, and she missed him. Missed her dad too, and suddenly Lauren's words bounced around in her head: *I can't tell you how much it means to me to feel like I'm part of a family unit again.*

Alice was sucking in some air and working hard at not crying when she heard it. Leaves crunching behind her, and she froze, all ears. A bear, or the boogeyman? Hmm, those were definitely human footsteps, heading her way. Unhurried, but not trying to be quiet either. Could still be the boogeyman, but her money was on Lauren, probably wanting to do what Alice had thus far managed to avoid—have a real talk about their past.

She'd have preferred the boogeyman. Regardless, she panicked. There was no other reason for what she did next, which was slide off the rock and duck behind the bush next to it. It was a manzanita, so it was prickly and itchy, and damn, there were bugs—none of which was enough to coax her out and into view.

Two big work boots appeared in the dirt in front of her. Then two long, denim-clad legs as the man they belonged to crouched down in front of her.

"You realize you're wearing white in the dark, right?" Knox parted the bush with his big hands and met her gaze. "You're lit up like a beacon."

She dropped her head to her knees, trembling from head to toe from attempting to hold on to the reins of her emotions. She'd thought Lauren finding her would be the worst thing, but nope, it was Knox. With Lauren she could've hidden behind her words, but Knox never let her hide. "I don't want to talk about it," she said maturely.

Knox scooped her up and sat on the rock, with her in his lap now. He picked something out of her hair. She decided she didn't need to know what. "Who said anything about talking?" he asked.

When he cuddled her into him, she pressed her face into his neck and gave up trying to fight the hot tears. If he noticed them as they slid down his throat and into his jacket, he said nothing. When she shivered, he unzipped his jacket and pulled her inside it, where his body heat engulfed her and the scent was all delicious Knox.

And still the tears came. Embarrassment had her skin hot, and anger had her so tense she thought she might shatter with it.

Knox just held her and let her be. No questions. No impatience over her silence. And she realized something. He was the first person in her life who didn't expect anything from her. Maybe that was why she finally stirred, shuddering out a sigh while keeping her face pressed into the crook of his neck. "Sorry."

"Don't be."

She sniffed and lifted her head. "Why aren't you running for the hills? Most men are terrified of tears."

"I'm not most men, and tears don't scare me. My mom used to cry a lot." He paused, and when he spoke again, his voice had some teasing in it. "I'm good at navigating the tricky, windy roads of the female psyche."

She shoved him. "You mean you *think* you're good at it. You *think* you're good at a lot of things."

He laughed. "Would you like to lodge any complaints?"

No, dammit, and clearly seeing her answer in her eyes, he smiled at her. Then cupped her face, swiping at her tears with the pads of his thumbs. "How did you find me all the way out here?"

"It took me a minute. I checked the barn first. Thought you might be taking a sledgehammer to one of the cars."

"Bite your tongue," she said with mock sternness. "I'm mad at Eleanor, not the babies in the barn."

He smiled at that. "My second stop was the saloon

set from *Last Chance Inn*. Eleanor's favorite. Thought it was possible you'd be setting fire to it."

She waved that away. "I liked the show. Plus, I cleaned all the sets. If I was going to destroy them, it'd have been before I spent eight hours working on them."

"Understood. Anyway, found you out here on the third lap."

Yeah. Hiding in a bush by the creek. Not her strongest moment, for sure, and while she hated to show her vulnerability, there was something about Knox that made it okay.

Terrifying in its own right.

She turned her head to stare at the creek she could barely see only a few feet from her. "I can't believe Eleanor was the unnamed eyewitness. She never once said a single thing about telling the police that Will was a reckless driver, prompting the investigation that blew up my entire life." She paused. Shook her head. "*Who does that?*"

"A nosy old lady who cared, a lot."

She closed her eyes. "A nosy old lady who didn't have a life of her own."

When Knox didn't say anything, she opened her eyes. "What do you think, Mr. Be Honest, Mr. Tell the Truth guy? You probably think she did the right thing."

"I think it doesn't matter that Eleanor spoke up, not when what she said was true, because the police would have figured it out with or without her. I also think"— Knox leaned in and gave her a very gentle, healing, comforting kiss—"that you're the strongest, most courageous, incredible woman I've ever met. I hate what happened to your family."

"We were talking about Eleanor."

"And now I'm talking about you," he said. "Eleanor should've told you what she told the police. Just like she should have told me about Nikki. Or tried to connect with Lauren. She had her faults and made mistakes, but loving us wasn't one of them."

Alice sighed. "I know." She paused. "Are *you* still mad at her?" She held her breath on his answer, watching him think over what he wanted to say. "Don't hold back now, Knox."

"I'm not. I wouldn't." He met her gaze evenly, openly. "I guess the truth is that I used to be mad, but at my mom."

"And . . . you're not anymore?"

"No. I think she did the best she could with what she had," he said. "And I think the same about Eleanor."

Alice shook her head. "I'm not sure I'm that evolved. I thought she had my back. I thought . . ."

"What?"

She shook her head, hating that the words, each one of them, felt like a slice of a knife as she uttered her darkest fears. "I'm just tired of love always causing pain." Even just saying it caused pain, slicing right through her heart and soul.

"Maybe it doesn't have to."

His words, uttered with more emotion than she'd ever heard from him, had her taking a deep breath and holding it before letting it shudder out of her. "You make me want things." She met his gaze, dark as the night around them. "Things I don't have any business wanting."

"Everyone deserves to be loved, Alice." He pulled her in tight. "Even you."

She gently put her fingers to his lips. She wasn't sure what he'd planned on saying, but she knew one thing—she wasn't ready to hear it. "Right back at you," she said fiercely.

Just as she had done, he gently touched the pads of his fingers to her lips to stop her words.

"Well, aren't we a pair," she murmured, nipping his fingertips. Rearing up, she kissed what she could reach. His bottom lip. Then she nipped it. "I tried to tell you, I require a lot of patience."

"I've got lots of that. Maybe I can teach you

some . . ." And there in the dark he smiled, then bent his head and gently bit her bottom lip too, and then the crook of her neck, and then her shoulder, slowly, sexily, working his way south . . . teaching her a whole new meaning of the word *patience*.

Alice woke up with a start, with no idea how much time had gone by. It was still dark, and she was in bed. Not hers, but the very girlie, frilly room from the show. She was wrapped up in Knox, the most masculine man she'd ever met, surrounded by more lace than she knew existed. It made her smile.

She felt utterly drained and exhausted, but oddly lighter than she'd felt in a long time, making her realize she'd been carrying around too much weight. Maybe it had to do with bad memories.

Or maybe it was the man who held her against him like she meant more to him than pizza.

Either way, she was going to soak up every minute. Turning her head, she eyed the clock: three thirty a.m. Then she realized Knox's eyes were open and on her. "Was I drooling?"

"No." He smiled. "Snoring a little bit though."

"Take that back."

"Make me," he said, voice low and husky, sexy as hell as he slid his fingers under the hem of her little pajama top and skimmed them along the soft skin of her belly.

Holding his gaze with hers, she came up on an elbow and kissed him. Softly. As tenderly as he'd treated her during her midnight meltdown at the creek.

"What was that for?" Knox asked.

"It's a thank-you." She kissed one corner of his mouth, then the other. "For getting me through high school without going boy crazy because I was just crazy for you." She kissed just beneath his jaw. "For getting me through being back here . . ." She kissed his collarbone, intending to kiss much more, but he wrapped a hand in her ponytail and tugged her back to his mouth.

"You sure, Alice?"

If she had enough breath in her lungs, she might have laughed, because as much as he flirted and teased her, when it came right down to it, he always made her confirm her choice. And her answer would be the same as it always was. "Very."

In the next beat, he rolled her beneath him and kissed her. Not gently. Not tenderly. "I'm the grateful one," he said. "I didn't realize I was missing something in my life. I'd shut myself down, just working, working, working. But now, you're making me feel . . ." He pulled back and smiled at her. "Alive, Alice. So damned alive."

And those were the last words either of them spoke until the sun came up.

Knox woke up wearing a still sleeping Alice and a smile. Very slowly and carefully, he slid out from beneath her, needing to get going if he was going to finish repairing the rest of the hardwood floors today.

Pickle, who'd been asleep on the floor, lifted his big head, trying to decide if there was going to be food or the dreaded run.

Knox pulled on a pair of jeans, grabbed the rest of his clothes, and tiptoed out, figuring he'd shower first and then make everyone breakfast.

Ever hopeful, Pickle followed him, letting out a sorrowful moan when Knox veered off course from the kitchen to take a shower first.

There was only one fresh towel in the bathroom. Knowing Alice would need a towel too, he went out to the hall closet in search of more. Just as he pulled the door open, someone came pounding down the hallway. Alice, sliding in front of him like she'd rounded all the bases and was stealing home base. "*Noooooo!*" she yelled, coming to a stop between him and the closet, just as a pile of colorful hats, scarves, socks, balls of yarn, packages of yarn, and more knitting needles than he could count tumbled down over her head.

As he worked to free her from the mess, he tried to speak, but Pickle was barking at the commotion, the pitch enough to pierce eardrums. "Pickle, zip it!"

Pickle zipped it.

Into the blessed silence, Alice—wearing Knox's T-shirt and possibly nothing else—tried to scoop everything up and shove it back into the closet, failing spectacularly.

But the heart-stopping view she gave him when she bent over . . . *Definitely* not wearing anything other than his shirt. Trying not to be a total Neanderthal, he crouched down to help, picking up a blue and green . . . thing. It was about two feet long, crooked, the stitches all mismatched. He had no idea what it was.

Alice snatched it out of his hands and clutched it to her chest.

"That's . . . a lot of supplies," he said carefully.

"Yeah, well, why buy something for ten bucks when you can make it yourself for a hundred dollars' worth of craft supplies."

He laughed, and she sighed. "I told you, I knit when I'm stressed."

Defensive tone. Shoulders hunched. Both breaking his heart. "And I sometimes marathon old shows like

Murder, She Wrote when I'm stressed," he said. "So what?"

She stared at him. "*Murder, She Wrote?*"

He raised a brow. "You judging?"

She grimaced. "No. Sorry. But take a good look at that scarf and try not to laugh at me."

A *scarf.* It was a *scarf.* He remembered telling her he liked blue and green, and a light bulb went off. "Did you make this for me?"

"No." She huffed out a sigh. "Maybe."

He took it back from her and set it around his neck, but it wasn't long enough, so it just sort of hung awkwardly, not quite to his collarbone. "No one's ever made me anything before."

"Take it off," Alice said, reaching for it. "It looks ridiculous."

"Stop. It's my new favorite piece of clothing." He lifted it out of her reach. "Who is the rest of this for?"

"I don't know." She looked sexily rumpled and adorably flustered. "It's easier to knit than take anxiety meds. Cheaper too, given my crap insurance."

Something about that was incredibly endearing. "Secretly?"

"I do a lot of things secretly," she said.

He took in the sight of her on her knees in front of him in nothing but his shirt, looking like a wet dream.

He wanted to ask about those secret things in great detail, but forced himself to stay on task. Her vulnerable stance and expression made that easy. He pulled her into him, pressing his lips to her temple. "So you knit, and then shove everything you make in the closet?"

"They're ugly."

"They're unique. Like you."

"You mean weird."

With a smile, he kissed her. "I happen to like weird." His eyes caught on something bright pink and he reached into the pile and lifted it. "Is this sock for Lauren?"

"No, because it's a *hat* . . ."

Knox bit the inside of his cheek. "She's going to love it."

"She's *never* going to see it and you're not going to tell her about it."

"Tell me about what?" Lauren asked, coming down the hall, still holding her keys and wearing her purse, clearly having just arrived. "Oh my God, do you two *ever* wear clothes?"

"Speaking of clothes, Alice made you a hat," Knox said, giving Lauren a look that he hoped telegraphed the thought: *love it.*

Lauren eyed the pink monstrosity and blinked. "Uh . . ."

Knox gave a small head shake, and clearly getting the message, Lauren pasted on a smile. "I mean wow. It's my favorite color. I'm sure I'll find lots of use for, um . . . *it*."

"Uh-huh," Alice said, crossing her arms. "What is *it*?"

"Well . . ." Lauren turned it over every which way, while Knox tried to surreptitiously pat the top of his head.

When Alice caught him, he pretended he had an itch.

"Clearly it's a mitten," Lauren decided with cautious optimism and slipped her hand into it and waved it around.

"It's a hat." Alice tried to snatch it back, but Lauren wouldn't let go of it, so they ended up in what looked like a very intense game of tug-of-war.

"Give. It. Back," Alice said through her teeth.

"Never." Lauren was breathless. "You made it for me and I get to keep it!"

Alice let go so fast, Lauren fell on her ass.

"Why? Why would you want to keep a hat that looks like a mitten?" Alice asked, offering her a hand up.

"Because I love hats."

"You thought it was a mitten. *Why do you want it?*" she asked again, voice baffled, body language braced for a blow. A verbal blow.

Knox held his breath, knowing this could go one of two ways: really good, or really bad, but he desperately wanted it to go good because he cared so much for both of these women, and knew they needed to repair their relationship.

After a heavy pause, Lauren came through. "Because you made it for me. And if you laugh at me and call me a princess, so help me, Alice, I'll . . ." She waved a hand around as she clearly searched for the worst thing she could think of to punish Alice. "I'll go kick Stella right in the tires."

Alice thought about that for a minute. "Knox is the princess. One of his hobbies is watching *Murder, She Wrote.*"

"Wow," Knox said.

"That's okay," Lauren said. "My hobbies include pinning pictures of home decor I can't afford, recipes I won't cook, and crafts I won't make. Also, I really like loading up my online shopping cart and not buying any of it."

Alice was looking befuddled.

"Is it that shocking to realize people care about you?" Knox asked.

Alice just stared at him, seemingly speechless for the first time in memory.

It made him hug her. "I'll let you think the question over while we work," he said.

Lauren laughed at that, and Alice narrowed her eyes as she studied them. "What if I said I was going to give away my wares to our guests, a little something from our home to yours? How funny would it be then?"

"Actually," Lauren said, "I think it's an amazing idea."

When Alice looked at Knox, he confirmed with a nod. "Me too." And perhaps his favorite moment of the entire day was the look on Alice's face as she realized that not only did they both care about her, but they also believed in her.

The day was long, so Alice didn't have much time to think about anything other than working on the inn. But after, when the day was done and she was showered and clean, her mind came back online.

She was still marveling at how an embarrassing start to the day had turned out to give her an odd sense of . . . belonging. She felt incredibly grateful to Lauren and Knox. She knew she still needed to apologize to Lauren for how she'd left after Will had died and for keeping her distance ever since, but depending on how it went, she could accidentally blow them up again.

So she'd face Knox first. Maybe because their past wasn't traumatic. He probably had no idea of all he'd done for her since they'd arrived. How he'd given her back some badly needed confidence in herself, soothing away her fears that she didn't have anything to offer anyone, making her feel wanted and special every moment of every day.

She owed him. She owed him so much.

And she desperately wanted to give him something back. It'd taken a while to figure out what. Hoping she was doing the right thing, she went in search of him. She found him alone with Pickle on the porch, watching the sunset, and nearly melted when he looked up at her and smiled like she was the best thing he'd seen all day.

"I want to show you something," she said.

Without question, he put Pickle inside, then offered Alice his hand, letting her lead him to the driveway. She pointed to his truck, because this was going to be a situation where he might need to feel in control of something.

A few minutes later, she was giving him directions, watching his expression, wondering when it would kick in where she was taking him.

No slouch, he realized the minute they got through town and over the train tracks. He slid her a guarded look, saying nothing.

She sent him what she hoped was a reassuring smile.

The sun was setting when he pulled to the curb in front of a small, mustard-yellow single-wide trailer. Black wrought-iron bars covered all the windows. There was no driveway and no fence. The grass looked like it was barely clinging to life.

Knox stared at his childhood home, then removed his seat belt and got out of the truck. Without a word.

Alice scrambled to follow, but she needn't have. Knox had stopped between the truck and trailer like he'd turned to stone. "What are we doing here?" he asked.

Assuming he was talking to her and not the trailer, she said, "You helped me face my past. I wanted to do the same for you."

The sound he made was a mix of pain, grief, and a long-buried denial. "I don't know why I bought this place," he said, "much less kept it. I guess I was trying to hold on to a piece of my mom."

"Maybe you were hoping something of her might still be here."

"No." He shook his head. "I know what I'll find." He moved to the front stoop and picked up a rock. Turning it over, he removed a key out of the fake bottom. "I just don't want to find it."

"It?"

"The reminder that I'm alone."

She understood this at a core level, much in thanks to him, so she murmured back the words he'd once spoken to her. "You're not alone."

He turned to look at her, and she held his gaze. A long beat later, he opened the door. There wasn't anything to see, the room was completely bare and dusty. He held out a hand. Alice stepped closer and took it, and they walked through the front room and into the kitchen together. Their boots made little sucking sounds on the cream-turned-brown linoleum that was peeling up and curling at all the seams. There was no stove, fridge, or any appliances whatsoever. The cabinets were open and bare. Knox walked to the small window over the sink and stared out. He remained there for a long moment, silent, at ease in a way that told her he had stood in that very spot a thousand times.

He appeared deep in thought, and she remained quiet, letting him be. But when his shoulders sagged, she came up behind him, softly rubbed his back.

"She used to make me blanket forts out there with our two chairs," he said. "We'd squeeze inside together and eat popcorn. She'd tell me stories about being a girl who wanted to grow up and build homes for people who couldn't afford their own. Then we'd lie down with our heads sticking out and look up at the stars.

She promised me that someday, she'd have a real home for us."

Throat tight, Alice smiled at the image of a young Knox quietly listening to his mom's every word, then growing up to take on his mom's dreams for her.

"She died out there," he said, and Alice stopped breathing. "Right there in the yard. She came home from God knows where and that's as far as she got. I found her there the next morning."

Her heart cracked for the horror of that, and then split wide open when he reached back for her hands, wrapping them around him, squeezing them gently, comforting *her*.

When *he* was the one who should be comforted. He'd found his mom, dead. "Knox . . . I'm so sorry—"

Turning in her arms, he wrapped her up, pulling her in close, dropping his forehead to her shoulder. He was silent, but she felt him shuddering, his grip on her like he was holding on for dear life.

They dropped to their knees right there in the kitchen, her holding him tight against her as she smoothed his hair and rubbed his back until his breathing became regular again.

After a long time, he sat back, as emotionally exhausted and drained as she'd ever seen him. He rose to his feet and offered her a hand. They walked through the place and out the front door, locking up behind them.

Back in his truck, he sat still, engine still off. "You were right," he finally said to the windshield.

"About what?"

Turning to face her, he leaned in for a soft kiss. "About me." He drew a deep breath. "I needed to come here to say goodbye. She was the first person to love me without reservation. She always loved me, no matter what she was going through. I'd forgotten that."

Alice smiled through unshed tears as she thought of Will.

"That kind of love is a gift," he said. "It's our core, and it makes us who we are." He looked at her. "And if we share it, pass it on, it only grows stronger."

Something to think about.

Chapter 23

On her very last shift at the library, Lauren sat behind the front desk, trying to enjoy every whiff of the thousands of books surrounding her, the hushed whispers of the patrons as they happily sat with their reads, the beauty of the large old building itself.

It was hard.

As of tomorrow, she'd no longer have a key. She wouldn't belong here, and then, as always, came the next thought rushing on its heels.

Where *would* she belong?

Not knowing, not feeling secure, felt terrifying. Tilting her head back, she looked up at the open-beamed ceiling and the fans whirling, gently swirling the air—and a few feathers—throughout. She was Mother Goose again today. Everyone loved Mother Goose, maybe as much as she loved this job. It'd saved her life after Will's death. Until recently, she'd really believed her life had been plenty full, that she was doing great. But the truth was, when she took the library out of the equation, she was left with nothing.

Okay, so not nothing, not entirely anyway. She had her partnership with Knox and Alice. But would that survive once they were gone, back to their own lives? Only time would tell.

She'd received a job offer from south shore earlier, to manage a B and B of all things. But she'd been brewing a better idea for a while now. All she had to do was raise enough courage to go after it.

"Oh my," Naleen said, stopping at her desk. "I know that smile. Is there . . . a new man in your life?"

"No." Well, maybe, but she needed courage for that too. In case she had to actually put it out there in the world for that to happen, she said, "I'm feeling hopeful for what's ahead."

"Oh, honey, that makes my heart so happy. I was talking to Clifford the other day, telling him how much I hate that we're losing you."

Lauren managed a smile. "The next time you talk to Clifford, make sure you tell him I'm going to be A-OK."

Naleen's eyes went misty. "You always did take after

Eleanor's side of the family. You're a good girl." She patted Lauren's hand and walked off.

Was that true? Did she have some Eleanor in her? She pulled a snack from her secret stash in her bottom drawer, one she rarely indulged in. But hey, some days required chocolate. Bending low over the drawer so no one could see her, she took a big bite, her eyes nearly crossing at the burst of pure pleasure as serotonin and dopamine flooded her brain. When she straightened up with a moan around that huge bite, she froze.

Ben and Hope stood on the other side of her desk with a stack of books.

Lauren tried to hide her mouthful of chocolate by not breathing. Only problem—not breathing was a problem.

Hope carefully set the books on the desk as if they were made of precious gold, and if Lauren hadn't already loved that kid, she'd have fallen for her right then and there. Too bad she was going to die from lack of air.

"Hi!" Hope said with great enthusiasm. "Can I check out these books? Is that chocolate? Can I haz some?"

Ben scooped Hope up into his arms. "Remember, baby, we whisper in the library. And we always say please and thank you. We also don't ask people for their food."

"I am whispering!" Hope grinned her toothless grin at Lauren. "Please and thank you!"

Still unable to speak, Lauren offered her a big chunk of the chocolate bar.

"Wow!" Hope exclaimed, and popped it into her mouth.

Ben chuckled, kissed Hope on the cheek, then turned to Lauren, "Morning, Lauren."

She smiled, feeling her heart skip a beat. Chewing furiously so she could swallow, she finally squeaked out a "Morning, Ben."

"Daddy, her name isn't Lauren, it's Story Time Lady. And I forgot to get a kitten book to read to Grandma!"

Ben set his daughter down and caught her before she ran back to the children's section. "What's the rule?"

"Don't try to tell everyone my favorite books, and never ever leave this area without you."

Ben kissed her on top of her head and she was gone. Then he leaned against Lauren's desk and met her gaze. "Hey."

"Hey yourself," she said, hoping she didn't have chocolate in her teeth, while also wondering if he knew her ridiculous heart was thundering nearly right out of her chest.

He smiled.

Yeah, he knew.

"We ever going to do this?" he asked.

"Do what? Go out to dinner?"

"Aw. I'd love to," he said, his smile still as sweet as it had been with Hope, but also more now, holding a level of heat that made her wiggle in her chair. There was also an easy affection that climbed right inside her and was like a balm on her personal demons.

But her personal demons fought back. What do you know about going out? they whispered. You've only ever dated Will, and his idea of going out had been driving up to Hidden Hills to drink beer and have sex.

"So," she murmured, mentally cracking her knuckles. "Is this dinner an actual date?"

"That would be a great start," he said.

The implication being that he intended for there to be much more than a single date. She sucked in a breath and inhaled a wayward feather, then proceeded to nearly cough up a lung. Ben came around the desk and patted her back until she spit out the feather and got her breath back.

Naleen rushed up, phone in hand. "Oh thank God. I called 911. Should I call them back?"

"Yes!"

Too late. Two EMS personnel burst through the

front doors. Naleen waved them over. "She was trying to impress this young man and nearly passed out."

Dear God. "No, I just inhaled a feather, that's all!"

"Please just let them check you out," Naleen insisted. She looked at the medic. "We had to let her go recently. That might be it too."

Lauren wondered if it was too soon to eat another chocolate bar . . .

By the time she convinced everyone she was okay, she was the definition of a hot mess. "You should be scared," she said to Ben when he'd let Hope go back for yet another book and they were finally alone. "Because that was me attempting to flirt with you."

He grinned. "I especially liked the choking-on-the-feather part."

"Hey, that part was real!" she exclaimed, then sighed when he laughed. He'd been just teasing her. "Look, I haven't been on a first date in . . . I don't even know. *Years*. I wouldn't even know what to do, or how to act."

He sat on the very corner of her desk and regarded her. "You do whatever your heart desires, no acting required."

"*Years*, Ben."

"I hear it's like riding a bike."

Her heart squeezed. She wasn't alone in the boat.

He'd lost someone too, someone who'd once been his entire world, and he'd been brave enough to try again.

With her.

"I'll hold your hand through the entire thing," he promised.

How was he both sweet and sexy? She hadn't realized the two could coexist. "I'd like that."

He smiled. "You ready for this?"

Lauren looked around. She'd drawn quite a crowd with the whole Mother Goose-nearly-choking-to-death thing. She eyed all the people milling around, people she knew from town and work. They were looking back at her with the same expression they'd been looking at her with since Will had died.

Concern.

Pity.

Well, you know what? To hell with that. Today, she would bask in the knowledge that there was a man who had the nerve to ask her out. She went to reach out her hand and realized she was still wearing her Mother Goose mitt. It took her a minute to pull it off. She had to use her teeth, but finally she tossed it aside.

Ben was grinning. Not laughing at her, but looking at her with genuine affection, which made it easy to make the first move and take his hand.

"Is that a yes?" he asked.

"If you're comfortable with all the baggage I come with, who am I to attempt to dissuade you? You sure you don't need to think about it?"

"Lauren, I've been thinking about it since you told me you were going to shower your indoor plant with so much love that it'd have the will to live outside."

Well, God help him. She picked up a Sharpie and wrote her number on his hand. Then she paused, pulling his hand toward her so that he couldn't see it. "*Wait.*"

His eyes never left hers. "As long as you need."

Completely undone, she nodded. "It's just . . . if we're really going to do this, you should have full disclosure. Like . . . I'm vegan, except for the very occasional dark chocolate, because, well . . . dark chocolate."

His eyes were smiling. "Of course."

This gave her some courage. "I'm also allergic to dogs." She grimaced. "I mean I'm afraid of dogs. Long story. I'm a bit of a hypochondriac. Oh, and the biggie . . ." She drew a deep breath. "I meant what I said before. I haven't been out with a guy in a long time. So if you really do take on the insanity and go out with me, everyone in town's going to have high expectations for you and that may get old."

He didn't say anything, and her heart sank a little. Actually, a whole bunch. She managed a smile and took a step back. "You need to think about it. I get it. It's a lot. Whelp . . ." She faked a bright smile. "You've got my number . . ." And then, even though it was her desk, she walked away, moving straight toward the back offices where she could hide.

About ten steps in, her cell phone rang. She pulled it out of her pocket and saw a number she didn't recognize. "Hello?"

"Hey. Long time no talk."

Ben, sounding amused. She whipped around and stared at him still leaning against her desk, his phone to his ear, casual as you please.

"I was wondering," he said, straightening to his full height, walking toward her as he spoke, "what you're doing after your shift." He stopped in front of her, took her phone from her hand, and gently ended the call.

She laughed, feeling lighter than she had in a very long time. "I'm busy. I'm going out with this guy I really like." She shifted closer and whispered, "That last part's sorta a secret."

He was smiling, which was good, but she had to ask. "Are you sure, Ben? Like *sure* sure?"

"I'm one hundred percent sure sure." He leaned in until his mouth brushed her ear with each word. "We've got quite the audience. Gotta admit, I'm pretty relieved you said yes."

She glanced around, startled to find it was true. Everyone was watching them, including Naleen. Buoyed by a courage she didn't know she had, she slid a hand to the nape of Ben's neck and went up on tiptoes. "Just in case they need a clue," she said against his lips and kissed him.

She didn't know what she expected, but it wasn't for the crowd to burst into applause. It had never once occurred to her that they were on her side, rooting for her.

"Isn't it lovely?" she heard Naleen say. "She deserves this more than anyone I know."

"That's my daddy!" Hope called out. "He's kissing Story Time Lady! Daddy! Daddy! Kiss me too!"

Ben pulled back to scoop up Hope and give her a smacking kiss on her cheek.

Lauren smiled at Hope. "How do you feel about dinner?"

"I love dinner! I want a french fry and a chocolate shake!"

"Just a single fry?" Ben teased.

"All the french fries, Daddy." She smiled at Lauren. "Do you like french fries and chocolate shakes?"

Lauren looked into Ben's eyes and grinned, because she knew she was going on the adventure of her life. "Love them."

Chapter 24

Dear Selfishly Selfish Sister,

If you were still around, and hadn't stolen Walter, and we were speaking, I know you'd have told me to tell Knox the truth about Nikki. And Alice that I'm the one who talked to the police about Will's speeding. And Lauren that her father could be a spoiled little shit who never appreciated what he had, instead always needing more. But I wanted to bring the three of them together, not tear them apart. Look, we both know I'm not good at this. You're the one who's good at keeping secrets . . .

Signed The Not Selfishly Selfish Sister

———

Three days later, Alice was in the kitchen finishing her last project—conditioning all the beadboard in the house. Lauren had come into the room and was sitting on the counter with legs crisscrossed, alternately working on her laptop and FaceTiming with Ben.

Mostly Alice was trying not to think about what next week would bring, and to do that, she distracted herself by sleeping with Knox. The good thing about that was Knox was a firm believer that a cup of Folgers should not be the best part of waking up. He preferred morning sex to caffeine, and she was a convert.

She realized she'd cleaned the last beadboard during her musings and stepped back to admire her handiwork. *"Fini!"*

Lauren whooped, jumped down, and together they went to find Knox, who was putting the very last piece of molding back on in the living room.

They all stared at each other.

"Did we just finish with a few days to spare?" Alice asked in a whisper, almost afraid to believe it.

Lauren beamed. *"Yes!"* She turned to Knox. "Right?"

He looked around at the homey, rustic inn and smiled. "Just about, yeah. There's a few tiny pickup items left, but we did a pretty damn amazing job."

Lauren clapped and jumped up and down. "You know what we need now?"

"A nap?" Alice asked. "For, like, a week?"

"No, a celebration!" Lauren said. "At the firepit with s'mores!"

"I was hoping you were going to say a vacation in Maui," Alice said.

Lauren rolled her eyes in what Alice thought was a great imitation of herself. It was a proud moment. "Okay, but I need a shower first."

"Don't take too long or I'll eat them all," Lauren said.

"She's not lying," Alice told Knox. "One time at summer camp, I had to leave the campfire for a few minutes and she ate all my s'more supplies. Didn't even bother to toast the marshmallows first."

"That's what you get for sneaking off to make out with Richie Emerson," Lauren said.

Knox raised a brow. "Richie Emerson? That guy was a tool."

"Yeah, he was," Alice said. "And from then on, I always chose dessert over a boy." She looked at Lauren suspiciously. "Do you have the real stuff for s'mores or the fake stuff?"

"Ohmigod, for the last time, vegan stuff isn't fake," Lauren said. "It's just plant based. And last time you never even noticed."

Alice blinked. "You cheated me out of *real* crap food?"

"Yes, and you're welcome."

Alice sighed and hit the shower. She had a whirlwind of emotions about the inn being done, all conflicting. They'd actually done it, pulled off the near impossible. Which was good. Hell, it was *great*. And so was the fact that after tomorrow's meeting with the management company, where they'd sign on the dotted line, she was free to go on with her life.

Except . . . that was also the bad.

A month ago, she hadn't wanted to come here at all, and now . . . well, now she wasn't even sure *how* to leave. How to walk away from Lauren again. How to not see Knox every day . . .

When she was clean and dressed, she walked out to the firepit. Lauren was wearing the pink hat Alice had made her, which was too big and fell nearly over her eyes. Knox was in the blue and green scarf, which was too small. Apparently things didn't have to be perfect to be loved or to be beautiful, and that was quite the revelation. "You don't have to wear them!"

Lauren lifted her chin. "Are you saying I don't look amazing?"

"You look ridiculous." Alice plopped down in the

chair between Lauren and Knox and shook her head again. "Ridiculously adorable."

Lauren beamed. "I knew it."

Knox gave Alice a look of warmth, affection, and a whole bunch more that changed her heart rate. He handed them each a bottle of beer. "We did it and we didn't kill each other," he said.

"Annnnnddddd . . . I think we even like each other," Lauren said. "I mean, not like you two like each other. You two *naked* like each other . . ."

"Seriously?" Alice said.

Lauren laughed. "I don't know, you tell me."

"You want to tell stories, let's start with you and Ben."

Lauren went as pink as her hat.

"Thought so," Alice said and lifted her bottle. "To surviving the last month together. I have no idea how we did it."

Knox laughed and lifted his bottle. "To making something of this place. I think we can all rest easy as we move on, knowing we did our best."

At the words *as we move on*, Alice's stomach did a nosedive, which was dumb. This was what she'd wanted. So she said, "Speaking of that, the hotel management firm emailed us the credentials for the three on-site managers they'd like to have on rotating shift here. We just need to approve them."

Lauren cleared her throat. "Actually, um, I've got a better option." She gave a nervous smile and waved her hand. "Me."

Alice blinked. "You?"

"I'm perfect for it," Lauren said, lifting her chin, as if expecting an argument. "I've got a business degree, I know this place inside and out, *and* . . ." She drew a deep breath. "I need the job. But more importantly, I *want* the job. So I'm suggesting we *not* hire the management firm and let me handle it. All of it."

Stunned, Alice looked at Knox, who lifted his hands. "Hey, she had me at 'I'm perfect for it,'" he said. "Because she is. She's the only one of us who's available and will for sure still be living here next week."

If Alice had thought her stomach had hit her toes before, she'd been wrong. It hit now, and she had to remind herself to breathe. That's what the thought of Knox leaving did—stole the breath from her lungs. Same when she thought about going back to her old job when there was so much for her right here.

"You don't think I can do it," Lauren said slowly to Alice, smile gone now.

"I—"

Lauren set her beer aside. "You still don't trust me, even after this past month."

"Whoa." Alice shook her head. "I didn't say any of that."

Lauren stood up. "You actually didn't say *anything*, which is the same thing as you not believing in me."

"I didn't say anything because you keep cutting me off."

Lauren sucked in a breath, took a beat, and then exhaled. "I'm sorry. I like to preempt disappointment. Talk. I'll try not to spin out of control while you do."

"I *do* think you can run this inn," Alice said carefully. "I just didn't want you to do it out of obligation to me or Knox, or Eleanor, for that matter. It should be for *you*. But I do trust you, Lor. In fact, I can't think of anyone better to handle this business than you."

Lauren smiled, looking misty-eyed. "Yeah?"

Alice smiled back. "Yeah."

So they drank to that too, and by then needed a second round of beers. After they'd all been cracked open and given a toast to their new manager in the pink hat, they sat back, Lauren looking so happy she could burst, and Knox . . . well, he was looking pretty damn satisfied with everything himself.

And yet here Alice sat, feeling decidedly let down and unable to put her finger on why. Oh wait, she did know. She was the only one of the three who had no idea what her life was going to look like next week.

Then there was the fact that she'd fallen stupidly, irrevocably, ridiculously in love with the man seated next to her, his warm thigh against hers. Which she couldn't even fully concentrate on because she was about to have her heart ripped out when they went their separate ways . . .

She closed her eyes. Lauren was telling Knox a story, and they were both chuckling. *Do not ruin this for them. You wanted this. Just keep smiling and putting one foot in front of the other, no matter what.*

Far easier said than done.

Lauren, toasty in front of the fire, sipped her beer, unable to remember a time when she'd been so . . . content. Alice was sitting, head back, eyes closed, but not asleep. This was Alice's thinking position. Lauren nudged her with the stick she was using to toast marshmallows. "You okay?"

"Yep." Alice opened her eyes. "Is Ben coming tonight?"

"If I have anything to say about it."

Knox choked on his beer.

Lauren grinned. She and Ben had been together three of the five nights this week. Hope had joined them for their first and also second date, where they'd gone horseback riding at a nearby ranch. Last night Ben had come over to the inn and had dinner with Lauren, Knox, and Alice. Lauren had never felt as at home with anyone in her entire life.

So she'd brought him back to her place.

He hadn't been able to spend the night. In fact, he'd been Cinderella, having to get home in time to relieve the babysitter, but the evening had been magical, and her fears about not remembering what to do or how to act had turned out to be unfounded. Ben had been tender and yet playful, managing to effortlessly bring out an equally playful side of her she hadn't even known she had. It'd been the most sensual, magical evening of her life.

Alice was watching all of it cross her face. "I'm happy for you."

Lauren met her gaze, feeling so much relief it was hard to even breathe. The two of them were really going to be okay, and she wanted to say that out loud, but Alice usually had to be dragged kicking and screaming into anything emotional and heartfelt, so instead she gave her something within her comfort range— sarcasm. And another poke with the stick. "Is that why you printed the pic that hit the local paper, the one of Ben kissing me as Mother Goose in the library, and then put it in a frame on the reception desk?"

"Oh, no, I did that for me." Alice let her smile fade as she eyed Knox and Lauren, whose stomach told her she wasn't going to like whatever came out of Alice's mouth next.

"We have one last letter from Eleanor," Alice said. "We need to read it."

Her stomach had been right. She didn't like it. "Do we have to? I mean, we all like each other right now." Plus there was that one pesky little detail Lauren had never shared, the one she hoped Eleanor wouldn't reveal, but Lauren had never been all that lucky.

"Your name's on the subject line," Alice said.

Yep. It was exactly what she feared. "I vote that we leave the past in the past. Who's with me?"

Knox shook his head. "The past *never* stays in the past. It will always come back to bite you in the ass. Always."

"Agreed," Alice said softly. "And plus, I don't think it's a good idea to walk away without knowing everything, every last one of Eleanor's little secrets. It gives those secrets far too much power over us."

Feeling more than a little panicky, Lauren stood. "You know what? It's my name, my letter. And the only one in the whole bunch of them too. So I should get to choose if we read it, and I choose no. Let's let the secrets die. *Please.* They don't matter anymore."

Alice stood too. She put her drink down and came to

Lauren, gently squeezing her hand. "She can only hurt you if you let her."

Lauren turned desperately to Knox.

He gave her a sympathetic look but a slow shake of his head. "Sorry, Pink, but she's right." He held out the iPad.

Lauren shook her head, refusing to take it.

Knox swiped his way to the draft emails, and Lauren tried to just breathe, but this was going to be bad, she could feel it to the depths of her soul. Dropping to her seat, she pulled her beanie all the way over her eyes as Knox began to read. "Hello, Horrible Sister. It's been quite a few days. Yesterday was Will Moore's funeral, which was sad and tragic. And then today, I got an engagement ring."

Lauren sank lower into her chair.

Alice gave her an odd look, but Lauren pretended not to see it. Apparently she'd gotten good at pretending, real good. She'd even fooled herself that this last secret could stay a secret.

"I'd like to say the ring was for me," Knox read on. "But I gave up on love and all that bullshit a long time ago. You remember why, don't you, sister? Anyway, although I was looking fine in my magenta tracksuit and new white Hush Puppies, the diamond wasn't for me. I was walking through town minding my own business, and you're never going to guess who approached me and started a conversation. Lauren. Yes, your very own granddaughter, the one you never got to know because karma came around and killed you too young. I have stayed away from her because they'd asked me to, but Lauren finally came to me."

Knox paused and, in unison with Alice, looked at Lauren with surprise. Probably because she'd told them she'd never spoken to Eleanor. As in ever. She pulled her hat lower—wishing it were the Hat of Invisibility— and studied her white sneaks. Huh. She had a chocolate stain over her big right toe . . .

Knox went back to reading. "She looks so much like you, Ruth. Beautiful, of course. The Graham genes are strong. But she was distraught. At first I thought she was upset because that boyfriend of hers had just died. But that wasn't it. She was panicked because she was carrying—"

"*Oh my God.*" Alice stood up and turned to Lauren, her face white with shock. "You were carrying Will's baby?"

Lauren stared up at her, stunned at the conclusion she'd jumped to. "What? *No!*"

"—an engagement ring," Knox finished.

Alice blinked and sat back down hard. "An engagement ring." She looked at Lauren. "Will asked you to marry him? *When?*"

"There's more," Knox said quietly. "Should I stop?"

"*No*," Alice said. "Keep going."

So Knox drew a breath and read on. "Lauren said Will had asked her to marry him, just before he drove off and decided to kill himself by driving too fast. Lauren was panicked because she was meeting Alice, who didn't know that—" Knox cut himself off with a sharp inhale, and clearly was reading silently to himself now.

"Out loud," Alice said tightly. "What *else* didn't I know?"

Lauren tried to sink farther into her chair, but she was as low as she could go, metaphorically and physically. So far, good ol' Great-aunt Eleanor was doing a bang-up job of destroying her newfound happiness.

Actually, you did this all by yourself . . .

Knox lifted his head and looked at Alice, his gaze filled with concern, worry lines tight around his eyes.

Alice took the iPad from Knox. Lauren closed her eyes, heart thundering in her ears. This was it. This was where her entire world blew up.

"She was meeting Alice, who didn't know," Alice repeated as she read out loud, "that Lauren had rejected Will's proposal. Clearly, the girl got my brains. But the boy had insisted she keep the ring and think about it. Only he died that very night. Lauren knew I'd been close to the Moore family and she thought I might be willing to hold on to the ring—which had been Alice and Will's grandma's. Lauren was hoping I'd hold it until she was ready to tell Alice the truth, that she'd rejected Will's proposal."

Lauren opened her eyes, and their gazes locked for a long beat. "I thought my grandma's ring had been lost," Alice said.

More than anything, Lauren wished she could go back in time and redo that night, making a cleaner, healthier break from Will. She wanted a second chance to be there for Alice in the aftermath, but she had no idea how to say any of that.

In the taut silence, Alice drew a deep breath and went back to the iPad. "Considering how distressed and guilty Lauren looked," she read, "I doubt she'll ever come clean. Which is a shame, because as you know, betrayal eats and eats at a family until it tears them apart. Those two girls were as close as sisters. Not like *us*, mind you, because neither of *them* are cheaters. As always, The Better Sister."

They fell silent, the kind you couldn't cut with the sharpest knife in the world.

Finally, Alice stood up and walked away.

Lauren implored Knox with her eyes to stay and let her go after Alice. Looking tense, he gave a short nod.

Lauren caught her at the stairs. "Alice."

She turned on Lauren, face pale, her body looking

tense enough to shatter. "Will asked you to marry him? And you said no? And then you let *me* feel guilty all these years for that accident, when *you* were the one who sent him away that night upset and devastated and distracted?"

Lauren opened her mouth, then closed it again. Because what could she say? It was the truth.

"Oh my God." Alice staggered back a step. "My dad used to tell me you thought you were too good for Will and I always defended you. *Always*. But all along, it was true."

Lauren tore off the hat. "No. I *never* thought I was too good for Will. Never, Alice." She paused on the edge of a precipice. She could tell the truth . . . or continue to hide. Either way, she'd lost Alice, so what the hell, she might as well try the truth for a change. "But I also knew it was never going to work."

"You don't know that," Alice said tightly, her eyes bright, shimmering with shock and pain. "You didn't give it a chance."

Lauren drew a deep breath. "Will wanted to leave Sunrise Cove. He wanted to go on the European racing circuit. It would've been an exciting, but vagabond, life for us, but I'm a homebody, always have been. You knew that. You also knew I wanted to stay here in Sunrise Cove and have a family."

Alice started to say something, but Lauren held up a hand. "He was going to go, Alice, with or without me. So tell me this—do you think I should've said yes and waited for him to get it out of his system, just hoping he would come back?"

"He loved you, Lauren."

"Yes. He loved me. But he loved his dreams more. He was never going to settle down, not for me, not for anything."

Alice softened her voice. "Why didn't you tell me any of this?"

That night had been a nightmare from start to finish, one that still haunted her. Lauren had raced to the hospital to see Will, but he'd already gone. And to her eternal shame, she'd then let the grief consume her and she'd turned on Alice. She had yelled at her right there in the hospital hallway. *"You know how he gets when he's upset, but you let him go anyway, what were you thinking?"*

Alice had looked shattered as she'd whispered, *"What did you expect me to do, stop all one hundred and seventy-five pounds of him?"*

Which was when Lauren had doubled down on her assholery. *"Yes! And if that hadn't worked, you should have called me. Or your dad."*

Alice's dad had been standing behind Lauren, stoically destroyed as he'd solemnly nodded his head in agreement with Lauren, and she'd never forget the look in Alice's eyes.

Devastation. *"He made me promise,"* Alice had whispered. And Lauren hadn't been smart enough to just hug her and hold on. Instead, she'd opened her mouth and spewed the poison that had broken them. *"That's the trouble with you Moores, you're so set on protecting yourselves from getting hurt, you chase everyone away."*

Now, looking at Alice, the chasm between them felt bigger than ever, and she knew it was just as much her fault as Alice's. "I'm sorry I didn't tell you, but you didn't give me much of a chance. After the investigation, you bailed, and I—" Damn. She refused to cry but her throat equally refused to let air pass, so she couldn't talk either. "I didn't know how to make things right. You're not the only one who's a hot mess, Alice."

Alice looked away for a long beat. "I'm sorry that you felt like I abandoned you," Alice said quietly, eyes dark and haunted.

She sat on the stairs as if her legs were too weak to hold her up. "I shouldn't have done that to you."

"And I should've understood." Lauren sucked in a relieved breath. "So . . . are we okay?"

Alice opened her mouth to say something, but then covered her mouth with her hand, as if she couldn't bear to let out her pain. "Yes, but I can't—" She shook her head. "I don't know how to do this. How to find my way back to you, to . . . everything."

Lauren looked into her best friend's pain-filled gaze and felt a calm come over her as she sat next to her on the step. "That's okay," she said. "Because I do." And she pulled Alice into her arms. "I've got you, Alice. And this time, I'm never letting go."

Alice stilled. Lauren knew she'd always felt uncomfortable with physical affection, an after-effect of being raised by a man who knew cars, not people. Of having only a male sibling who'd been a chip off the old block. Yes, she'd had Eleanor, but that woman had been colder and harder than even Alice's dad.

But maybe it'd been the time away without letting anyone too close, because suddenly Alice was holding on to Lauren right back, letting out a shuddery breath, setting her head on Lauren's shoulder.

"I missed you, Alice."

Alice tried to pull back but Lauren tightened her grip. "Say it back. Say you missed me."

"Can't. Breathe."

"*Say it.*"

Alice sighed and gave in. "Okay, maybe there was once or twice I missed you, like the time I went into a library—"

"You went into a library that wasn't mine?" Lauren

cried. "How dare you!" But she didn't want to joke this away, so she met Alice's gaze straight on. "I need you to know something. Ever since we've been here working on the inn together, my life's felt . . ." She lifted her hands, searching for the right words. "Right. It's felt right, Alice, for the first time in a long time."

"That's the sex. You should be thanking Ben."

"That's not it! And we've only been together like that once so far!" She felt herself blush as she thought about how great that one time had been. "Okay, maybe it's partly about the sex," she allowed. "But it's mostly about *you*. I've loved having you in my life again. Are you really going to try and tell me you haven't felt the same?"

"Fine. It's been . . ." Alice's eyes suddenly went suspiciously shiny, and then filled. "*Dammit!* You're contagious!"

"Say it," Lauren demanded. "Finish that sentence!"

"Okay, okay, it's been amazing to have you back in my life!" Alice swiped her cheeks. "There. You happy? I said it and I mean it, but it doesn't change anything. Too much time has passed. We've moved on. We've got very different lives now. And mine isn't even here, wasn't ever meant to be here." And with that, she hugged Lauren once more and then . . . headed up the stairs.

With her stomach back at her feet, Lauren turned

and found Knox leaning in the doorway to the living room. "I think she's really going to leave," she said, shocked. "I mean, she always said she would, but I'd hoped . . ."

"I refuse to believe it," Knox said. "She's no longer the same person she was. She can't just walk away, not this time. She'll work something out, where she comes and goes, she won't just walk away from us."

But Lauren's heart was cracked in two. "I know you love her, so for your sake, I'm going to really hope you're right." She rose to her feet and hugged him. "You're one of the good ones, Knox. No matter what happens, I'm glad we're stuck together as friends and partners."

"That sounded like a goodbye."

She gave him a look.

"No," he said. "First of all, you're our new manager, you're not going anywhere."

"No, but you are."

He shook his head. "I'm sticking right along with you."

Lauren felt so grateful for that, even as they both looked up the stairs. "Are you okay, Knox?"

"TBD. But I do know it's not over."

Lauren *really* wanted to believe him, but she wasn't a naive kid anymore, and dreams didn't always come true.

Chapter 25

Dear Sister,

You might have noticed the lack of adjective in my greeting. Too tired to come up with a good insult. Our dear mother used to say that I needed to pick my hill to die on because I couldn't die on all the hills. Well, guess what? I think I'm finally starting to understand that.

Your sister, Eleanor

Knox climbed the stairs, not sure what he was walking into. A month ago, he'd have agreed with Lauren wholeheartedly, that Alice was indeed about to walk away from them. But after all the time he and Alice had spent together, practically 24/7, working their asses off, getting to know each other, sometimes laughing, sometimes fighting, sometimes not saying a word but making love all night long . . . she wouldn't just take off without talking to him, without making plans for how to keep this undeniable connection between them, no matter where their jobs took them.

At the doorway to her room, he stopped short. She had her big duffel bag on the bed and was shoving things into it.

Trying to control his racing heart, he walked over and looked inside. Yep, all her stuff. He pulled out a small bag containing what looked like her current knitting project, a migraine-inducing mix of yellow and green. "Where we going?"

"*I'm* going." Taking the knitting back from him, she shoved it into her duffel again. "We're done with the inn. Lauren's going to manage things for us. We're finished here."

He pulled the knitting back out.

She met his gaze for the first time, and in hers he saw a very carefully banked grief that stole his breath. "Alice." Stepping toward her, he cupped her face. "Why are you running?"

"I'm not."

What a devastatingly gorgeous liar. He brushed a

kiss to her temple and was gratified to feel her lean into him. "Can we go for a ride?" he asked. "Talk?"

"We already went for a ride, a month-long one. And it was . . ." She closed her eyes for a beat. "*Amazing.*" She stepped back. "But it's time to go back to solo."

It wasn't often that anxiety gripped him by the gonads, but it did now. "Why?"

She just gave him a look.

"So you're going to let the email of a dead woman chase you out of here? You're tougher than that, Alice."

She turned the laptop he'd left on her bed to face him. That morning, he'd woken up to her already in the shower, and he'd spent a minute running through his work emails and his accounts before joining her.

Alice made the screen live, revealing the spreadsheet he'd left open, with the balances of his bank accounts showing.

Well, hell.

She was watching him. "That's a whole lot of zeros."

He wasn't sure what to say to that. "You're mad because I'm not broke?"

"Nope. I'm mad because you lied."

He shook his head. "I've never lied to you."

"On day one, I asked you—No, I *begged* you and Lauren to think about buying me out. I didn't want to be here and you knew that."

"I did." And back then, maybe he hadn't taken her wanting to leave seriously. But in the weeks since, he'd come to take her *very* seriously. She was clutching a T-shirt in her hands, ready to add it to the duffel. "Is that my shirt?"

"Yes. I'm stealing it. I'm not a liar like some people, but I am a thief."

She had that right. She'd also stolen his heart. "Listen, I—"

"No, Knox, you listen. There were so many options. We could've gotten the lawyer to redo the partnership without me, worked out a deal where you didn't have to pay me anything until the inn was in the black again, *anything*. Only you wouldn't even consider it. So I had to stay, and that's fine. I learned a lot about myself. I also learned who I can trust, who I can't, and that's fine too. But I never thought you'd be one of them." She brought his shirt up to her face and inhaled.

He was pretty sure she had no idea she was even doing it. "Alice—"

"I *don't* care that you have money," she said. "You work your ass off. You're smart and resourceful and successful. I'm not surprised by any of that. But you know what I *do* care about? That you let me think you couldn't buy me out, when you clearly could, probably without losing most of those pretty zeros. Why not just be honest? That you enjoyed making me stay here in my own personal hell this past month."

"If that's what you think, we have a bigger problem than I thought." He stopped and looked at what appeared to be his deodorant, also in her bag.

"So I want to smell like you, so what?"

Damn, he loved her. "Alice, you can take everything I own. And what I said that first day was that I wouldn't buy you out. Not that I couldn't."

She took this in with heartbreaking uncertainty, then tossed his shirt into her bag and zipped it. "You know what? Forget it. I don't care anymore. I put in my time, and now I'm out."

As she shouldered her bag and turned to the door, he felt panic sink like a stone in his gut. Catching her hand, he very slowly pulled her around to face him. "You have to trust me when I say this. I never meant to hurt you."

"Trust you?" She let out a mirthless laugh. "As it turns out, there's no one I can trust anymore, and it doesn't matter anyway." Belying those words, her eyes filled. "I'm best off on my own. Goodbye, Knox." And with that, she walked out the door, pausing only to grab his ball cap from the dresser.

He was still standing there when Stella started up with a rumble, watching out the window as she vanished down the driveway.

Lauren came running into the room, stopping at his side. She looked into the yard, now empty of one 1972 Blazer. "Oh, no. Knox, I'm so sorry."

He exhaled but didn't speak. Wasn't sure he could.

"Do you know what my biggest regret is?" she asked. "It's not when I turned down Will. It's that after Alice took off because she was so hurt—me being one of the ones who hurt her—I didn't go after her."

Knox tore his gaze from the window and looked at her.

"I mean, yes, we talked occasionally, but it wasn't the same. For her, going is easier than giving anyone another chance to hurt or disappoint her."

"You want me to go after her."

"You would be the first," Lauren said. "And if you told her how you feel about her, how much you love her, that would be another first for her."

"And if she still wants to run?"

Her eyes were shimmering with tears at the thought. "Well, then, at least you gave her the chance to choose love."

Chapter 26

Alice drove, her heart left back at the inn in Knox's pocket. She adjusted Knox's pilfered hat and tried to channel his calm energy. Failing, she turned onto Lake Drive, heading for 80 before she had to face the question.

Okay, *two* big questions.

One, why hadn't she put the top back on Stella, or grabbed her jacket from her duffel bag in the back, because it was *maybe* forty-five degrees with a storm brewing and she was already half frozen to death?

And question number two . . .

Where was she going?

Was she really going to run away like she'd been doing for most of her life, and certainly all of her dubious "adult" life? She *hated* the idea of that, hated what it said about her as a business partner, as a friend, as a human being. After all, she had an obligation now to the inn and her partners. But more than that, she cared too much about those partners to do this to them.

But. If she *didn't* run, she'd have to face the elephant sitting on her chest, and once she let those emotions loose, she wasn't sure she could ever bottle them back up again.

So she kept driving. The lake was churning like the sea beneath the turbulent sky that matched her mood. And then suddenly Stella coughed and sputtered, making Alice's pulse skip a beat. Sure, Stella had been around the block a time or a hundred, but Alice had just given her a bunch of TLC.

Stella sputtered again.

"No, no, no, no, not now," she murmured, stroking the dash. "Baby, this isn't a good time. I'm in the middle of falling apart, so I need you to hold it together. Is it the oil? I had to give you a different brand because the store was out of our usual, but I swear it came highly rated."

Another sputter, and she knew.

It wasn't the oil. It was Alice. She'd once again forgotten to put gas in the tank. Talk about sabotaging herself. *What was wrong with her?* Probably too many things to name at this point. "But why? *Why* would I do this to us?"

Stella didn't have a response to that. Not that it mattered. Because deep down Alice knew what was wrong with her. In this case, she was the big, fat chicken who made a regular habit of screwing up her life. She was simply bailing before anyone could bail on her.

When Stella died, Alice managed to steer off the road. But thanks to no emergency lane and a steep slant leading directly into a ditch, she had to angle in, her front end up to a line of trees, bending to the wind's will.

The lake was on her left. Nothing but woods on her right that she knew would lead her to gorgeous trails, but no civilization. It was at least a mile to the closest gas station, maybe more. Leaning back, she stared up at the sky. "Do you think this is funny?" she asked. When no one answered, she blew out a sigh, pulled her phone from her pocket, and stared at it. She could call Lauren, and she would come. But she'd bring more questions than Alice had answers for.

Who else?

She knew who else. The man who she didn't want to admit owned her entire heart. Her entirely broken heart.

Well, whose fault is that . . . ?

She never should've come back. This place had wrecked her once and she'd barely survived. Why had she expected this time to be any different? And this time it just might kill her, though clearly, before she died, she was going to have to pump gas.

She drew a deep breath and tried to figure out what her heart wanted.

Run.

Okay, so *that* wasn't a surprise. It'd been silenced for so long that now, when she'd finally lowered her walls, the poor organ actually thought it was in charge. But shouldn't important life decisions be made by the brain?

Naturally, her brain chose that moment to be silent.

What does your gut say? Knox had asked her. Well, her gut said she was an idiot. Letting her head fall back on the headrest, she closed her eyes. She'd made both Lauren and Knox think that her leaving was all their fault. Who did that to the people they loved?

So this was what rock bottom felt like. But the joke was on her, because she felt the first drop of something icy cold hit her face. And then another. Opening her eyes, she watched snowflakes begin to fall from the sky in slow motion. "You've *got* to be kidding me."

The words weren't even all the way out of her mouth when the sky opened up. She was still sitting there swearing the air blue when a dark gray truck angled in to park directly behind her, blocking her in.

Knox got out of the truck, followed by Pickle. She

watched the man and his dog approach in her side-view mirror, annoyed that the warning printed on the mirror—OBJECTS IN MIRROR ARE CLOSER THAN THEY APPEAR—was *not* true, because in a single blink Knox was at her door; big, solid, sexy as hell, his expression dialed to unhappy.

Join my club . . .

Something bubbled in her belly. Nerves? Oh, yeah. But it was something else as well. A teeny tiny itty little bit of . . . *hope?* He'd come after her. No one had ever done that, not even Lauren.

But you're mad at him, that self-destructive voice deep inside her whispered. Yes. Yes, she was. Very mad. Only . . . deep *deep* down she knew the truth—that Knox had done absolutely *nothing* wrong. He'd made something of himself, become successful, and she was thrilled for him. So why was she so upset?

Because you're scared.

Ding, ding, ding, we have a winner . . .

Knox stood at her door, Pickle sitting sweetly at his feet, blinking up at her through the falling snow. Alice's window was rolled up, but with the top off, it didn't much matter. Knox met her gaze, his own solemn as he carefully looked her over, like he was making sure she was okay. "Nice day to hang outside," he said, getting dusted with snow as he lived and breathed.

"How did you find me?"

"It's one road in and one road out. I guess for the first time ever, I was hoping you'd run out of gas."

She sank in her seat a little bit. "I used to be unpredictable. Mysterious."

"If it helps, you're still a complete mystery to me." He opened the back door. "Up," he said.

Pickle jumped into the back and sat politely, then proceeded to tip his head back and play at catching snowflakes as they came down around him, his jaws snapping audibly as he amused himself. Snap, snap, snap . . .

Knox went back to his truck and reappeared carrying a gas can, no doubt full.

She tried—and failed—to ignore the little flutter that gave her.

Setting the can down near her tank, he came back to her. He opened the driver's door, then crouched at her side, easily balancing on the balls of his feet. "Ready for that talk yet?"

"I'm pretty busy having an existential crisis."

His mouth twitched, but he didn't smile. He wasn't going to let her joke this away.

And he also deserved better. Way better. "Look," she said. "I'm sorry. Your financial affairs are none of my business. It wasn't your problem to bail me out.

I, um . . ." She looked away. "I used that ridiculous excuse to run like hell. Out of fear."

Snap, went Pickle's jaws. Snap. Snap. Snap.

Knox's expression didn't change. Nor did he move a single inch, but Alice could *feel* how much he hated what she'd revealed. "You're afraid of me," he finally said softly, almost as if to himself.

"Of what you make me feel." She adjusted his hat low over her eyes. "I know that people think I'm so tough, but I'm not. I'm a big faker. I mean, look what happened when I was faced with real emotions. The first chance I got, I lashed out and pushed you away. Lauren too." She swallowed hard. "You both deserve better, and I'm sorry. I'm sorry about a lot of things. Being back here stirred up all sorts of bad stuff, and I let it all get mixed up with the now. Which is dumb, I know, but so was making a bunch of stupid promises to myself about not letting myself get involved so that I couldn't screw anything up. But then that's exactly what I did, so—"

He readjusted the hat so he could see her eyes and then gently set a finger to her lips. She nearly collapsed in gratitude because she'd probably have kept babbling forever.

"You haven't screwed anything up," he said.

She gave him a get-real look. "I screwed *every-*

thing up. Me and Lauren. The car inventory that I let sit because it paralyzed me, which is basically like taking money from both of you. Eleanor would be so disappointed in me." She paused. "And then there's the biggie."

"The biggie?"

Damn. He wanted her to say it. "Me and you . . ."

Knox just looked at her for a long beat. "First, you and Lauren are going to be okay."

She sucked in a breath, hoping that was true. "And second?"

"The inventory will still be there whenever you're ready. Or if you decide you're never going to get there, we'll figure something else out, the three of us. Also, Eleanor always had faith in you. You won't disappoint her."

She stared at him, wanting to believe. But it sounded too easy. Plus, there was one thing left, and there would be *nothing* easy about it. "And the me and you thing?" she whispered.

Snap. Snap. Snap . . .

"*Pickle*," Knox said.

The dog gave a sigh, then turned in a circle three times, plopped onto the seat, and closed his eyes.

Knox hadn't taken his eyes off Alice. "As for you and me . . . I'm right here."

"But?" she whispered, because there was *always* a but.

"No buts, not between you and me," he said, eyes still very serious. "We're just talking. And then after, if you still want to go, you'll go. I want you to be happy, Alice. As for what *you* might want, whatever it is, please know it's of the utmost importance to me."

She hadn't had a warm fuzzy in years and years, but she got one now, all the way down to her toes.

"I'm sorry you felt blindsided by what you saw on my laptop," he said. "I wasn't trying to hide it from you."

She grimaced. "I know. And it doesn't matter. Again, not your problem."

"No, but I still could've told you." He drew a deep breath. "The truth is, I didn't because I didn't want you to leave. But if you still want to, I'll deal with it and try to understand. I meant what I said, Alice. I want you to be happy, whatever that looks like for you. Will you tell me what *you* want?"

She turned to fully face him where he was still crouched at her door, her knees bumping his chest. She found the contact comforting. "I want a partner who's in the trenches with me. Someone I can let my guard down with. Someone who doesn't see that as me being weak."

"Tumbleweed, there's nothing weak about you."

She gave a slow head shake. "We both know that isn't true. Honesty, right? That's one of our things? So here's my truth—I want to learn how to stop running away when I get scared."

He reached for her hand and squeezed gently. He wasn't quite as calm as he'd like her to believe. There was a tension in every line of his body, and his mouth was set in a grim line. "I get that," he said, then almost smiled at her surprise. "You think you're the only one who gets scared?"

"I scare *you*?" she asked, incredulous.

"Hell, yeah you do. When you left, I was afraid I'd never feel happy again." He drew a deep breath. "Alice . . . what does your gut say?"

Shockingly, she found a smile. Because yeah, her heart and her brain led with fear, but her gut didn't have an ounce of it. "It says I should stay. I mean, you do make a mean breakfast, so . . ."

That finally got her a small smile. "Do you need a bribe?" He pushed her wet hair from her face. "Because I'm not above it. I'll vow right here right now to make you breakfast every day of the week for the rest of your life. I love you, Alice. I'm *in* love with you. I'm never going to stop loving you and thinking about you, wherever you live. I choose you, and if you let me, I'd spend the rest of my life proving it to you."

She was pretty sure her mouth was hanging open because she could taste the snow. It was coming down in thick white lines now, covering them both. It was sitting on Knox's hair and shoulders, and yet he remained still. He had to be cold. He was wearing only a T-shirt and jeans, like maybe he'd come after her so fast he hadn't thought to grab a jacket for himself. She slid over into the passenger seat.

Knox got in behind the wheel, the snow still drifting down on them. He tugged her hand, getting her to come back and right into his lap. "Whatever you want, Alice."

And he would give it. It both humbled and thrilled her to the core. She cupped his jaw. "As long as you let me prove to you that you are enough, exactly as is."

He let out a breath. "You could prove that with the next three words that you say."

She grinned. "You. Are. Enough."

His gaze didn't waver. Still not playing.

"A relationship with me will be hard," she said softly. "I'm no picnic."

He dropped his head to her shoulder, then turned his face to kiss her neck. "I don't know about that. You sure taste good."

With a quiet laugh, she adjusted herself so that she was straddling him, then wound her arms around him.

"When I first got here, I was scared to see you again, so scared to let my secret crush on you renew itself, because I knew of all the people I've ever met and pushed away, that you were different, that I couldn't scare you off or pretend not to feel things for you." She drew a deep breath. "I love you, Knox. So much. I think I've been waiting to tell you that for just about my whole life."

She didn't know what she expected his reply to be, but it wasn't for his eyes to remain incredibly intense as he nodded. "Then you should know something."

Oh, God. She started to climb off him, but changed her mind. Nope. Hell no. She wasn't going to run. For once, she was going to go toe to toe with him and hold her own. "What?"

"You live your life unapologetically. You're fierce and passionate and incredible, and the way you look at me . . ." He shook his head, looking marveled. "It humbles and surprises me every time. You're everything to me, Alice. I can only hope to be the same for you."

Relief had her collapsing like a balloon against him. "Are you kidding me? You're everything to me too, and *more* than enough for me. You're so much that I can hardly take all of you."

He snorted, and she felt heat warm her cold face as

she pressed it to the crook of his neck. "I didn't mean it like that."

"How did you mean it?"

She lifted her head and held on to the rest of her life by fisting her hands in his wet shirt. "You're going to make me say it?"

"Damn straight I am."

She looked him right in the eyes as she gave him a soft kiss, then pulled back slightly. "You're the best thing that's ever happened to me. I promise to stop running, Knox."

He kissed her gently, tenderly. "How about this instead—if the urge hits, I'll run with you." He cupped her face, held her gaze. "You are the most important person in my life, Alice."

As she glowed with that, a Nissan LEAF pulled off the road and parked behind Knox's truck.

Alice's stomach dropped.

Lauren got out of her car and, hugging her jacket close to her body with one hand, the other holding her hood up, ran toward them. "I knew you'd be out of gas."

Alice drew a deep breath, not sure how to fix things, only knowing she had to try. She knew that what Lauren had done hadn't been to purposely hurt her. Unlike what Alice had done.

Knox reached around Alice and opened the passenger door for Lauren. Climbing in, Lauren shut the
door, then let her head fall back. "Oh. My. God."

"I know," Alice said. "Crazy storm."

"I meant you!" Lauren reached over and hugged
Alice tightly, clearly not minding at all that Alice was
still in Knox's lap. "I want you to know if I get any new
gray hairs from today, even a single one, you're paying
for my next set of highlights."

"Done," Alice said into Lauren's hair because Lauren
hadn't let go. In fact, her hold on Alice was strangling.
She tried giving Lauren a little pat on the back.

The woman still didn't let go. "And . . . ?" Lauren
demanded.

Alice took a deep breath. "And I'm in love with your
other business partner."

Lauren rolled her eyes. "Well, duh. I knew before
either of you two knew, but even if I'd somehow managed to miss the long looks and sizzling chemistry hot
enough to light up all of Tahoe, you sitting on his lap in
a car without a lid in a storm is clue enough. But that's
not what I meant, by the way. I was asking why the hell
we're sitting in your car without a lid in a storm."

"Because I'm a slow learner," Alice said. "Lauren,
I'm so sorry—"

"Stop!" Lauren commanded, and Alice froze.

"Me first." Lauren pulled something from her pocket—an antique gold diamond ring, which she handed to Alice.

Her grandma's, and overcome at having a tangible reminder of the family that once was, Alice closed her fingers around it and brought her hand to her heart.

"It was in the box the attorney sent me," Lauren said softly. "I was always going to give it to you, I just didn't know how."

"It's okay. I understand. I made things harder than they needed to be. I'm sorry for leaving the way I did. I never meant to hurt you." She drew a deep breath for courage. "I meant to stay in touch more. I wanted to. You were . . . you *are* so important to me, Lauren."

Lauren was slapping her pockets, clearly looking for a tissue, muttering about having something in her eye.

Knox hauled out some napkins from a stack he had tucked into the pocket of the driver's door. Alice took them and handed them to Lauren. "Please don't cry, Lauren."

Lauren blew her nose. "It's a good kind of cry."

"There's a good kind of cry?" Alice asked Knox.

Knox shrugged. "Apparently?"

Alice drew a deep breath for courage. "I talked myself into the idea that I didn't need love in my life. I mean, all it ever seemed to do was hurt me. I didn't realize until I came back here how wrong I was. My life is better off for being loved by you, Lauren."

"Oh my God, and now you're flinging the *L*-word around." Lauren hugged her again, hard.

"Did you just wipe snot and mascara on me?" Alice asked.

"Maybe. Just a little. But I love you too. I'm so sorry I didn't tell you about Will's proposal. I was afraid you'd be mad at me for breaking your brother's heart. Just because he wasn't a good fit for me doesn't mean I didn't care about him, because I did."

Alice believed that. "Maybe we both agree to agree that we were both young and dumb, and move on."

"No." Lauren shook her head. "Not if it means you're still leaving."

"You know I was always going to leave," Alice reminded her gently. "But . . ."

"You'd better tell me that *but* involves you changing your mind, or I'll cry *buckets*, I swear it, *and* make *you* cry buckets too, and—"

"I'm changing my mind," Alice said quickly. Yes, she'd come to Sunrise Cove with the goal of getting in and back out as soon as possible. But somewhere along the line, that need had changed. And at the end of the day, the Last Chance Inn was the only place to ever feel like home to her. But it was more than that. She wanted Lauren in her life.

And Knox.

She wanted it all. "I'm staying."

"You're staying," Lauren repeated, staring at Alice as if she didn't trust her own ears. "Is it at all possible for you to, I don't know, maybe use *more words faster*?"

Alice took Lauren's hand in hers, but it was Knox's eyes she looked into, Knox who'd gone still as stone beneath her. "I came here and found what I didn't even know I was looking for. Forgiveness. Acceptance. Self-worth. Love." She paused. "Family."

Lauren let out a breath and nodded. "Me too," she whispered.

"We have Eleanor to thank for that," Alice said.

Knox didn't look surprised at the revelation. Clearly, he'd gotten there first. "I think she knew *exactly* what she was doing."

"Agreed. She masterminded the whole thing," Alice said. "We were her second chance, just like she's ours." And how she missed the old broad. "The truth is, I can't walk away. I mean, okay, so I tried," she said, gesturing at Stella. "But it turns out that I can't, because I want to stick for once. I want to be here, with you guys. I know you're going to build a business here in Tahoe," she said to Knox, then turned to Lauren. "And you're going to run the inn. You both have your lives sorted out." She hesitated because this was a hard admittance. "But I don't, not even close. You need to know that going in."

"Oh, we do," Lauren said dryly enough to make Alice laugh.

Alice squeezed Lauren's hand and with her other, reached for Knox's. "I didn't know where my place was." She gave a small smile. "But I know now. It's with you both. I want to stay, and while Lauren manages the inn, I'd like to manage the actual property. Fix up the TV sets. The barn. The cars in the barn. We can sell some and keep others, like the ones that have ties to the TV show. Maybe we can renovate to what it looked like back in the day, go all wild, Wild West, you know? Use it to enhance and expand our guests' experience. And then, when I'm finished with all that . . ." Be brave. Say it. "I want to open my own mechanic's shop." At that, she forced herself to shut up and take in their reactions, so she would know if this could really be her future.

Lauren was working her way through the stack of napkins. "Happy tears," she cried, waving a hand in front of her face. "I promise!"

Knox cupped Alice's face and pulled her closer,

pressing his forehead to hers. "I can't think of anything I'd love to see more."

"Well, *me*, right?" she quipped.

He smiled. "Always."

"Always," she repeated softly.

"You know what we need now?" Lauren asked. "Food." She pointed at Alice. "*You're* buying." She got out of Stella, then poked her head back in to look at Knox. "Oh, and your dog did number two in the front yard. If he wants to be our mascot, he needs manners."

In the backseat, Pickle tried to look guilty, but he didn't have it in him.

"I'll get it," Knox promised.

An hour later, they were all in the living room of the inn, in front of a roaring fire, eating takeout. They sat in comfortable silence for a while, looking into the fire. Alice felt herself drift, the crackling of the fire lulling her into relaxing. She looked around at her two favorite people and her favorite dog and her favorite inn, and felt so incredibly proud. Lauren had her eyes closed, maybe asleep, maybe just enjoying herself as Alice was. She glanced at Knox and found him watching her. "Hey."

He smiled. "Hey."

"Thanks for . . ." *Loving me like no one else ever has.* "Letting me in."

Catching her hand, he gently drew it up to his chest. "It was about time."

"No kidding," Lauren murmured and opened her eyes just so she could roll them.

Alice snorted. Standing, she walked over to the wall and lifted the last piece of beadboard and set it in place.

Hiding their lists.

She nailed it in, and when she turned, Knox and Lauren were right there. "To us," Lauren said.

"To us," Knox repeated.

Alice smiled, feeling more at home and more herself than she'd ever felt before as the last piece of her heart fell into place.

Epilogue

The Last Chance Inn stood proudly in the distance while Alice watched Lauren attempting to get up out of a wooden chair, unable to help from laughing. They were in the yard off to the side of the barn on the saloon set, which was now used almost exclusively for weddings, and also, since they'd found a stash of Wild West wardrobe in boxes in the barn, family photo shoots.

They were booked nearly a year out, and felt successful beyond their wildest dreams. Alice had just put a deposit down on a small warehouse just outside of town for what would eventually become Woman Auto Know, her mechanic shop.

Who'd seen that coming? Not Alice, that was for sure.

Lauren gave up fighting her way out of the chair and sat back with a heaving sigh.

Taking mercy on her, Alice offered both hands and dug her feet in, bracing herself.

"Seriously?" Lauren asked breathlessly. "I'm not *that* big."

But Alice couldn't talk because hoisting Lauren out of the chair took all of her concentration and every ounce of strength.

"Okay," Lauren huffed, finally on her feet. "So I'm as big as a house."

"You're eight months pregnant, you're allowed." Oh shit, Alice thought as Lauren's eyes went suspiciously shiny. When would she learn to keep her trap shut?

"So I *am* big as a house?" she cried. "Why didn't you tell me to stop eating?"

"Uh, because I like breathing? Please don't cry. You got all dehydrated the last time you cried, which was just this morning when your husband suggested you *might* want to *slightly* cool it with the two inches of cream cheese you were layering on your bagel."

"Ben thinks I'm fat too!" Lauren wailed.

"You're supposedly vegan, *and* you've got a dairy intolerance, remember?" Alice was frantically searching for the tissues she'd taken to keeping in her pockets at all times and shoved them at the pregnant sobbing chick. "And Ben thinks you're perfect. That's why he married you. That's why he knocked you up."

"It's true."

At Ben's voice, Lauren stopped sobbing to whip around and face her husband of a year and a half.

Smiling with love and laughter in his eyes, Ben pulled her in close, nuzzling her temple. "How's my baby?"

"She's sitting on my bladder and kicking the air out of my lungs."

He huffed out a sympathetic laugh. "I meant you."

"Oh." Lauren smiled up at him. "I'm good. Where's Hope?"

"Right here!" Hope came skipping across the yard, Pickle right on her heels. "When's the wedding?"

"That's the thing." Ben looked at Lauren. "It's canceled."

Lauren's mouth fell open. "Today's bride and groom . . . canceled? But they paid us a small fortune up front for everything, including the food, and Alice and I are almost all set up. I was going to marry them in . . ." She pulled out her phone. "Three hours."

"They eloped." Ben shrugged. "They called as they were boarding a flight for Fiji. Something about meddling mothers and irritating friends not RSVPing, and the bride not being able to fit into her dress because she's three months into a surprise pregnancy."

Alice chuckled, then received a dirty look from Lauren because her pregnancy had been a surprise too. A happy one. And it looked great on her.

Alice heard Knox's truck pull up. The Tahoe branch of his eco-building company had taken off. But the pro bono work was his favorite. He'd renovated his childhood home and given it to one of the families in the area who'd lost theirs in a fire. He'd then purchased as many in that same trailer park as he could and had done the same for each one. And somehow, he'd also managed to build a house for the two of them.

They lived in relative harmony. Relative, because Alice wasn't all that good at harmony, and every once in a while, her contrary side liked to buy into her anxiety. This consisted of her having a freak-out about being too happy, so therefore something must be wrong.

Calm, unflappable Knox had been able to talk her through each one so that they came out even stronger on the other side. It was a miracle.

He was her miracle.

As was this new life of hers, one she knew she'd never take for granted.

"Heard the wedding got called off," Knox said as he

came close, stopping to pull Alice into him for a hello kiss.

"How did you hear that already?" she asked, holding on to him because he was warm, smelled amazing, and was looking good enough to eat. "We just found out."

"Ben called me a few minutes ago."

Alice and Lauren went brows up at Ben.

Ben just smiled. "Knox had an idea."

Everyone turned back to Knox, who just held on to Alice and smiled down into her face.

"What?" she asked self-consciously, running a hand over her mouth since she'd been noshing on a bag of M&M's while working with Lauren. "Am I wearing chocolate?"

"Nope."

She stared up into his face, his eyes warm with love and affection and something else. A question. She blinked, then looked at Lauren to see if she had a clue.

Given the way Lauren gasped suddenly and put a hand to her mouth, she absolutely did have a clue.

"I'd like to buy a vowel," Alice said.

"Maybe you'd do better to buy a dress," Ben said.

"Dress not required," Knox said, never taking his eyes off Alice.

"Oh please, please, *please* say yes!" Lauren said, jumping up and down.

Well, not exactly jumping. She was too unwieldy for that. But she did bounce a few times. "Crap," she said. "Now I have to pee. Hurry up, Alice, say yes!"

Alice finally got that clue, and stared up in shock at Knox. "You want to marry me? Today? Here?"

"Well, we're already all set up with flowers and food and everything," Lauren said. "And because the bride said she didn't know what kind of food she wanted, you helped her pick, remember? You picked all your favorites. You've even got pigs in a blanket. How perfect is that?"

Alice couldn't take her eyes off Knox. He'd asked her to marry him a year ago. She'd agreed. She even wore a ridiculously gorgeous engagement ring, the nicest thing she'd ever owned, and she loved it. But every time they'd tried to figure out a wedding date, something had come up and taken them off track.

Maybe . . . Maybe because she had subconsciously been waiting for something just like this. "Are you sure?" she whispered.

Knox cupped her face. "I've never been more sure."

Which was how she ended up getting married on an old Wild West TV saloon set, complete with a pregnant officiant in a *Little House on the Prairie* dress the size of a tent, Pickle as the ring bearer, Hope—also in a *Little House on the Prairie* dress—as a flower girl, and a groom in his best jeans and an old cowboy hat they'd found on the set.

As for the bride, she'd picked a simple sundress she had in her closet but had never worn, and cowgirl boots, because hell, why not lean into the theme *and* her new life, the one that wasn't perfect, but was perfect for her.

HARPER
LARGE PRINT

We hope you enjoyed reading
our new, comfortable print size and found it
an experience you would like to repeat.

Well – you're in luck!

Harper Large Print offers the finest in
fiction and nonfiction books in this same larger
print size and paperback format. Light and easy to read,
Harper Large Print paperbacks are for the book lovers
who want to see what they are reading without strain.

For a full listing of titles and
new releases to come, please visit our website:
www.hc.com

HARPER LARGE PRINT

SEEING IS BELIEVING!